MW00489589

Moment of Inertia

Moment of Inertia

A Novel

Jason Montgomery

VERSE FIVE

Verse Five Publishing
Bellvue, Colorado

This is a work of fiction. Names, characters, and incidents are the product of the author's imagination or are used fictitiously, and any resemblance to actual events, organizations, or persons living or dead is entirely coincidental.

Moment of Inertia
A Novel

All contents copyright © 2018 by Jason Montgomery

All rights reserved.
No part of this book may be reproduced or transmitted in any form or by any means, electronic or mechanical, without express written permission from the publisher.

Published by Verse Five Publishing
A division of Verse Five LLC
Bellvue, Colorado.
www.versefive.com

ISBN 978-0-9963173-2-0
eBook ISBN 978-0-9963173-3-7

Cover and interior design by Jason Montgomery.

First Paperback Edition v.1.0.0
2020

Printed in the United States of America

PAUL'S LETTER TO TITUS,
CHAPTER THREE, VERSE FIVE

CHAPTER SIXTY

Go ahead and eat another cupcake, you cow. He would never actually say it to her, but he felt safe thinking it.

She sat across the table from him, phone clamped between her ear and shoulder, mindlessly peeling the corrugated wrapper off her third cupcake.

Too bad prattling to Whatserface all night won't burn off those calories for you.

"...no, I thought she was kidding," Kate was saying. "You would think with a comment like that she would have to be kidding. No. I know." A long pause with tinny garbling out of the earpiece. Kate giggled. "I know! Well, you heard her and..."

Tom poked at his cold dinner. It was cold before he even made it home from work.

That meeting... His shoulders slumped at the memory. *If we've gotta sit through a browbeating like that, he should at least try to wrap it up by five-thirty. But at least there were cupcakes. Our consolation prize.*

He looked up toward Kate and winced, feeling his own barb at her.

She was still attractive—the kind of attractive about whom strangers whisper, "If only she'd lose some weight, she'd be really pretty..." And when she bemoaned the weight she wasn't losing, she wasn't just seeking compliments. She meant it.

When she and Tom were dating, she really turned heads. He had been drawn to her pretty face, her ready smile, her cute little curvy figure, her ivory complexion, and what could be called her 'ample femininity.' *All guys are drawn to that, really. Not their fault.* But Tom never dreamed how soon after offspring began springing off that Kate's voluptuousness would begin to multiply and migrate in search of uncrowded pastures.

But that's not when it started. His attraction for her had begun to wane mere months after their wedding, even before her figure began to change. The superfluous curves she had picked up only added fuel to the fire. Or lack thereof.

I should've known, Tom thought. *Evaluated the genetic potential.* He shook his head, remembering the day before. *But I never should have said it. Never be honest to a woman.* He had, in a moment of diplomatic dementia, told her she was starting to look like her mother.

While she grazed on cupcakes, he gorged on his stupidity. He would eat his words for days, maybe a couple of weeks. Whatserface couldn't possibly sense through the phone lines the smoke still hanging in the room after yesterday's grenade volley.

I never should have married a redhead. "Auburn," she would correct him. *Same thing. Same temper veiled behind her smiling sunshiny goodness, her painted splendor the folks at church get to see. They all think she's flawless: the perfect wife, the perfect mother.*

Tom stared through his food.

Sure, the perfect wife, except...

He glanced up at her for the briefest moment, almost a twitch.

Except...

Except for the chasm growing between them.

It had started as newlyweds: Her stratospheric expectations. Her holding him responsible to meet needs he didn't even know she had, only to snub him when he asked her what's wrong. Her jealousy. Her hypocrisy.

Then the kids came along.

It was easier to be happy back when we were allowed to have fun, back when it was just two of us, with two full incomes and only two mouths to feed.

But now… Tom frowned. *And still she takes the cash we were saving to replace that barbed-wire mattress of ours, and instead dumps it into that weird table thing we don't need. And she was surprised that another battle followed.*

Tom sat motionless with a forkful hovering above his plate, his eyes hollow.

Sure, the perfect wife, except…

Except for the coldness growing between them.

He had started needing her less. No—not really; he had started wanting her less. She sensed this, but she assumed her weight had caused it, when really everything—all of her, *all of life*—had caused it, exacerbated by the vicious cycle of his own unharnessed thoughts. But she became more and more self-conscious, less and less flirtatious, and they drew further and further apart, and it depressed her. And when depressed, she ate like her mother. Her own vicious cycle. His attempts to help, in his analytical, clinical, surgical manner, didn't help. He only stirred up her fight-or-flight instinct—except she was Irish, so the flight part was missing, and he would find the scalpel turned on him. Rewind, replay. With each replay a deeper rut gouged into the routine, a more searing pain carved into each other.

Suddenly Coby howled out in his high chair, thinking he was done or something. Tom didn't hear him, his mind already back on the afternoon's meeting. He remained frozen, staring through his food. Abigail tried to shush Coby, but she was only a big sister, not even that much bigger, very easily ignored. Coby hurled his little plastic bowl overboard; the clatter threw orange spots up the wall that wouldn't be discovered until thoroughly petrified. He arched his back and shouted again.

Kate covered the phone and glared at Tom. "You just gonna sit there?" she barked in her angriest whisper. She tilted her head toward Coby. "Get him. Can't you see I'm busy?"

Tom shoved his plate back, rose to work his way down the tiny space between the chairs and wall, knocked a photograph askew, and grumbled, "Hannah, move."

Hannah tried to scoot her chair forward, but it was big and she was little. He scooted her himself. Low enough so Whaterface wouldn't hear, Tom growled, "Jacob, quiet." He snatched up a napkin and commenced the impossibility of scouring coagulating food off Coby's face, from between his fingers, out of his ear...

"Of course," Kate said into the phone, giggling again. "No. I don't even know what I did. Yeah, I guess I'll have to, but only because..."

Jacob, dangling by the ribs, happily kicked his legs as his father carried him out of the room. Tom's unfinished plate sat until it also petrified; he would chisel it off an hour or so later.

But the photograph stayed crooked just a little while. As she carried on an unbroken chat with her friend, Kate walked around to straighten the frame, and stood before it reminiscing on the day the photo was taken. Typical family portrait: uncreatively composed, cheaply framed. There they all stood behind the picture glass. No, not all: Jacob was not yet; Hannah was in Dad's arms. Abby stood by Mom holding her hand. Cabbage sat in front, looking the wrong way, her leash taut, clearly held by someone off camera. Somehow Kate had the ability to laugh over the phone while her eyes grew distant over the picture.

Tom looked happy in it.

CHAPTER FIFTY-NINE

MacMillan Robotics
Tom Ericson
Mechanical Engineer

Tom lowered the business card and smiled up at the secretary. "Yep, it's all correct."

"Thanks, Tom." She returned a few little boxes from the corner of his desk into a bigger box under her arm, then she headed to the next cubicle.

Tom chuckled under his breath. *Engineer…* he thought. *Yeah, right.* He examined the card. *I do hold a couple of engineering degrees. I'm pretty good at engineering. I work at an engineering company. Maybe I am an engineer.* He returned his card to his own little box, opened his bottom drawer, and tossed the box into the back. *Maybe next year we'll hire a new guy, and I'll unload this busy work and get back to designing stuff.* He nudged the drawer shut. *At least I've already got a couple hundred business cards. Won't have to reorder for, say, fifty years or so.*

One bonus of his job at MacMillan was his short commute from his home in midtown Fort Collins to his workplace in south Fort Collins; he could leisurely bike to work in a quarter of the time it took others to drive Interstate 25 all the way down to Denver.

But they can probably pay all their bills on time.

Another bonus was that he had a cube with a view. If he stood on his desk and leaned over his cubicle wall, he could see a sliver of Horsetooth Mountain through his boss's window, as long as the boss's door was open.

"How's it lookin'?" Tom heard behind him as he teetered over his wall checking the sky above the mountain. "They said it was supposed to rain." He turned to find Tara draped on his cube door.

"Nah, looks pretty good," he answered as he dropped to the ground.

"You gonna run tonight?"

"I think I might. You?"

"No. I got a few miles in this morning." She glanced at her watch. "Shoot. Gotta run now, though. See ya, Tom." She spun and hurried away. He watched her from the corner of his eye for a few seconds, then he wrestled his gaze back to his computer.

CHAPTER FIFTY-EIGHT

Kate poked her head around the corner. "Hey honey, time to tuck in the kids. You coming?"

Tom glanced up from his computer, raised his eyebrows, and showed a wooden smile. "Yeah, one sec."

He hated working at home, at night, *again,* but he at least wanted it over with. Bedtime rituals would break his train of thought, which would delay getting his work done, which would delay doing something he felt like doing. He had no particular plans, but he'd rather start his non-plans as soon as possible.

Jacob was first. The crib rail was too high to kiss him without picking him up, but picking him up would chase off his sleepiness. Bad idea. Tom instead kissed two of his fingers and lightly touched the smooth, warm, cushiony forehead. Coby grabbed them and said, "Da."

"Yes, Daddy loves you. Coby's a sweet boy."

Kate whispered, "Mama loves her Jacob so much. Nighty-night."

Tom added tenderly, "Poop real soon so Mommy will come right back."

"Tom!" She choked back a laugh. "You're awful." They darkened the room and stepped out. "Don't teach him that," she whispered, chuckling, as she silently closed the door behind her.

"He already learned it. It's his favorite trick."

Kate went to rescue Hannah and the bathroom floor from tooth-paste foam, and Tom found Abigail already in bed, gazing at Hamlet in his glass cage as he ran like mad on his little wheel. Abby thought he looked like Piglet, but announced she couldn't name him Piglet because he wasn't a pig. She still knew nothing of Shakespeare.

"How do you sleep with him doing that all night?" Tom asked as he sat on the edge of her bed.

"Does he do it all night?"

"I don't know. Does he? He's your hamster."

"I can't tell when I'm asleep."

Tom shrugged and conceded. Hamlet ran and ran, then he would freeze and swing back and forth a moment, then he would run some more, then freeze and swing. The others entered the room, a wet spot the size of a football down the front of Hannah's pajama shirt. Kate started stripping it off, Hannah's floppy arms and head forming a logjam in the inside-out shirt.

"Just let her sleep in it," Tom said.

Kate didn't even look up. "No, we can't sleep in icky, cold ladybug jammies, can we, Booger-Bear?" Hannah shook her head really big.

"*Booger-Bear* sounds gross, Mama," Abby inserted.

"It's her fault," said Tom. "She needs to learn to brush carefully."

Kate cut her eyes at him. "Tom, really."

"Or at least make her brush before she changes. Or something."

Kate simply kept to her task. She began to work off the little pants.

"Really, both?" Tom asked.

"She has to match." Kate poked through the drawer for a new set. "Nobody wants clashy jammies, do they?" Hannah shook her head really big again. But it didn't bother her to stand there mostly naked.

Tom said, "You're kidding. Who's gonna see her?"

"Hamlet will," Abby inserted.

Tom gave up.

They tucked Hannah in, said a fairly mediocre prayer that the girls only cared about because it kept their parents in the room longer, and gave kisses.

Tom was closing the door when Abigail called out, "Daddy?"

"Yes, baby?"

"Is Hamlet cold without a blanket at night?"

"No."

"I think he gets cold. That's why he has to exercise."

"He has fur all over him, and he crawls under his stuff."

"What stuff?"

"His stuff. The fluff-stuff. With his poop in it."

"What stuff?"

Tom's shoulders drooped. He walked back to the shelf next to Abby's bed, where Hamlet's aquarium sat. The night-light was enough to see the wheel still turning and Hamlet's beady little eye bobbing around. "That stuff, in the bottom. That's his blanket. He doesn't get cold."

"Why does he run then?"

"'Cause he's an idiot."

"Daddy!"

"I'm just kidding. He's very smart. He runs because it feels good. Hamsters think running is super fun. They just run and run all the time and never go anywhere, and it never occurs to them that they've accomplished nothing, and that their whole life is just a complete wa..." Tom thought better of it. "...a complete—uh—a complete—ly fun time of running and sleeping and playing with little girls."

"Is that why you run?"

"Because it's fun? Yes. And it keeps me from getting fat."

"Hamlet is fat."

"Hamsters are supposed to be fat. It makes him cute. People aren't supposed to be fat. They look better, um, un-fat."

Hamlet's wheel still quietly spun when Tom escaped the girls' room. He backed out and pulled the door closed, and his foot landed on something that yelped and leaped away.

"Cabbage, you moron, what do you think is gonna happen when you're...?" Cabbage shuffled up to Tom's knee and humbly apologized for getting injured. Her tail cowered under her droopy bottom as she made tentative eye contact once or twice, hoping with all her might for restored fellowship with Great and Noble Master Tom Ericson.

"You're fine, you doofus." Then he scratched behind her ear, and she knew that all was right in the world and she sprang up and her tail got back to work. "Hold on. I'll take you in a bit."

"How long do you think we've got?" Kate whispered from behind him. He turned to find her down the hall leaning against their bedroom doorframe.

"'Til one of the kids bothers us? About five minutes."

"That's long enough."

"I've gotta walk the dog, and I really have to get that stupid proposal done for Roger first thing."

Kate quietly said, "Okay." She smiled at him on purpose. "Try to hurry."

Tom dragged Cabbage along as she tried to smell everything in the entire world to determine if any smells could be added to her library of smells. She had to make sure. Several intriguing smells smelled identical to doggie piddle, but she confirmed that she had smelled all these smells before, so they only needed smelling for thirty seconds or so apiece. "Come on, would you go?" Tom pleaded.

He soon found himself back in his tiny makeshift office away from the bedrooms. His dim lamp illuminated a scatter of papers which he kept shuffling to find the figures he needed. His computer screen glowed cold and indifferent and made his face look blue. Tom would type a little on his keyboard, and some pixels on his screen would turn from white to black, and he would type a little more, and a few more pixels would change color, and he would shuffle papers again, and he would type a little more and shuffle a little more. And across the house Hamlet would run and stop and run some more and stop some more.

When at last Tom left his office and made his way to the bedroom, he found Kate fast asleep. He was disappointed and glad at the same time. He wouldn't have to try to be anything for her. He decided to watch something on TV until he decided nothing was on and that he was far too tired to watch nothing anymore.

CHAPTER FIFTY-SEVEN

Here it is the new millennium, Tom thought, *a new era of progress and achievement—but instead of facilitating my work, my computer is making it stupider.*

For the moment, Tom's CAD software and an unfinished project sat idle, loitering around their virtual water cooler, whining to each other about how tough it was to not actually exist. Tom had no time for them because he had to wade through emails from customers making dumb requests. "How 'bout we bolt a full-size copy of the Hubble telescope onto our spot welder, in case we want to take pictures of ants in Manitoba? What do you mean, it will raise the cost?"

If it weren't for customers, work would be ideal.

Not five minutes after Tom shook his project awake again, a paper-clipped stack of 8½ x 11's landed by his keyboard. He turned to find Roger reclining his squishy hinder parts against his desktop. "Looks good, Tom. Nice work. Except I don't think this is gonna fly. Deltek is balking about the money."

"They already got back to you?"

"No, last week they started acting sketchy. I doubt they even glanced at that yet. Hope it doesn't scare them worse."

Tom paused a bit longer than expected. "I worked on it until ten-thirty last night. You said it was 'vital' for this morning."

"It was, sort of as a contingency. If we lose them it sure as heck won't be our fault."

Tom almost said it, but bit his tongue. He studied his pen for a moment. It looked pretty sharp.

If it weren't for customers and supervisors, work would be ideal.

Roger waddled off to go wheeze on another of his underlings, leaving Tom to wake up his straggling project again. He jiggled his mouse twice, three times, four times. He tapped a few random keys. Not even a system message popped up this time. Completely frozen. *Dang, I hope I hit 'Save' recently.* He forced a manual reboot.

If it weren't for customers, supervisors, and computers, work would be ideal.

As his computer crawled to life again, Tom saw his reflection in the blackness of the monitor. The curved screen made his nose look big, like Hamlet's.

I am Hamlet. I am Hamlet and this is my cage. I am trapped in this rectangle of glass, running and running and getting stinking nowhere. "Hey, Tom, why don't you do this super important project really late at night at your own house so we can feed it through the shredder first thing in the morning? You see, your cage is a lot bigger than this cubicle here. Your cage is everywhere.

You want five minutes of freedom? No way! Time to change a diaper—better yet: a blowout, so you can scrub the entire nursery. You want five extra bucks so you can buy a decent lunch? No way! Time to swap out the tranny on your wife's car. Maybe she should come to a stop before shifting into reverse. You want five percent more job satisfaction? No way! You're smart, but not enough to take over work from Don the Fluid Dynamics dropout: he's got seniority."

The screen finally turned blue, and Tom stopped gazing at his dim reflection to recline back and find the ceiling. *God, if you would just show up. Just do something. You put me here. Make it make sense.* The ceiling didn't answer.

"Busy, huh?" Tara strolled up.

Tom waved his pen toward the monitor. "Computer. Crashed again."

"Nice."

"I think it's powered by a hamster, somewhere inside. He gets awful tired. Needs a rest every so often."

"Ha ha. Like me on my run this morning," Tara said. "I felt it the whole time."

"Man, I hate that. You're not sick, are you?"

"No, I'm pushing it. I'm training for a marathon in August. Back home. My dad is doing it for like the hundredth time, and he wants me to run with him. It'll be my first."

"Gotta keep up with the old guy."

"No kidding. Does your dad run?"

"Never did. It wasn't his thing, I guess."

Tara sensed the implication. "Oh, is he…um…"

"Yeah. Died a few years ago. I didn't get running from him or Mom."

"I'm sorry. I didn't…"

"No worries." Tom changed the subject for her benefit. "I'm in training too. Same reason: can't let the old guys beat me. I am hoping to do Longs Peak."

Her mouth fell open. "*Run* Longs, you mean?"

He nodded a little, a bit sheepishly. "I'm gonna try to run the whole thing, up and down. It's not as far as a marathon. Not near."

"Tch. Yeah it is. Even if it weren't…" She laughed at him. "What on earth for, Tom? Are you insane?"

He swiveled in his chair to face her more directly. "Okay, so, the last time I hiked it, there's this skinny old guy practically jogging up the Homestretch. That's at the very top."

She acted slightly shocked. "I've been there."

"You know what it's like, then. The rest of us are hanging on for dear life, and this geezer comes loping up the Homestretch, upright on two legs, like some kind of mountain goat, not caring that one misstep and he's got a real long time to think about how many pieces his body's gonna be in. He passed all of us clambering up the cracks. He wore these vintage, 70's-looking running shoes, like his pair never wears out. Finally I summited, and he's up there *smoking*. He's at fourteen-thousand feet, where all these young bucks can barely breathe, and he's smoking an un-filtered cigarette. That's when I decided I would run it one day."

"You're insane."

"Maybe. But not an hour later on my way down I see these two ultra-runner-looking guys running up the Trough. Not jogging—running."

She shook her head in disbelief.

"I *know*." He winced his face. "So I decided I was gonna try it."

She moved to rest against his desk just like Roger had, but he didn't mind so much this time. *Not at all, really.*

"You said you've done marathons, right?" she said.

"A few."

"This will be way harder. *Way* harder."

Tom chuckled. "I know. I'm stupid."

"Yes, stupid." She cocked her head. "But I get it. I could use somebody stupid to push me a little in my training. It's so hard to stay motivated by myself when this marathon seems so far off. So—theoretical." She shrugged and drew a strand of hair behind her ear. It was blonde and cut so she could pull it back into a tiny ponytail, like an athlete. It framed her face nicely.

"You don't ever run with anybody?" he asked.

She shook her head.

"Me neither. Hardly ever. It's sort of a drag."

She brightened and sat up a bit straighter. "We could run together," she offered.

Something quickly knotted in him. He suddenly thought about the ring on his left hand. Almost wished he weren't wearing it. *Of course that doesn't matter; she must know I'm married.* Several things in him, all at once, started telling him to run. *Away*, not *With*. But something else, something a little darker, a little more selfish, told him, *It's fine. It's no big deal. It's nothing. She's just a co-worker.* That same dark thing didn't work very hard to ignore the image that popped into his head of how she must look in her running clothes. Her legs were about a mile long and lean and tan, and this moment her narrow hips were perched on his desk not three feet away from him, like a Fabergé egg on a spotlit pedestal in a museum somewhere. Somehow that image, as incongruous as it was with *no big deal* and *just a co-worker*, lingered all day like a song stuck in his head.

"Yeah, maybe." It just came out of his mouth, as if he were a ventriloquist's hideous dummy. "My schedule is pretty nuts, though. Finding a good time would be...you know." *Good save,* a part of him thought, though it had been an accident. He swallowed.

"Of course. Let me know," she said. "Well, I guess I should actually do a little work today. See ya, Tom." She vanished and he was safe. Except the song kept playing over and over, juxtaposed over his 3-D model on his monitor.

CHAPTER FIFTY-SIX

As if gravity was tilted in this one spot, Kate had to pause to straighten the same photo on the wall again. Had Tom cared whether the picture was always crooked, he already would have devised a permanent fix. Kate did care, but her mind never leapt quite that far.

The kids were down for their nap, though lately Abby was rarely sleepy enough to sleep; she lay quietly in bed because Mama made her. She wished Hamlet weren't sleepy so she could watch him play. Daddy was right: he did crawl under his stuff.

Kate stayed busy around the house. Somehow always busy. A family provided plenty to do. It would get worse in a few weeks when Abby resumed homeschool, especially since she would start big-girl school with real grades. Kate couldn't imagine schooling three at once; at least she had a few years to prepare.

Kate smiled at the picture, level again. Of course Cabbage looked distracted; cameras don't smell interesting at all. Baby Hannah didn't look terribly interested either, and her pretty Sunday dress had bunched up around her ears as an awful wad. Tom had argued for an outfit more practical for a baby. Of course he was right, but Kate didn't care—she still was glad Hannah wore a pretty dress. Hannah was the only true redhead among them, a real Irish girl. Tom's blonde mixed with Kate's auburn made sense in Hannah, and she got Kate's wide face and short nose. On the other hand, Abigail's golden braids made her look like a beautiful Viking princess; Kate thought they should get her a horned helmet and fur boots for Halloween. Abby acted how a princess ought: reflective and reserved, always looking out for the welfare of her people. Jacob had somehow landed brown hair from some branch in the family tree, though in the photo he was nothing but a twinkle in Tom's eye. None of them had any hope but to inherit brilliant blue eyes from both mom and dad.

Kate's eye fell on her own image with a little sigh of discontent. Even then she had already gotten much heavier. Ounce by patient ounce, she had grown. *And that was then…* she thought. *I've really gotta do something.*

Her eye shifted to Tom cradling Hannah. *Ah, I love that man. Still just as handsome. Still a great father. Moodier, maybe, but who isn't moody sometimes? A little too moody lately, perhaps. But he's under a lot of pressure, always so preoccupied with work.* Her brow subtly furrowed. *I miss him. He should be more preoccupied with me.*

PROLOGUE THREE

Tom Ericson had met Katherine Kiernan in a parking lot. She got out of a car, he did a double-take, and a miracle happened: he thought of something to say to a pretty girl, and he said it. "Hey, nice car."

After having earned his Bachelor's degree in Mechanical Engineering, a dearth of jobs and a surplus of debt convinced Tom that a stint in the Army Corps of Engineers would be an ideal way to further his education and reverse his financial situation. But he discovered too late that very few civilians need employees skilled at blowing up bridges and riding in trucks through the desert. He figured that returning to school for a Master's would be his best shot at a bright future.

His bright future first appeared in the form of a pretty redhead *(auburn)* who, besides turning heads, turned out to be pretty level-headed. Plus, she was outgoing, bubbly, popular, funny, entertaining, and a good, sweet person. And she owned the same junker model of car as he did.

Five years younger, she was flattered to receive attention from such a guy. Plenty of guys paid her attention, but usually just chumps with inch-deep one track minds. Tom, on the other hand, was mature, kind, disciplined, thoughtful, handsome, honest, hard-working, wanted to be with *her*, and best of all, a Christian from a good family. To the dismay of all the frat boys (though she never told them), she would only date demonstrably sincere Christians.

18

Things went well. Tom spent as much of his college money on Kate as on college, and his debt grew like fingernails: too slowly to notice, but eventually reaching a point when the realization struck him: *Houston, we have a problem.* In the meantime, however, she agreed to marry him. Things went well.

Because Tom felt like the oldest virgin on earth, he suggested they marry at Christmastime rather wait five additional plodding, brutal months until their graduation. Kate jumped aboard with starry eyes.

She declined to reenroll for her senior year so she could work and save up. It wasn't a huge loss; she was only a moderately talented art major studying in a program that mainly taught her how valuable her opinions on the world were and how to expose the world to those opinions in abstruse ways.

Kate landed a job somewhat related to her major, in that she worked as the receptionist for a medium-sized HR firm with a signed and numbered limited-edition print hanging on the lobby wall. This print had been signed by an artist with neither great talent nor anything valuable to express, and Kate was lucky enough to have #297 right there in her lobby for all her visitors to ignore.

Meanwhile, Tom toiled away over problems tough enough to flummox his teachers. Then, when the sun went down, he toiled away at a job which allowed him to transfer the stress from his brain to his lower back. He rarely had time enough to both sleep well and study well on the same day.

The wedding date drew near, and the happy couple effervesced with anticipation. Tom chugged antacids to counteract his diet of coffee, and Kate bubbled with excitement that her dream would soon come true.

She worked tirelessly planning her wedding—even at work, occasionally pausing to do her job. No one seemed to mind, for she was friendly and attractive and made people feel welcome and knew how to look up information in ring binders and could consistently make mediocre coffee. As always, she was universally well-liked. Fortunately she kept her job; she needed much of the money she was earning by dropping out of college to ensure their special day would provide a lifetime of precious memories.

Tom finished that fall semester just in time to rush to Stapleton Airport in order to wait for relatives on weather-delayed flights while his car accumulated hourly parking fees.

The wedding ceremony was to be held at Kate's church in Colorado Springs, her hometown since second grade. But first, everyone gathered at her parents' house to celebrate Christmas. With so many in town for the wedding, they had a wonderful, noisy, frenzied holiday. It was the first time the extended families were together. It would not be the last.

For Tom's side of the family, important social events always seemed to trigger important sewage events in distant places. When his dad's pager buzzed on the morning of Christmas Eve, they all groaned and shook their heads. Roland Ericson was the state's leading expert on wastewater treatment equipment. This time the failed facility was in the town of Craig, clear over in northwest Colorado.

As Roland was folding a few items into his suitcase, Tom's mother Maggie begged her husband not to leave. "Can't you wait a few days?"

"Nobody wants a stinky Christmas," he declared. "And it's only a five hour drive. So don't worry—I'll be back in time for the rehearsal, come hell or high water. If we can't fix it, I'll just point Craig in the right direction and get out."

"But you'll miss Christmas with the family," she whined.

"That doesn't bother me so much. Christmas is an annual event." He winked at her and chuckled. "Let's hope Tom's wedding isn't."

When at last his tenacity wore her down, she suddenly brightened. "Oh, darling! As long as you'll be up there anyway, you can swing by the house and pick up my dress."

Roland froze and glared at her. "Oh, no. Are you serious? That's a two-hour-long 'swing by the house.' Of all the things to forget to pack…"

"I know," Maggie whimpered. "I know. I didn't want it wrinkled. I remember right where I hung it. Please? There's no way I'll find another dress for Tom's wedding on Christmas Eve. Probably nothing's open anyway. Darling, *please?* And everyone's already here. And we can't *both* abandon the party. And darling—it's for *Tom's wedding*. Oh, please? It would mean so much."

When at last her tenacity wore him down, he agreed.

When no one had heard from Tom's father by the time of the rehearsal, the worst anyone assumed was he was late. No one knew he was dead.

Anxiety mushroomed into festering worry when he still hadn't shown up by the next morning, and the Craig facility reported that he'd already left. Regardless, they decided *the show must go on.*

Roland's absence overshadowed the wedding. Tom's mother neither smiled nor cried. Instead she incessantly and conspicuously glanced back toward the doors, expecting every moment to see a sheepish husband quietly slip in. Tom went through the wedding day motions, feebly trying not to worry. Kate's joy was stripped from her; though the ceremony was beautiful, she only saw the pain behind Tom's brave act, and she only heard echoes of Maggie's torment. Even the crowd felt the tension; the rumors had spread as they mingled beforehand, and no one failed to notice the groom's mother alone and upset.

Meanwhile, far to the north, the Fort Collins police got no response to their knock on Roland and Maggie's door out in rural Masonville, and their phone calls produced only an answering machine.

Not until many hours after the ceremony did policemen show up at the right door. After Tom called Craig and Fort Collins to report a missing person, word at last made its way to officials in Colorado Springs.

The long way round to pick up Maggie's forgotten dress proved to be the mistake; one for which she would long blame herself to the point of madness. The long way round led Roland, on the day after Christmas, over Cameron Pass, a place where winter liked to visit as early as August. He intersected a blinding white-out racing down from Wyoming. The next morning a plow operator discovered a lone vehicle in a trailhead parking lot with snow drifted up to the windows. A victim was inside, dead of carbon monoxide poisoning. The gas tank was dry. *He just went to sleep,* the grieving families were told, *He just woke up chilly, started the car, and went back to sleep.* It comforted, but only a little.

Tom and Kate missed their honeymoon in Cancun. No refunds were issued: not for airfare, not for hotel, not for rental car. Tom had missed the 24-hour cancellation deadline by several days; he tried to explain his distraction, but he learned that policy is policy.

He found himself strangely busy all week. Arranging a funeral involved way more than he would have expected. He had to do it all; his mother was more than incapable, she was incapacitated. His sister Emily simply wasn't the right person for the job.

Kate shuttled back and forth between her parents' home, his parents' home, and their new apartment in Boulder, where Tom determined to return in just a few days to finish his Master's degree.

They didn't even sleep in the same bed until four days after their wedding; several more before they did so like married people. At first they could only hold each other and cry or fall immediately into exhausted sleep.

It was Tom's first funeral. It wasn't his favorite. Already all cried out, he watched the whole thing, expressionless, from the bottom of a well a thousand miles deep. He was glad his mom and sister and Kate were there. He was glad he was there, mainly so he could be there for his mom. Most other people were unnecessary. He felt terribly awkward, like the star of a show for which he was unprepared, a show neither he nor his audience wanted to attend. He had no words to exchange for all the words self-conscious people struggled to produce for him—the comfort pills they had to hand him so he wouldn't add their names to the *People Who Are Heartless Jerks* list. Many quoted to him Bible verses he already knew, platitudes; they might as well have opened fortune cookies and tucked the little strip of paper into his suit pocket.

The open casket had been a bad idea; he didn't need a portrait of some sleeping person—a wax sculpture of some *thing* supposed to resemble his father—burned into his brain. His father wasn't there; his father was gone. He had lost his father in a parking lot.

CHAPTER FIFTY-FIVE

The Ericson family left for church in *The Haitian Wagon*—Tom's nickname for Kate's car—a hospital-green 1984 station wagon with fake wood paneling. Except it wasn't quite a station wagon; it was an econobox with an extended interior instead of a trunk.

Perfect for trapping heat on summer days like today, Tom thought as he backed out of the driveway. Both their cars sat outside all year because somebody had converted their garage into a dining room. *Helps us remember the three times we tried to fix the air conditioning. If Thanksgiving were in August, we could handle all the turkeys in the neighborhood.*

This was the very car from which Kate had emerged when he first saw her. This had been advantageous for Tom, for it gave him something to say to her: he had the exact same car (except his was white, lacked the wood-toned vinyl stickers along the sides, and had a real trunk). They joked that the cars were a sign they were made for each other. How else would a grad student in engineering and a junior art major ever meet on a sprawling campus? Except now, years later, both cars threatened to come to their demise at the same time, leaving family members stranded at opposite ends of town, perhaps forever, without enough money between them to dream of a new car.

By the time they rolled into the parking lot of Powder River Community Church, they all were sweating profusely. Coby alone didn't seem to mind; he kept wiping sweat from his forehead with his fingers and putting them in his mouth. The kids looked as if their adorable outfits—ready for military inspection just moments before—had been used by a family of marmots as the lining of their burrow all winter. All except fussy little Abby, who issued plaintive remonstrations each time Coby brushed the tip of his drooly finger against her finery.

Reflections of the morning sun glinted off the parked cars, and small groups of stragglers streamed between them toward the sanctuary. *Running late,* Tom thought. *Shocker. Making sure the children look their best requires a great deal of emergency preparation. Every stinking week.* At last they found a parking space, seemingly closer to Wyoming than to the church.

Kate worked to get Hannah out of her booster seat; apparently the harness had been designed to be child and gorilla proof. Tom untangled Jacob from his car seat, threw him in the crook of his arm, put on his game face, and made for the sanctuary. Abby was last out because she had to sit in the middle because she could fasten her own belt; she had to jog to catch up.

Dave the garrulous greeter met them in the foyer. Beyond him, group singing sounded through the main auditorium doors. He stretched out a hand to Tom. "Hey, Doubting Thomas. How's the family today?"

"Hey, Adulterous King David. Couldn't be better." Tom switched Jacob to his left arm and shook his hand. He wore a believable smile. Kate was glad for at least that.

Dave reeled a moment, then he brightened and pointed at Tom. "Ah, gotcha. Adulterous King David. Yes. Ha, ha!"

They split up, Tom for the nursery, Kate for the Sunday school rooms. They rejoined at the usual spot and headed into the auditorium, finding once again that parking spaces furthest from the auditorium also meant seats closest to the stage. They self-consciously made their way to front and center right under the worship leader's nose, who took the time while singing and strumming to nod at them.

Church was good. Mostly it was much the same as before, Tom noticed, with Pastor Mark talking a lot about God and faith and stuff, but overall it was good. The air was on nice and high. Nevertheless, Tom's mind drifted. *Since we're always the people who arrive late, why can't we also be the people who get to leave early?*

At last it ended. Tom waited under the sun in a somewhat oblique proximity to Kate as she chatted with friends. *I'd even be okay with leaving when the service is over.* Kate inevitably ran into Megan or Shawnda or Natalie or Pam, and Tom would wait, and Kate would eventually interrupt herself to remind him to go get the kids so the nursery workers could come stand around and talk to Kate and Megan and Shawnda and Natalie and Pam.

After Tom retrieved the kids, he allowed the girls to run around the courtyard though they would end up soaked through with sweat, and he shuffled little Coby, who was like holding a toaster, from arm to arm until he could bear it no longer. He finally escaped to the air-conditioned foyer at the risk of getting cornered by Dave, who never seemed to have anywhere to go after church, and who always had plenty to say. He kept one impatient eye on Kate through the glass door.

At last Kate came and rescued him. "You ready to go?"

As if I could possibly want to finish our gripping conversation about ice fishing in Wyoming. Tom grinned apologetically at Dave. "Sorry, gotta run."

Kate and Tom hunted the girls for about ten minutes. They found them back in the nice cool sanctuary darting about like greased pigs through an obstacle course made of brittle old ladies.

They easily found their car in the now sparse parking lot. *It's never too hard,* Tom thought. *Ours is the only hospital-green car left in any first-world countries. Even junkyard owners paint them to avoid dragging down their property value.*

"You know," Tom mentioned as they neared home after church, "it would be a lot easier to have faith if God would sometimes do something that made it seem like he were there."

Kate stared a moment, processing what she heard. "What brought this on?"

"Nothing, really, I guess. Or everything. Like this piece of junk we drive. I'm thankful and all that it still runs, and that we have a car—some people don't even have that—but if we prayed for a new car (not 'new' new, just new to us), and God actually did it, you know, somehow miraculously, we would say, 'Wow, there sure is a God, isn't there?' But we pray for, you know, ten bucks, so we can buy diapers, and we get nothing. Not that God is obligated or anything, but it would be nice, once in a while."

"Tom, he comes through all the time. When's the last time any of your kids went a day without food?"

"True. I know. But I'm talking about something really—different. It doesn't even have to be about money; I know there's more to life than money." Tom chuckled with a timid grin. "It would just be sort of reassuring if God would just—*Pow!* One time. 'Here you go guys, here's a blessing that could only come from me'."

"I see that all the time in our lives. Each other. The kids. Your job. Where we live. Even being forgiven is a miracle. Especially that."

"Yeah, I know." Tom shrugged. "But could you really tell some atheist that you're convinced there's a God because you have kids? Or because you think you're forgiven? Lots of people have kids and jobs. What does that prove?"

"It is not about proof, Tom," she said sharply. "It is about faith. That's the whole point." She studied him. "What's bugging you? What Pastor said?"

"What did he say?"

"Mama?" Abby said quietly.

"One minute, baby. That we don't have to know why God does what he does; instead we trust who he is. That faith is a choice. That it isn't easy. That the choice is what pleases him."

"Why, though? Why does God want people to force themselves to believe something that doesn't seem true? Every religious nut goes that far."

"Why is this so hard for you, Tom?" she said harshly. "Does it not seem true? Maybe you've been around truth so much that it's dead to you. People come to Christianity because it's got answers their religions don't. You were born in it; you must be taking it for granted."

"You don't have to get upset about it."

"I'm not upset. I just don't understand what you're talking about."

"Mama?" Abby said quietly.

"One minute, baby. Tom, really. It doesn't seem true?"

"That's not what I said. Hold on, let's at least get inside."

He pulled into their narrow driveway. His white car was on the street, along the stretch of curb void of tree shadows. They maneuvered the kids out of the car. Cabbage happily met them at the door, squirming around and blocking Tom from getting through the door as he awkwardly lugged Coby in his car seat. A few minutes later the kids were situated, and Kate met Tom as he donned cooler clothes.

"You did say 'it doesn't seem true'."

"Are you wanting to fight? Gosh, Kate, I'm just asking questions."

"No. No. I just want to know what you're saying."

"Well then let me just say it, and don't tell me what I said. All I'm saying is I wish God didn't feel as if He always has to be so sneaky and invisible, so our faith is this big deal, this hard thing we have to try and *do*. Shouldn't we believe the things we do because they make sense, instead of forcing ourselves to believe them because we're scared to do otherwise?"

"So, Christianity doesn't make sense to you?"

"Dang it, Kate, that's not what I'm saying. I'm just…"

"Then stop saying it if it's not what you're saying."

"Hold on. Hold on and let me finish. Stop being so defensive all the time. I just had a thought, that's all. I wanted…"

"All the time, Tom? Gimme a break. Look who's talking."

"I'm not trying to fight about it. Why the heck are you upset? What did I do?"

"Mama?" sounded quietly from the hallway. It went unheard.

"I don't understand you, Tom. Right in front of the kids you're acting like there's no God or something. What do you think that'll do for their faith?"

"*Their* faith? What? They believe in Santa Claus, for crying out loud. We're talking about real things here, but you wanna make this a bad thing I'm doing. I'm the bad parent. As usual it's my fault."

"Oh, yes, suddenly it's all about you. Are you all you see? You always…"

And on and on it went, and it went nowhere at all, and it helped no one. Especially Abby, who quietly closed the door to her room and laid on her bed, not even glancing at Hamlet though he ran and ran on his little wheel.

CHAPTER FIFTY-FOUR

"I guess you ran it, huh?" Tom said.

Tara gingerly made her way toward her desk on a Monday morning. She grinned broadly back at him. "That bad, huh? I'm trying not to waddle. I almost called in sick."

"It's weird, huh? It hurts just the same no matter how you walk; seems like you could just walk normally. So how'd you do?"

"Twenty-six point two. Not very fast, but under my own power."

"Congratulations."

She gave him a sly look. "Two seconds in front of my dad."

"Nice. Time to start training for the next one."

"Aw, don't say that." Tara grimaced as she lowered herself into her office chair. "Not unless you'll help me figure out how to train, like you promised."

"Uh…" Tom started.

"My dad is probably dancing around this morning. He's amazing."

"That's good." Tom nodded, his eyes distant.

"What about you? You do your Longs run?"

"Yeah. I summited. I made a good time, but I couldn't run the whole thing. It was too hard. Kicked my butt."

"You're not even limping."

He shrugged. "I feel all right today. I thought I might be able to actually run everything but the sketchy parts…"

"Oh, the places where people fall to their deaths? Just those?"

"Yeah." He chuckled. "I thought maybe I'd slow down there. But I basically oozed up the Homestretch. I had no pride left in me at that point. I did run down though, starting at the Ledges. I was completely blown by the time I got to the car. I just slept in the driver's seat for like half an hour. Didn't even bother to eat first."

"You're awesome. I would have just laid down and died. How are you not sore?"

"No, I'm sore, all right."

"Barely."

He waved it off nonchalantly. "It's in the preparation."

She threw up her hands. "You said you were going to help me. Really, I mean it. I would totally run with you if you just name the time. I'm completely free."

Yeah, well I'm not, he thought. "We'll figure it out."

CHAPTER FIFTY-THREE

Cabbage was always first to know when Tom got home. Kate spied her wiggling by the front door, and she paused her chopping to wait for him. The door opened, and Tom squeezed past Cabbage and smiled at Kate. "Hi, honey."

"How 'bout that? You're on time for dinner again."

"I know. It's crazy, huh?"

Well, he's in a good mood, thought Kate.

He made his way around the delaminating laminate countertop to give her a cordial peck. She received it, holding her knife and messy hands out of the way.

"Brought you guys something. This for you." He revealed a long-stemmed rose and held it toward her.

"Aww. So sweet." She smiled at him, then gestured toward a cupboard. "You'll have to—uh—my hands…"

"Yeah, oh, hold on. Where's the girls?" He glanced toward the hall.

"Playing. How's your day?"

"Okay, I guess." He shrugged. "Wait 'til they see what I found at the thrift store. There were no jackets my size except dork jackets, but check this out." He laid the rose on the counter, then held up a large cloth sack and opened it for her to peer in.

"Oh, toys."

"Not just toys—*Legos!* Real ones. Only ten bucks for this whole bagful."

"Ten dollars! Tom! For *that?* Geez!"

"Do you know how much all these are worth? Some idiot just *left them there.* It's like I stole them."

"Daddy!" came a pair of voices from down the hallway. Not a moment later his legs were bombarded by huggy girls. He hoisted the sack up out of their view and bent to kiss them.

After dinner he gathered the kids in the girls' room and prepared them for his presentation. The girls waited with bright-eyed anticipation while Coby started to crawl back out into the hallway. Tom wore a Cheshire Cat grin as he dumped the Legos out into the middle of the floor.

Abigail's eyes lit up. Hannah looked bewildered as she knelt to inspect them. The clatter made Jacob turn and look, and he slowly wheeled around and made his way back.

"They're Legos."

"What's Legos, Daddy?" Hannah said.

"Toys. You build stuff with 'em."

"What stuff?" Abby asked.

"Anything you want. Everything in the world."

"Okay," Abby said thoughtfully.

"JACOB, NO!" Tom cried out. He grabbed up Coby and fished five slimy pieces out of his mouth. "Not in your mouth."

Coby immediately grabbed another piece and aimed for his sinkhole. Tom deflected it. Coby glared angrily at Tom and grabbed another piece.

"You can play, just not in your mouth."

Coby turned his face away from his father and tried inserting another one.

Tom took it away again. "I guess this was a bad idea." He rose and scooped up Coby, set him in the hall, and closed the door between them. Angry screaming immediately came through the door. "He'll choke to death," Tom explained to a worried Abby.

"Look Daddy, a fow'er," Hannah said. She had a few pieces arranged on the carpet in what she thought must look like a flower.

"You're supposed to stick them together, like this." Neither daughter glanced at his example. Abby was busy trying to get her Barbie to cradle a little Lego astronaut in her arms. "Is that her baby?" Tom asked.

"Yes. His name is William."

At that Hannah bounced over and grabbed William. "I need dat."

Abby cried "Daddy?" her eyes pleading.

"Hann, Abby's right. She was playing with that."

Hannah frowned and scooted away with William.

"Hannah, give that back to your sister, right now. There's probably twenty more people in the pile; you can find your own."

"I need dis one," Hannah asserted.

"What's wrong with Coby?" Kate's voice sounded through the door.

"He's trying to eat them. He'll choke. Hannah, give that to Abby. Abby, hang on a sec."

Hamlet started running on his wheel.

The door opened to Kate with Jacob in the crook of her arm. "What am I supposed to do with him?"

"I don't know. Just stick him in his crib or something. He can't play in here." He raised his voice. "Hannah!"

Kate closed the door and Coby's wailing receded.

Tom fanned his fingers through the pile in search for another person. "Hannah, look. There's got to be more in here. Now give me the astronaut." He snatched it from her and tossed it back toward Abby. "Look for your own person."

Hannah stood and kicked the pile, shooting pieces into every nook and cranny. "Okay, you're done too. Out!" He pointed at the door.

Hannah flopped onto the floor and cried. Tom picked her up by her shorts and hauled her into the hallway, leaving her in a heap on the floor. She wailed dramatically.

With the door shut again, Abby triumphantly had the whole room to herself. She sat cross-legged and returned William to Barbie's arms. Meanwhile, Tom scoured the room for all the scattered pieces, so Coby wouldn't play chipmunk with them later. In a few moments Tom glanced over to find William's legs sticking sideways out of Barbie's shirt.

"Oh, gosh, Abby. What's he doing now?"

"He's hungry, Daddy, like Coby does."

Tom looked defeated. "Now Abby, he can't—oh, gosh. At least take his helmet off. Poor guy. Listen, Abby. Um…"

"William," Abby said sternly, mimicking her mother, "stop fooling around and eat."

"Well, you know…" Tom muttered. Then louder, "Okay, Abby. He's done now. Let's find all these pieces and make something. C'mon. Put baby William down now."

Ten minutes was all Tom could tolerate. All Abigail made was a "diaper bag" out of two mismatched bricks. She added a Lego policeman and race car driver to the family, and the daddy ended up being a lop-sided teddy bear who left for work while Barbie homeschooled the kids.

CHAPTER FIFTY-TWO

"No team has a shot against them, as long as this kid keeps it up." Barry leaned against the break room counter stirring a coffee. His coworker Kevin grunted and took a sip.

"What's that? What kid?" asked Tom, approaching with his empty cup.

"Holy smoke, Tom," said Kevin. "You crawl out from under a rock?"

"What? Why?" said Tom.

"He's this new fullback," said Barry, "and he's nuts. Some Hispanic kid, Henry Caravaggio or something."

"It's not Caravaggio," mumbled Kevin.

"Caravaggio was an artist," Tom added. "Italian."

"Whatever. Henry Something."

"What school?" said Tom.

"Poudre High."

"Of course." Tom rolled his eyes. "Ugh."

"What?"

"I went to Rocky."

"That's right, you grew up here, didn't you?" asked Kevin.

Tom nodded.

Kevin added, "He's not exactly new; he got moved from linebacker this season. Their star graduated, and the backup hurt himself this summer, rock climbing or something stupid."

"Anyway, he was a brutal tackler," Barry said, "but now he's killing it as a running back. He's in the paper every week. I guess he always played defense, but they just tried him out. He ran over a hundred yards his first time out."

"I hate it," said Kevin. "My son John plays DE for Fossil Ridge, and I had to sit there and watch this kid either crush him into the ground or make him look like a fool, hugging air. He's real good. Two-hundred yard games every week."

"He's like six-four, but runs like a rabbit," said Barry.

"Defenders are scared of him. Sometimes he'll juke and then run right through the poor tackler anyway, like it's fun. He toys with them."

Barry said, "Well, he's a senior, so he's gone next year anyway. My neighbor Charlie is on coaching staff at CSU, and he says they're already gunning for him. If he keeps it up, he'll get a scholarship there, or CU, Boise State, anywhere."

"Shoot, I don't even—" Kevin paused and motioned with his head toward the doorway, "—really, uh, think that tools like that can be ready in less than a month. I'll check to see if GSC has any bandwidth."

Their manager Roger stepped into the break room. "Hey, fellas. Mornin'."

"Hey, Roger."

"Hi."

"Mornin.' Well, I…"

The three engineers nonchalantly headed out toward their desks.

CHAPTER FIFTY-ONE

"Tom?" He felt a feather come to rest on his shoulder. Kate's voice was soft and fragile behind him. "Tom, baby?"

"Yeah?" He sat like a stone.

"I'm sorry. I'm so sorry. I know you're mad. I deserve it." She waited a little while for him to do something. "I just want you to forgive me. I'm so sorry."

Of course, there she goes again, he thought. She was usually first to do the right thing, to resolve it, to make him feel bad, to make him feel like a jerk. Sure he was still mad. They'd had another brawl. She had jumped all over him about some other thing. *She just needs to suffer a while. She needs to learn.* Immediately something inside accused him. Here she was doing the right thing. She was trying to be humble, to apologize, even though he had jumped all over her just as much. It had been over something stupid. Bread crumbs, if he remembered correctly.

Not really. It had been over dozens of unresolved bitternesses toward one another, bitternesses which arose because they were both human—pathetic, self-centered, arrogant humans who let something like bread crumbs drive them to cruelty to each other, cruelty toward the human who loved them the most—or who at least was *supposed* to love them the most.

It's not like I can help being human. It's not like I signed up for it. God just expects me to act like something I'm not.

Another thought materialized in his brain, but it was so foreign to his own thoughts, it seemed to enter from outside. *You sure expect Kate to act like something she's not. You have no trouble holding her accountable for her actions, though you have no shortage of excuses for your own.*

And here she was: being nice first. *Dammit, Kate.* He wouldn't cuss out loud in front of her; she wouldn't like it. Yet, how many damnable words had he enjoyed stabbing into her just two hours earlier, words such as *two-faced* and *parasite?* But he wouldn't speak aloud a certain word she didn't enjoy—a word he wasn't even sure was a real cuss word— because he didn't want her to think him a bad person. *Who's the two-face, Tom? You hypocrite. You liar.* Tom tensed, fighting it. *You strain at a gnat and swallow a camel.*

He turned and glanced up at her for half a second, for as long as he could bear. Her eyes were red and puffy. "I'm sorry, too," came out of him, almost mechanically. *How many times will we go through this drill? How can she trust I really mean it? For that matter, how can I trust her? We'll do it again, no doubt.* He took a breath and held it for a second. "I need you to forgive me, too."

She started bawling and took his hand. "I love you so much, Tom. I'm so sorry." She stood shaking and wiping her eyes. He felt an odd little satisfaction, as if somehow he won. Then a word rang out inside him: *Pride.*

You aren't winning, you're losing.

"Can I hug you?" she sobbed. "Please?"

He rose to his feet and allowed a hug. She laid her head on him and shook. He started to break a little. Genuine love, genuine compassion, began to stir in him. He really had hurt her. He didn't even know why. He pulled her close. *Poor thing. Why am I always such a jerk?* Finally he squeezed her tightly.

She could tell he meant it.

CHAPTER FIFTY

Kate was puttering in her bedroom when suddenly she felt hands sliding around her from behind. "Oooh, who is this?" she said with a coy little smile. She felt her hair moved to one side and a delicate kiss by her ear. She tilted her head to receive kisses ambling down the side of her neck. She closed her eyes and slowly exhaled. Tom paused and retreated to close and lock the bedroom door.

"The kids are up," she whispered.

"Coby's down. The girls are playing. It's fine."

He returned to face her, started kissing her ear, her jaw, her neck, descending. Their pulses quickened. They soon were hindering each other as they hastily battled her tricky, recalcitrant buttons.

At that moment Hannah screamed out, immediately followed by a loud crash, then utter silence—the utter silence every parent knows is worse than intentional crying. "This is gonna be bad," Kate said.

Abby's wail began. Soon it reached the level of a tornado siren, even with a closed door between them.

Tom growled, "God, are you kidding me?" It was a real prayer, albeit not a very respectful one. He did not look happy. Kate quickly restored her blouse as she followed Tom out the door and down the hall.

They entered the girls' room to find Hannah terrified and staring, pressing herself back into the corner, howling, face red, tears gushing. As soon as her parents appeared she cried out, "I didn't do it."

Abby sat on the floor opposite from Hannah, by the toy box. The tornado siren issued from somewhere inside her. Blood streamed down her face, into her left eye, down her shirt, onto the carpet.

Both parents rushed to kneel by Abby, who looked up at them with her unbloodied eye. She immediately screamed something unintelligible and pointed straight at Hannah. Her blond hair on the left was filling with red. In a flash, Tom had the odd, detached thought that Abby's long hair, due to its immense surface area and its adhesion to viscous liquids, was probably keeping most of the blood off the carpet. He scooped her up and carried her across the hall to the tub. Kate followed.

"Get some rags," Tom said without taking his eyes off of Abby. "Clean washcloths or something. Make sure they're clean." Kate didn't budge, but stared with both her hands over her mouth. Tom turned, caught her eye, and commanded, "Get some clean washcloths. Now!" Kate vanished. Abby continued to wail.

Kate quickly returned and knelt by Tom. He snatched a cloth from her, located the gusher in Abby's scalp, and applied direct pressure.

"Ow, Daddy! Ow, Daddy!" Abby kicked her legs, thumping the tub.

"Tom, careful," Kate pleaded.

"Trust me, okay Kate?" Then, more gently, "Abigail, you need to be still. Please hold still, baby."

Hannah's screaming remained constant. The sound of Coby's cry rose to join the other two.

Tom said, "Go do something with Hann. She's freaking out."

Kate went and gathered up Hannah into her lap. Still terrified, Hannah kept repeating, "I didn't do it. I didn't do it." At last Coby grew the loudest wail in the house. Kate went to retrieve him, reappearing into the girls' room with him in her arms. Like a mother, she had an uncanny strength to also lift Hannah in one smooth motion and to gently rock both of them, alternately kissing both of their heads. "It's okay. Abby's gonna be fine. It's okay. It's okay."

Tom appeared in the doorway holding several towels, two of them soaked with cold water. "Abby says Hann hit her with the music box."

Hannah panicked and shrieked again, "I didn't do it."

Tom glared at her and barked, "Hannah, stop it. Stop lying." He turned to the toy box and pointed toward the floor near it. "Yep, there." Lying among several toys strewn about, the music box lay with its lid wrenched back and its mirror broken. It was large—a rectangle about six inches wide, and heavy—solid walnut enclosing a cast metal mechanism. Tom dumped the towels on the carpet by the blood spots. "Kate, you need to work on those spots right away." He hurried back to the bath.

———————

Abby specifically asked for Mama to accompany her into the room with the doctor. She didn't know where the stitches were on a person, but one time Mama had to fix the stitches on her stuffed bear, so Mama must be good at it.

Daddy spent the evening in the ER waiting room supervising the other kids, a wall of glass panes separating him from Kate and Abigail. Coby squirmed a good deal and practiced his repertoire of cries. Hannah calmed down sufficiently to want to climb everything. After what seemed the life cycle of a redwood, Abby and Mom reappeared. Abby wore an embarrassed grin and a shaved spot above her hairline with a white bandage taped onto it.

When they made it home at last, Kate began soaking Abby's hair to remove the dried blood. As Tom passed by the girls' room, he found the towels where he left them and the blood spots now feeling quite at home. "Aww, Kate!" he called. "Now look. Dang it, Kate!"

Incredibly, they had both fallen out of the mood.

CHAPTER FORTY-NINE

Abigail was not a Viking princess for Halloween—only a regular fairy-tale princess. Though she didn't know what a Viking was, she did not want to be one: apparently they don't wear pink clothes or elegant plastic tiaras. In the end she had to leave her tiara at home because it either hurt her healing wound or slipped down over her eyes, but she was brave and didn't cry over it, just like a Viking princess.

Hannah was a ladybug, a spotted red ball topped by a smaller black ball with a circular hole for her face, just big enough to look like an olive giving birth to a toddler. This was crowned by springy antennae with lights on the ends that whirled around with the slightest movement, and few of Hannah's movements were slight.

Jacob was a candy bar with arms, though he didn't exactly care and wasn't allowed to eat candy yet anyway. Later they would trade his Halloween windfall for animal crackers, which he would undoubtedly liquefy in his mouth and fling on the curtains.

Kate was sort of a cat, though her costume had been last-minute; it came into being by popular demand from the girls and consisted of nothing but black clothes, eye-liner whiskers, and crooked paper triangles for ears that refused to stand up. The girls said she made a perfect, beautiful cat just like a real cat. Kate said she wished she had a handsome Tomcat of her own.

Instead, Tom went dressed as a father of three, complete with umbrella stroller, diaper bag, flashlight, extra coats, and a really heavy ladybug on his shoulders who was tired of walking, but who kept insisting she didn't want to fly away home.

In November, Tom began occasionally running with Tara during lunchtime. He told himself he was only coaching her—though she ran capably with little need of coaching. The colder weather meant she ran in tight black pants, hiding her legs ever so slightly, which the two halves of Tom found either an advantage or a disadvantage. She had been "accidentally" brushing against him from time to time, but somehow these slight touches were occurring more frequently and were becoming less slight.

Kate and Tom couldn't choose whether to be lovers or fighters. She slowly improved at showing him unearned gentleness and respect, but it generally went unnoticed. More and more he viewed her through a lens of his own design, obscuring the person that loved him, loved his children, was kind to others, and worked to make life good for her family—but magnifying her whining, her neediness, her spending, her defensive little half-truths, her hypocrisy, her short temper, her impatience, her nagging. Yet Tom had a rose-colored filter for himself, making every bloodied thing appear clean and white. He became the nobly suffering victim, the deserving but deprived. And despite his acute introspection, his filter blocked him from seeing who actually built his dissatisfaction, brick by brick.

Thanksgiving landed Tom, his family, and his mom at his sister Emily's apartment in Denver.

Perhaps *apartment* was not the right word: bigger than Tom's house, it overlooked the snow-dusted high peaks of the Front Range from the twenty-sixth floor. His brother-in-law Jonathan had dropped out of college to start some random software business with a friend and had made his first clean million within three years.

Although Jonathan's bank ledger would hardly notice a debit for Thanksgiving dinner for five adults and three tiny kids, Kate insisted on bringing half the food. Tom was on edge the entire time, his kids every moment threatening to leave a smudge on some pristine surface somewhere. But Hannah was discontent with mere smudges—instead she careened into a lamp and sent it through the glass top of the coffee table. Of course Tom insisted on replacing them both, though either of them appeared to be worth more than his car.

In early December, Tara finally found the nerve to make a real pass at Tom. It came in the form of an unmistakably intentional, lingering touch, and a sultry hint about how lunchtime is too short and that they should consider getting together later.

Tom failed. He should have slammed the door on her, cut her off, made it impossible for her to want him. He didn't. For opposite reasons, both halves of him filled with anguish, leaving him indecisive and uncommunicative. He intended to discourage her, but his phantom response left the door wide open and the conflagration inside him raging.

Tara: the mysterious forbidden, the untrodden ground to explore, the ego builder, the inflamer. All Tom knew of her was paint and flash, those things easy to maintain for a half hour per day. He blinded himself to the immense likelihood that a willing adulteress hid a dark center that could swallow Kate's own imperfections like an abyss. Too often he told himself that marrying Kate had been a mistake; he was fool enough to believe his self-indoctrination, and blind enough to overlook the wound from which his happiness was hemorrhaging: the inside of his own head.

CHAPTER FORTY-EIGHT

The hard drive was the first insult of the day. The drive home was the worst insult of the day. Tom's pessimistic prediction turned out false: his car didn't die the same day as Kate's, it died the same day as his work computer. His failed hard drive took with it two sizable projects not retrievable from backup.

Other insults quickly followed. The bosses surprised the company with news about Christmas bonuses: *Out of the question this year.* Then, in an unsurprising display of paranoid psychotic scapegoating, Tom's supervisor Roger called him into his office and chewed him out, essentially blaming him for the company's poor performance. If the office was glum, Tom was glummer.

After work, under threatening skies, Tom ran an errand to return a Christmas present he had purchased with his soon-to-come bonus money. Stepping back outside, he found the parking lot already half white with snow.

At last, while heading home on an increasingly dangerous I-25, a tremendous squeal under the hood killed his car. He precariously threaded his way through heavy traffic and coasted to a stop on the shoulder, the corner of his rear bumper toeing the line of the freeway, taunting other drivers to be inattentive. A couple turns of the key made clear the car was dead. Wisps of smoke escaped from the seams of the engine bay. Fat snowflakes clung to his windshield and quickly turned to water. Tom brooded, impatiently waiting for something to go right. His inner voice took its stand, furious.

What now, God? Can't you go one week without piling on some new headache? So what's your point?

Tom slapped the steering wheel three times and shouted a curse, then he threw himself back in his chair and stared through the headliner.

They keep blathering on that you're working some good. If so, I guess having wheels isn't part of that plan anymore.

Oh—except the one, big, meaningless wheel I can't get rid of, the hamster wheel that is this worthless life. Well, I'm not interested.

He groaned and threw his hands onto his forehead. After several seconds he relaxed, staring at nothing, slowly shaking his head.

You know, if you care at all whether I believe that you care at all, you could try doing something that makes it seem like it.

A fierce glower appeared.

Or maybe it's just that you get your kicks jabbing at all your little test animals through their cages. You love seeing the fear in their eyes.

So is that your point? To keep me trapped in this cage? Trapped in this stupid car, trapped in that stupid job, worst of all, trapped in my own stupid self with my own stupid brain that can't find a way out of this stupid pit I've dug myself.

Tom paused and took a lingering glance through the glass at the traffic speeding by. A semi flew past, and it rocked his car with a wave of air.

Or, I guess—not 'necessarily' trapped in my stupid self. Not if I end it.

Tom froze, stunned by his own suggestion: by its immediate feasibility, by its attractiveness, by how smoothly it offered its hand to him.

To Be or not to Be... He swallowed. *That's what the stupid hamster would ask. We all die in the end anyway; how does it matter whether it's in fifty years or fifty seconds? At least—I think it doesn't. But maybe it does. Can I even make myself not—Be?*

He stared blankly through the blur of vehicles.

No doubt Kate and the kids would be better off without me. At least after the—the bad—the gut-wrenching time I would put them through wears off. It always wears off.

Tom exhaled through clenched teeth. He leaned his head back on the headrest.

I can't do that to them. I'm not that much of a snake; not quite. So God's using them to keep me trapped. His plan for me is to dump every last ounce of my time and energy into all this nonsense. It's such a waste. All of it. And nothing to look forward to.

Well, I don't want it. You can have it back. Life's supposed to be a blessing, but I hate it. Just end it. You'd do a better job at taking care of my family than I am anyway—if taking care of them is something you care about.

So just kill me.

Tom shook his head almost imperceptibly.

But God won't do it. That's for sure. And I won't kill myself because I've got them. And of course they're sticking around. I can't get untrapped.

It's not even their fault they exist; it's mine. Or God's. Why did he even make us? If he wanted me to be a hero, why didn't he make me somebody else? I'm not even a decent husband or father. I'm certainly no hero. Not like Kate; everyone just adores her. But they don't get it; her brightness starts to wear off after you live with it a while. Or it starts to burn out your retinas.

Oh, and apparently, I'm also not a decent employee. I'm the guy who blows everybody's Christmas bonus because I'm so stupid I respond to customers with honest numbers.

Well, thanks, sir. Exactly the job satisfaction I was shooting for.

Yeah, I was gonna be big stuff, do big important things, change the world. But no. Trapped in the endless nightmare of the American Dream.

No—nightmare isn't the right word. Nightmares have significance; they shake you. Instead I am dragged awake by an alarm every day: 'I must have dreamed something. I can't remember for sure.'

Oh yeah, dreams. 'Follow your dreams,' they tell you. 'It's your life. Do what you love. Never settle.' Yeah, right. It's inspiring 'til you watch your unfollowed dreams shrink to a pinpoint on the horizon.

'I wanna explore Antarctica!'

Sorry, you've got a family to feed.

'I wanna live under a bridge!'

Can't do that either.

'How about the dream of investing a penny a year in some kind of future? Or the dream of not existing at all?'

Sorry, pal.

Tom gave the steering wheel one more slap.

Why did I sign up for this? I never dreamed of—of this. What did I dream? I don't even know. But it felt big, important, fulfilling. But along the way, I guess I assumed marriage was my predetermined role, the thing people automatically do, like breathing. I wasn't smart enough to think through what it really meant: prison.

Yeah, that's better: it's not a nightmare, it's a prison. You can never choose: When to eat. Where to go. What to do. It's all about what you're not allowed to do. No escape, no way out. I volunteered for prison.

What was I seeking? I could have skipped the ball and chain. I could have taken a hint from the phrase 'ball and chain.' Why did I need Kate in the first place?

Cleavage. Idiot.

Our mindless, inescapable need to ensure our race's survival deludes into thinking us that we'll be fulfilled if we sign up for bondage. And we find someone willing to trade her body for a lifelong meal ticket. 'Hey, Mister! You lookin' for a good time? Well, you gotta pay for it.' And pay for it you will, the rest of your life.

Yep. Can't live with 'em, can't live without 'em. You sure find that out the hard way. Sucker.

And there's plenty who'll give it to you for free.

Tom lifted his head and stared through the windshield into the darkness.

There's plenty who'll give it to you for free.

Just then, right on time, God sent an atheist to crash Tom's pity party. Almost literally. A car skimmed past him onto the shoulder and slid to a crooked stop. It was a junker, mostly blue but with one white fender. Out jumped a young man, maybe college aged, wearing shorts and a t-shirt, and he ran back through the falling snow up to Tom's window. Tom cranked the window down.

"Dude, I saw your hazards. Lousy day to be stuck. Need some help?"

Tom nodded. "Thanks. Yeah. Check this out." He turned the key in the ignition. No sound but a raspy buzzing.

"Oh, not good. C'mon, I'll drive you wherever. Just got off work, so I have time. First, let's push it into the grass so it doesn't get nailed."

Tom raised the window then got out and pushed, steering through the open door while the kid muscled it from the rear. Once satisfied, they headed for the other car. Tom noticed a Colorado State University bumper sticker on the left side of the trunk, and on the right side, a plastic fish with legs containing the word *Darwin*.

Tom squeezed in the passenger side. The kid climbed in opposite and shifted the stick into first. He glanced back for less than a second and gunned it, groping for traction as he crawled sideways into the wash of a massive SUV blurring past. He fishtailed and straightened and picked up a little momentum. Watching his rear-view he muttered, "Noooo, don't hit me, don't hit me, don't hit me."

Tom white-knuckled the armrest. Suddenly he wasn't so thrilled about dying.

"Yesss. We're good," the kid announced, rowing through the gears. He offered his left hand to Tom, stretching it across the center console. "Hi, name's Chuck."

"I'm Tom. Nice to meet you." He awkwardly shook Chuck's hand. "CSU, huh?"

Chuck nodded.

"Me too, a few years back."

"Cool." Chuck had a mop of sandy hair, scruffy sideburns, and dark, quick, friendly eyes.

The conversation on the way to Tom's house was strange and interesting and pleasant, with exchanges about majors, student cars, and snow. Tom stayed alive the whole way home. He climbed out and began to shut the door, but he poked his head back in. "Here, let me give you some money." He dug around for his wallet.

"No way, dude. You stop that. It's my pleasure. You'll need your five bucks to go replace that car of yours. Ha ha!"

"Alright, then. Take it easy. And thanks again."

"No worries. Later, Tom." Tom shut the door, and Chuck pulled out and did a sloppy U-turn to get it pointed in the right direction. Tom waved as he passed, and Chuck returned a two-fingered salute. Tom had forgotten his misery long enough to be smiling. As he turned for the door he remembered.

CHAPTER FORTY-SEVEN

When Tom saw Tara's little red two-seater, he knew he had found the right condos. He swung Kate's station wagon into a space marked *Visitor* two down from Tara's car. Though the sky was already black and the temperature close to freezing, conditions weren't yet harrowing enough to hinder a couple of serious runners.

Tom climbed out of the car, glanced left and right, and checked his watch. He scouted around for a moment but found no one. He tried to lean against his car to wait, but the icy metal quickly bit him through his running clothes. The streetlight turned his breath into glowing clouds drifting about his head.

For a couple minutes, he paced and scanned the area and checked his watch and glanced toward his car. Finally he double-checked the number on the parking block in front of the red sports car: *E204*. Second-floor lights in building *E* were on. He started for the stairwell.

Tara beamed as she pulled open the door, but her smile wavered for a heartbeat as she sized him up. "I'm sorry, Tom." Her smile had returned, but it was plastic. She wore elegant clothes, and her hair and face were made up. "I completely lost track of time. If you can wait a few moments, I'll be ready."

"Uh, sure, I guess. I'll be down by your car."

"No, no." She grabbed his hand and drew him in over the threshold. "It's too cold to just stand around. Just come inside. I'm fast."

The breath suddenly caught in Tom's chest. "I, uh…" He nervously glanced around the condo. It was upscale. A couple of dim lights were on, and a couple of candles were lit. And it smelled good.

"Hey, you've never seen my place, have you? Remember I mentioned I moved, right?"

He shrugged.

"So, this is the entry, of course. Living room. Kitchen over there. Hey, there's those weird masks I got in New Zealand. Roger and Frank. Roger's the one on the left. Ha ha! Pretty funky, huh?"

"It does look like Roger."

"Only cuter. Here." Tara grabbed his hand again and began leading him toward the hall, which would include, he imagined, the bedroom. She felt him resisting and turned to face him. "I'm sorry. I'm already late, and I keep yakking." She had not released his hand. "Listen, if it's too late, we don't have to run tonight. It's pretty cold anyway. You can go, if you want." She held his eyes and lowered her voice. "Or, you can stay, if you want. We could just hang out here a while and chill. Unless you really want to run. Whatever's fine with me."

Tom withdrew his hand and looked away. The top of the stairwell showed through the narrow window by the front door. "No, I just…" He looked back at her face, then his eyes slid down toward her blouse. It was fitted. He quickly regained her eyes. "If you don't feel like running…"

She grasped his hand again and laid her other hand over it, drawing it up toward her. "I'd rather stay in, really. You can stay as long as you like."

"You sure?" he said awkwardly.

"In fact, I'd like it if you'd stay." She reached around his shoulder and pulled him a bit closer. "*Whatever* is fine with me."

His eyes slid down again, and he moved his free hand to her narrow waist. His heart thundered inside him.

"Well, then," she began. "We could…"

"Tara, no. Tara, please no. I can't." He forced her hands away and stepped back. "Tara, please."

"Tom, it's fine. Come on. You're just out for a run—that's all anybody needs to know."

"No. Tara, I like you a lot. I do. But you know as well as I do—I'm—um… I can't—uh—stay. Tara, I'm sorry."

"Tom, I don't get it. I like you more than a lot. And it's just a little fun. I don't see…"

"I've strung you along. I'm being a jerk, I know. I can't tell you how bad I—never mind. I can't run tonight, or hang out."

"You're serious? Well, that's the deal, I guess. It sucks."

"I know. But you've got to understand. I can't do this."

"Whatever, Tom. Fine. I'll see ya, I guess."

"Right. I'm so sorry." He turned for the door and made his escape.

CHAPTER FORTY-SIX

"I wonder if I'll ever be able to do this and not feel—um—this feeling," Tom mentioned after a long silence. The humming of tires and an occasional ticking of the turn signal had been the only noise for many minutes. He glanced up to see a sliver of Abby in the mirror: her distinctive subtle frown hovered over the top of her picture book, and he knew her lips were silently forming the sounds. Coby faced the rear in his car seat, but his silence made clear he comfortably snoozed. Hannah looked anything but comfortable as she slept, slumped awkwardly as if her neck were broken. Cabbage probably slept as well, curled up among wrapped presents way back in the wagon part. She was leashed to the inner liftgate handle so she couldn't jump the seatback onto the kids.

Kate turned soft eyes to Tom. "I know," she whispered. "Probably not, I guess." She didn't have to ask what he meant. He found her hand and gently squeezed it.

Christmas Eve traffic was surprisingly light as they headed south toward Colorado Springs. Because it was an even-numbered year, they had spent Thanksgiving with Tom's mom, and would spend Christmas with Kate's parents.

Understandably, Christmastime at the Kiernans evoked a strange, detached poignancy in Tom. But he went. His mother Maggie, on the other hand, had never returned to their house.

Every other year the Kiernans invited Maggie to join them for Christmas; each time she coughed up limp excuses. No one wondered why or failed to sympathize, but they all felt she would begin to heal if she would pluck up some courage and face her husband's death. Years hadn't smoothed the edges. She had been wounded deeply—of course—but her state was worse than grief or sorrow: something in her had broken. She was unstable. She had become increasingly paranoid and doleful. She made irrational, impulsive decisions, such as hastily selling off the family's little ranch so she could move closer to Emily, into an ostentatious apartment in a depreciating neighborhood.

Tom checked up on her often. He and Emily whispered between them that their mother was increasingly hard to like. They whispered that her frail mind was what had failed her body—had opened the door to her cancer. And though she had tested clean for over two years, they sensed that her health continued to fray.

But because Emily and Jonathan were in Omaha with his parents, Maggie would likely spend this Christmas alone. Tom worried, but nevertheless preferred to be smothered by noise and bustle at Kate's parents' than to be smothered by his mom's melodramatic pathos.

At last they pulled into the sweeping driveway of the Kiernan house, the place rising before them like a cover photo for the *Elegant Holiday* catalog. Kate's niece Brooklyn was plastered against the front window. While Tom negotiated a parking spot among three other vehicles, Kate watched Brooklyn vanish and the curtain waft back into its place. Before Tom even opened his door, the driveway filled with outstretched arms and boisterous greetings.

Grandparents and uncles and aunts had the kids out and peppered with kisses before their parents could lift a finger. Tom found himself tasked with liberating a hysterically wagging Cabbage, just in time for her to race inside and barrel around the house. Tom crossed the threshold last, arms full of presents charmingly wrapped by Kate, crumpled by Cabbage, and made possible by the slim funds he had gotten from the wrecker for his dead car.

A Kiernan Christmas never varied. First, the children were distracted with stocking stuffers while the parents and grandparents slowly whirred to life. Afterwards, as the adults reloaded their coffee cups, the kids played with cheap little stocking toys and had a sip of juice and whined a bit.

Breakfast was next. Over at the kids' tables—a wobbly card table and a miniature plastic picnic table for the little ones, with Jacob hovering over them in his perch—antsy children wiggled and giggled. Only Abby ate patiently or tidily. Cabbage and the Kiernan's dachshund Michelle volunteered to post themselves underneath for floor cleaning duty.

Nobody who ever sat at Mom Kiernan's table ever blamed her for being fat. Though she considered her breakfast "a little something to tide you over until Christmas dinner," it looked like she was trying to hide her table under platters of food. All of it was superb.

Especially her barmbracks—postponed from Halloween to Christmas each year for the family. And the opening of gifts was postponed until after breakfast because each child who found a cherry in their slice of barmbrack would receive an extra gift. This year, only Abby did not find a cherry, yet she conjured a smile and shrugged. Kate was proud.

The adults also had prizes in their loaves, but theirs were the traditional objects. They laughed when Tom's slice produced the small strip of rag. "Ha ha! Poor Tom!" someone jested. He conjured a smile and shrugged.

Kate found the sixpence in her slice and proudly displayed it.

"Looks like she's gonna leave 'Poor Tom' in the gutter."

"I would never." Kate cried. Not a minute later she muttered, "Uh, oh," and held up the wedding ring before them. Everyone at the table erupted.

"Two prizes? Are you kidding me?"

"Ha, ha, now we know her plan: she's got a wealthy man on the side."

"It's alright Tom, you can come live with us."

Kate clutched Tom's arm and laid her head on his shoulder. "No. Don't even say that," she playfully protested. "I'm keeping him 'til the day I die."

The nightmarish pace of grown-up breakfast made the kids feel like they would detonate. But at last, the squeal of Grandpa's chair sounded out. "Alright, let's do this," a brother-in-law offered. As the other kids vanished from the kitchen, Coby, trapped in his high chair, had to appeal to Mom. He rocked and called out, "Down! Down! Down!" until Kate could get him cleaned and set free. By the time he toddled into the great room to rejoin the others, they were packed around the tree, squirming like puppies fighting for a place to nurse. Poor Coby had to play runt on the outskirts.

"Coby, you sit here," said Abigail, offering him her spot. "I'll help hand out presents." She hoped someone would commend her because she could read the labels; Kate was proud, nonetheless.

The great room soon resembled a bombed-out city made of wrapping paper. Everyone got too much stuff. The adults carefully tucked the return receipts into safe places. The children whined a little bit because someone wasn't letting them play with such-and-such.

Mom Kiernan made her way back to the kitchen to clean up breakfast so she could kick off her gargantuan dinner. The daughters and daughters-in-law joined her so they could help and chat.

The children and dogs played.

The men happened across some football on TV, which got in the way of their intentions of helping in the kitchen.

Tom went on a little walk by himself and thought about his dad.

Then dinner.

Afterwards, the children watched claymation holiday specials in the basement while the adults settled down with mugs of eggnog and a black-and-white Christmas classic.

Tom nestled with Kate on the loveseat and took her hand. She wrinkled her nose at him and wriggled a little closer. As they watched, he would occasionally whisper in her ear and she would nod, or smile, or giggle, or gaze at him a moment, and she would whisper back to him and he would nod, or smile, or gaze back at her a moment. The room around them began to grow distant.

And the movie played on. *...and spending all your life trying to figure out how to save three cents on length of pipe. I'd go crazy. I—I wanna do something big and something important.*

You know George, I feel that in a small way...

"...but Andrew put on the bug movie," Abigail was whispering to her mother.

"So? You love that one," Kate whispered back.

"But it's not a Christmas movie."

"That's okay, baby. There's no rule that you can only watch Christmas movies on Christmas."

Abby twisted up her mouth and thought for a moment, then she shrugged and said, "Okay Mama," and tiptoed back to the stairwell.

Kate turned to Tom and rolled her eyes. He grinned and leaned close to her ear and said something. She chuckled.

By the final act, Kate had melted into Tom on the loveseat with her head on his shoulder at such an angle that she was watching the movie sideways. He held her hand and caressed the inside of her forearm with the other. A contented smile played around the corners of her mouth, and she only vaguely tracked the movements on the TV. She glanced up at him to find moist eyes staring at nothing. She moved closer and whispered, "Everything okay?"

He quickly raised his sleeve to his eye before turning to her. "Yep."

"You sure?"

"Oh, yeah. Quite okay." He smiled broadly at her.

"Brooklyn's a piece of work, isn't she?" said Kate. "Even Mom started to lose it toward the end."

Tom snorted. "Yeah, she's a blast. She made Hann seem calm."

Their view was of little more than snowflakes materializing in their headlights and racing toward the windshield. Apart from their murmuring and the hum of the Interstate, the car was silent.

"You handled it pretty well." Kate added. "You even seemed to have a good time."

"Yeah, it was…" He thought a second. "…pretty fun, actually. Once I got in my zone. I had to sorta think of Brooklyn like white noise."

"Just tune out the noise and eat."

"Yeah, no kidding. I'll still never get how your mom…"

"Oh, shoot, Tom, was that the Harmony exit?"

"Uh, yeah."

"Aw. I was wanting to stop by the store before we get home. There's nothing for breakfast."

"Seriously?"

"Well, there's Mom's leftovers we could…"

"No, no, it's fine," chuckled Tom. "Yikes. We need to rest up before we hit that again. I'll just swing around on Mulberry."

He let their usual off-ramp scroll past him. Up ahead red taillights appeared through the gauzy air, with a group of three lights way up high. As Tom glided into the left lane to get around the semi, an array of bright amber lights came into view along its side. The truck drew thin streams of snow behind it along the chalky road as if ghostly serpents were chasing its flaps.

"Uh oh," Tom mumbled. "I forgot how fast Mulberry comes up." He let off the gas to glide back behind the truck, but it seemed to be slowing as well. "Are you getting off or not?" Both of them drifted past the Mulberry exit. Tom grunted. He accelerated to pass.

"Tom…"

"It's fine, I just gotta get around this truck or I'll miss Mountain Vista too, then it's forever before we can turn around."

As he ascended a man-made hill lifting the freeway over some train tracks, he changed into the right lane. No one would ever wonder whether his maneuver was too hasty.

The trucker alone saw them leave the road. Nobody in the next few cars noticed the deformed guardrail at the train overpass—they only saw a big rig lined with red and amber lights parked beyond it on the shoulder. Few people would consider pulling off in a snowstorm for a stopped truck. Several minutes passed before someone did: a police officer, who added her cruiser's roof strobes to the truck's light show.

Only after the officer emerged to inspect the truck did she notice the dancing beam of a flashlight down by the frontage road a hundred yards back. The beam fell on what appeared to be a wheels-up vehicle with a lone silhouette frantically circling it.

The trucker glanced up to see red and blue lights bouncing off the back of his trailer, then his eye caught a bobbing flashlight descending the slippery embankment on the near side of the train tracks. He began waving and calling.

The officer ran up and confirmed what she had feared. The trucker's panicked voice added foggy pieces to the puzzle: "taillights flying… there's no… I can't see…" was the only sense he made. Her radio was in her hand transmitting the pertinent details. *Accident, single vehicle, Northeast Frontage Road, I-25 mile 270, unknown…*

The vehicle lay upside down on the far side of the frontage, half in the drainage ditch, half on the driveway of a commercial building sitting just back from the road. Snowflakes were faintly hissing on contact with the exposed engine bay. As the officer circled, her jittering beam came across what appeared to be the front half of a dog lying motionless among red-spattered snow just behind the vehicle. The dog's leash snaked toward the back of the pancaked roof and disappeared inside the crushed metal. Fifteen or twenty feet further back, her light revealed a spray of dark soil cast across the whitened frontage road, apparently thrown by the vehicle from the embankment. Her beam landed on something resting on the road among the soil. It appeared to be made of yellow and blue plastic. It was some kind of toy.

"Please God, no," she muttered, as she hurried around to the side of the car and knelt in the snow.

CHAPTER FORTY-FIVE

There's a lot of white. I feel terrible. It's a ceiling. Heads. Heads around the bottom of the ceiling. My stomach hurts. Many blurry heads. Something is wrong. My throat hurts. I feel terrible.

"What...?" Tom croaked. "What...?" The blurry white world with blurry heads wavered and spun. He lifted his head enough to see blurry bodies attached to the heads, and they were bustling about, or maybe something in his brain made them seem to move.

"Hello, Tom," said a female voice by his ear.

His oscillating eyes found the voice. Her face was close to his. A pleasant face attached to dark blurry hair and white things and boxes and strips on the blurry white ceiling. His head wallowed in the pillow as his eyes tried to find things. Find things that when lined up in the right order would make a sentence that would tell him why the world was white and painful and filled with blurry strangers. At last he found an I.V. bag on a chrome rod with twisty ends on top of a chrome pole, with a blurry hose snaking down toward him. The hose terminated under a piece of tape that was biting his arm. And a lizard or a bat was eating the back of his throat and burying its claws inside his sinuses, so he reached up to shoo it away, but instead he found smooth plastic tubes crawling out of his nostrils, so he tried to get his fingers around the tubes to yank them out, but instead a hand grabbed his wrist and pinned it to his side. It was the hand of the pleasant face with the blurry dark hair. She sat

61

next to him, and he lay on his back in a bed dressed in white sheets. He flopped his head to the other side to find a woman in an ugly turquoise shirt holding his other wrist, which was encased in some kind of stiff sleeve.

"Hello, Tom," said the voice. It was calm and pleasant. "You are safe. Please just relax. We've got you." The voice continued to hold his wrist.

Tom groggily tried to lift himself, but a flaming meat hook started to yank on his intestines. He growled through his stinging throat and had no choice but to submit to gravity. A firm hand on either shoulder ensured he remained against the bed. "Please, Tom," said the voice.

The pleasant face spoke again, more urgently, "Please relax, Tom. Lie back as comfortably as you can. I know it hurts. We will help you with that as soon as we can."

Tom wheezed, "What? What did—ow. Oh—ow, ow, ow."

"I know it hurts, Tom. Please try to relax. You are very safe here. We are taking very good care of you."

Tom's eyes glazed over, and little puddles formed at the outside corners and overran. His breathing came in tiny, labored puffs. A few long moments passed. His unfocused eyes regained the pleasant face.

She said, "Tom, you've had an accident, but you will be fine. We are taking very good care of you."

Tom's head remained against the pillow, but he shook it weakly. His eyes rolled back to find the ceiling again. "Please, God. Oh. What…" Each word was an effort, more a hissing than a voice.

"You are going to be fine. We are…"

"My gut. What is…ow. Ow!"

"Please don't try to sit up. It will only hurt more. Lie back and relax. We've got you, dear."

Tom risked a deeper breath, but immediately he winced and shuddered. "What's in my gut?" he rasped, barely audible.

"Nothing is in there. You've just had another surgery, but you are healing, so it will be very sore for a while."

"A surgery? Why? I haven't had a sur... a sur..." He had to pause to draw in a few breaths. He felt the pleasant lady remove her hand from his wrist and gently grasp his hand.

"You've been injured in an accident, but you are going to be fine. You are..."

"Another—another—surgery? What? How many have..." A grimace cut him short.

"No need to worry; you're doing great. You are healing very well. You've just needed some stitches and things."

Tom looked nauseated and pale, and his eyes wavered and blurred again. He turned to Pleasant Lady. "What happened?"

She maintained her grasp on his hand, but lifted an eyebrow toward one of the men.

The man turned to one of the nurses seated by the machines. "Lauren?"

Lauren answered, "Strong and steady."

He motioned to some other nurses. "Thank you all. Stay close."

Three of them silently stepped out of the room. Pleasant Lady, the man who talked, and nurses Lauren and Beth remained. Beth held Tom's other hand, seated on the opposite side of his bed from Pleasant Lady.

She returned her gaze to Tom. "I am Dr. Pozzi. This is Dr. Keyes. You were injured in an accident. You needed a bit of work to patch you up, and you've needed a little while to heal. But you're doing so well, it's time for you to wake up now."

Tom stared blankly at the ceiling. After a long pause, he whispered, "Thank you." Several groggy minutes passed as he slowly began to look about a bit more alertly, as if the pieces were falling into place. "Hospital."

"Yes, Tom. Very good."

"Wake up? You said..." He faded a moment, then he revived again with rapid, shallow breaths. He caught Dr. Pozzi's eyes. "Wake up? You said 'time to wake up'."

"We've kept you asleep for a little while." Pozzi tried to sound as cheerful as possible.

Showing no alarm, Tom whispered, "Medically-induced coma?"

Pleased with Tom's lucidity, Pozzi glanced at Keyes with a smile. He returned it with a nod.

"Excellent, Tom. Yes, we needed to perform several surgeries, with some time to heal between and after."

"I still feel terrible."

"I know, Tom. I am so sorry. But you are healing very well. You will begin to feel better and better each day."

"How long?" rasped Tom.

She glanced at Keyes. He said, "You'll need to stay here a bit longer. Depending on how quickly you progress, we'll make a decision."

Tom shook his head. "I mean, how long is 'a little while'?"

Pozzi cocked her head. "I'm sorry?"

"The coma. 'Asleep for a little while.' How long?"

Keyes answered, "About seventeen weeks." Pozzi shot him a subtle frown.

"Weeks?" Tom glanced between Pozzi and Keyes, then from Beth to Lauren. Lauren still had her attention on the equipment. "Sevent…" His head fell back to the pillow, his eyes focused on nothing. Several long moments elapsed with Tom struggling to breathe and lie still and stay alert. Dr. Pozzi rubbed his hand and cooed reassurances to him while Lauren and Keyes studied the machines. Beth remained silent, gently touching Tom's hand and shoulder. Finally, he looked in Pozzi's eyes. "Seventeen weeks."

"Yes." She said, "Do you remember the accident?" He stared blankly. "The car accident?" she clarified.

He shook his head.

"Can you tell me your name?"

"It's Tom. You just told me."

"Very good. Your full name?"

"Ericson. Thomas Roland Ericson.

"Excellent. Do you remember driving on a snowy night two days after Christmas?"

"Christmas?" he wheezed. "Last Christmas? Or—uh—not next month?"

"You were in a car accident shortly after Christmas. Since then, you've been here for these weeks. Do you remember Christmas?"

Tom's eyes filled with fear. He shook his head, almost imperceptibly.

Pozzi shot a knowing glance at Beth. "That's fine. It's nothing to worry about. Sometimes the memories take a little while to speak up after you've bumped your head."

"Okay."

"What is the last thing you remember?"

Tom's eyes whirled for a moment, then he looked at Dr. Pozzi uncertainly. "There's a donkey," he mumbled. "No. No, wait. That's dumb. Um…"

"Take your time."

"That was long ago. Stupid." His eyes focused a bit and he glanced at Pozzi. "Halloween? Hann was a ladybug. No, Thanksgiving. Thanksgiving is after Halloween, right? Yes, Thanksgiving is November. Hann broke the lamp."

Pozzi flashed Keyes a wide smile, and a bit of tension left his shoulders. "Correct. Very good."

"Then I…" Tom shook his head. "Wait—I couldn't have a car wreck; I sold my car."

"Excellent," she continued. "When was that? Do you remember the date you sold it?"

He paused, frowned, then shook his head again.

"Do you remember anything after that? After you sold your car?"

Tom scanned the air for a moment, then pain suddenly crossed his face. Recoiling with worry, he stared at Dr. Pozzi.

"It's okay. It'll come back."

He let out a weak groan and melted back into the pillow. "I don't— uh. I—um."

"Anything else, Tom?"

"I—I—uh—visited a friend. Yes. I was—um—with a friend. I think it was December." Tom sheepishly avoided eye contact with Pozzi. He remembered being inside Tara's apartment with his hand on her waist, but the memory vanished after that.

"Very good. You are doing so well. What about Christmas? Any details there?"

After a long pause, Tom whispered, "No. Nothing."

"Well, don't worry. It should come back to you soon. It's not important for today. You got yourself quite a bump on..."

"Really?" Tom rasped. "Asleep for seventeen weeks?"

Pozzi smiled thinly and nodded, giving his hand a gentle squeeze.

"Is my wife here?"

She paused a moment before answering. "No, Tom. Your sister has visited, but she couldn't come today. Your wife is not here. Can you tell me her name?"

"Of course, it's Kate."

"Well done. You should be..."

"Did you tell her you were gonna wake me today? She would have come."

Lauren no longer paid attention to the machines. All eyes were fixed on Tom.

"No. I'm very sorry, Tom," Pozzi said softly. "Is the pain in your abdomen tapering off?"

He laid his head back and his eyes closed slowly and out of sync. "It hurts a lot."

"I know. We'll get you something to help with that as soon as we can. For now, try to lie very still so you don't aggravate the pain. Let us move you if you need."

"Okay." Tom tensed his brow. "Could you–is it okay if you—my legs are really hot. Could you take the blankets off?"

Pozzi looked genuinely troubled. "There's just one sheet over your legs. I'm certain taking it off won't help you feel cooler."

"Please, Doctor?" Tom lifted his head to look at the sheet, and tried to move it aside with his feet. His feet didn't budge. He tried again with no result. His head seemed to weigh a thousand pounds; he dropped it to the pillow.

He turned to Pozzi. "You strap down my legs?"

Pozzi sighed deeply, and grabbed his hand again.

"What? No? You know something. Why…"

"Tom, we have some bad news." She paused for too long, brow furrowed. "Your legs are paralyzed. I'm so sorry."

Tom flashed surprise, then slid to worry, then disbelief. "Then why are they hot?"

"It's phantom—uh—false sensation. You are paralyzed in your lower body. There was nothing we could do."

"It can heal, right Doc? Is it temporary?"

"No, Tom. You will never heal. Your spine was irreparably damaged."

He lay there with his eyes closed, shaking his head, his chest twitching with silent gasps. Finally he lifted his eyes to Dr. Keyes. "I'll never walk again?"

"I'm sorry, Tom," he said quietly. "That is correct."

Tom lay there for several minutes in silence, shaking his head in disbelief, punctuated by occasional waves of pain crossing his face. Pozzi rubbed his hand, and a couple of times she spoke whatever soothing words she could think of. At last, without opening his eyes, Tom spoke. "I need my wife. Can you get her?"

"You need to rest first. It's important that you rest now."

"I'm—I slept for weeks. I need Kate here. Please go get her."

"Tom, you are in Boston. And Kate cannot come now. You need to rest. It's very important."

Tom gurgled a little around the tube down his throat. A tiny cough sent a spasm through his face and shoulders. "Ow. Gosh, I feel rather…" He grimaced again. "Can't you see that I need her? I want to—Ow. Oh. Sorry. Why…"

"It is best if you…"

"I don't understand. We can call her. Give me a—give me—oh, ouch. I'll call her myself. She needs to know."

"Tom, please…"

Dr. Keyes wheeled another stool up from behind and sat. He gave a resigned nod to Pozzi.

She gripped Tom's hand a bit more tightly before she spoke. "Tom, I'm so sorry to tell you this. Your wife passed away in the accident."

Tom's face went blank, but his eyes stayed fixed on hers, unmoving.

"Do you understand what I told you?"

Tom scanned all the faces around him. All were grave. Keyes reached forward and laid his hand on Tom's next to Beth's below his plastic splint.

"Do you understand, Tom?" Dr. Pozzi said softly.

Tom's glassy eyes had returned to the ceiling, but she detected the tiniest nod. His mouth began to quiver.

"I'm so sorry. We are all so sorry, Tom."

Tom stared into space for a minute or more, tears rolling down over his temples. At last he spoke, "Who's got the children?"

The tears filling Dr. Pozzi's eyes finally overflowed. "Your three children also passed away in the accident."

Tom's eyes squeezed shut and his mouth fell open, slowly pulling down into a hardened, alien shape. That shape fought him as he tried to form words. "They're all—dead?"

"Yes, Tom. I'm very sorry. You alone survived the accident." Pozzi's shoulders shook, but she fought it bravely. Lauren trembled and held her hand over her mouth, though she faced the machines.

Tom began to shake his head as he struggled to speak. "Seven... Seventeen weeks... You didn't..." He wheezed between words. "You never told me. Seventee..." He choked, and the coughing sent him into torments as the red-hot meat hook began to twist and tear. Tom writhed his head back and forth while Pozzi and Beth held his wrists and shoulders to the bed. His groans turned to inhuman howls as all the pains overcame him.

Dr. Keyes snapped to his feet and barked, "Lauren!"

Lauren snatched up a vial, tore off the cap, jammed the needle into the I.V. tube, and depressed the plunger. In a few seconds Tom stopped writhing, then his eyes rolled back, and at last all went dark.

CHAPTER FORTY-FOUR

Footsteps entered Tom's room. They stopped, followed by shuffling and the click of a ballpoint. Then another click, more steps, and the sound of weight compressing the padded vinyl seat of an armchair. Then the sliver of a sigh, a female.

Tom drunkenly rolled his head over on his pillow to find nurse Lauren seated by the wall. She studied something in her hand.

"I didn't do it," Tom croaked.

Lauren startled and stood. "Tom. You're awake." She quickly stepped to his side, pausing to press a button.

"I remember now. I left her," he said.

"I'm sorry?"

"I didn't do it."

"Are you remembering more?"

"What I told you. Nothing happened. I just left her condo."

Lauren looked puzzled, then she rolled up a stool and sat. "I don't think you..." she started, but thought better of it. She took his hand. "How are you feeling? Is there anything I can do for you?"

"Not too well. I..." Tom lifted his head an inch or so, grimaced, and let it fall. "I'm sorry. I don't know how—I can't really—um—I'm sorry."

"It's okay, Tom. You just let me..."

"I'm sorry." Tom started to weep again. He drew her hand to his shoulder and rested his cheekbone on it. "I'm sorry. I'm sorry. I'm so sorry."

"It's okay, Tom," Lauren whispered. "It's okay. Go ahead. It's okay."

At that moment another nurse entered and announced, "Hey, Lauren. A call?"

Lauren turned and mouthed to him, *Get the doctor.* He nodded and disappeared. She leaned close to Tom and gently cradled his head with her free hand, pressing his forehead against her cheek.

He submitted to her gesture. Though his eyes were squeezed tight, the flood readily escaped. He silently shook.

"Go ahead, Tom," she whispered. "Go ahead. It's okay, dear. It's okay."

Tom's will withered. His lungs filled with gravel, his head thudded, and the muscles in his legs turned to molten slag. Other, less intuitive pains also crowded his body in strange ways. No one could have noticed him slacking, but he felt it. He allowed it. Then he passed out of dense trees into a vast opening and spotted Bill Blue only forty yards ahead. Bill Blue the senior from Poudre High. Bill Blue who had won the last six meets. *Blue Ribbon Bill.* Tom knew he could overtake him. He stuffed the pain in some compartment in the deepest part of his brain, slammed shut and latched the iron lid, and picked up his pace.

I will win, or I will die.

A few spectators lined this section of the cross-country course, waiting in the long grass next to the freshly mowed path. They whooped and clapped as the runners passed.

One more section of trees, then the final straight. All the families will be there. Cheering. Dad and Mom and Emily. And the Blues. They will watch me win.

He paced himself to pull up near Bill by the time they reached the woods. Hoping Bill wouldn't sense pressure behind him along the winding trail, he held his pace a few yards back. As soon as they broke from the trees the crowd erupted. Tom saw the flags marking the finish.

Now.

Tom's pain raged against him. He drew within two yards of Bill. Bill glanced back. Tom matched the new pace.

He'll watch them hang that First on my neck.

Tom saw himself. Future Tom, the winner. The fastest. He saw it as if it were already on video. He drew up alongside Bill. Two hundred yards to go, max. The crowd was wild; shouting, clanging bells, whistling. But Tom saw only the video. Bill fell back two paces. Tom knew. He nearly smiled. His head, his lungs, his legs; they all just obeyed. Tom cranked even harder until he no longer felt Bill. Bill was gone. Tom found enough to sprint the last hundred. He knew better than to glance back until after he crossed the line. He had Bill by nearly three seconds.

Tom refused to lie down. He paced with hands on hips until Emily flew up and almost knocked him over with a hug. Next Dad and Mom approached. Dad said nothing, but he shook Tom's hand with a look on his face that meant more than words. He was holding back tears.

During the car ride home, Mom talked loudly about how proud she was, how exciting it was, how well Tom ran. Dad only said, "What do you prefer, running or winning?" He caught Tom's eye with a smile.

Tom gazed at his medal a few seconds before looking up. "Today?" His grin widened. "Winning." He studied the medal, turning it over and over. *And there'll be more. Not even Blue has the guts to beat me.*

CHAPTER FORTY-THREE

"How's your pain this afternoon?" Dr. Pozzi asked. She held no clipboard or chart as she sat by Tom's bed. She had no intention of taking any notes; she'd been briefed anyway. Her question was part courtesy, part psychological probe.

As Pozzi spoke, Tom's fingers gently traced the scars on his head with his left hand. He had already begun the habit of mindlessly running his fingertips along the bald, jagged C shape where half his scalp had been flayed open in the wreck. His hair was still only about a quarter of an inch long. His right forearm and wrist remained in a plastic splint. "Hard to say," Tom answered her, his voice still hoarse and weak. "As long as I don't move, it's like a stomachache, but lower. It's pretty uncomfortable when I move." He frequently paused for thin breaths. "But at least now the pain is dull enough that I sometimes forget to hold still."

"That's a good sign," she said.

"And the phantom sensation is gone. There's nothing at all now. I think my brain has accepted the paralysis. This morning they poked my legs and feet a few times to help prove it." He shrugged. "It's really weird. Very surreal." He stared into space for a moment, expressionless. "And as weak and spent as I feel, I'm getting cabin fever; I'm desperate to hop out of bed and just move around. Do jumping jacks or something." He wore an intentional little smile.

She gave him a sympathetic look and gently squeezed his shoulder. "I know it's very difficult. You have been so brave."

He made a face as if to say, *I've done nothing brave.*

Pozzi said, "As soon as you can manage it, we would like to start you on some simple exercises. Begin rebuilding some muscle mass in your arms and torso. That should help mitigate your restlessness a bit. Then we'll get you sitting up."

"And these tubes are really irritating," he added. "They're horrible."

"I know. I'm sorry. It won't be long. We'll soon be able to start you on some liquids. If your digestive tract responds well, some soft foods will follow shortly."

"How much of the intestine did they have to take out?"

"Altogether, a little over twenty percent. But that last surgery removed just a small section that was refusing to heal. I believe it should be the last one. Everything else has healed quite well. I think those new incisions are the primary cause of your pain. And they're doing great. It won't be long and you'll be moving about."

"I'm sure there'll be tons of therapy."

She raised her brows and offered a thin smile. "Of course. And we're talking to a hospital back in Colorado so you can be closer to home. That'll help you begin the transition to living as independently as possible." She reached out and touched his arm. "But we'll discuss those details later."

Pozzi picked up a sheet of paper from a tray nearby. "Now—visitors." She smiled broadly and caught his eyes. "You've had some visitors come and sit with you while you slept." She glanced down at the sheet. "To date, Emily Bonneau, James Kiernan, and Rosie Kiernan have been here to see you."

"James and Rosie came?" Tom looked surprised and glad. Suddenly his face fell, and he closed his eyes and groaned. He glanced at Pozzi. "They're my—*were* my—in-laws." He sighed deeply, scanning the fragmented pictures in his head. At last he focused back on Dr. Pozzi. "That's—that's—I can't believe they came all the way to Boston just to sit around and watch me sleep. I don't know. They probably needed…"

He grimaced and stared at the ceiling for a moment. "I don't know. Closure? Or..." He looked at Pozzi. "Emily's my sister. I feel bad they all came this far."

"You're deeply loved. I'm sure their presence helped you heal, though you didn't consciously know they were there."

He shrugged.

"Anyway," she continued, "since you're awake and starting to feel better, we would like to help you contact friends and family. You may want to speak with them, and some may even want to visit. Let us know who we can arrange to call or invite to come."

"So, my mother never came out, I'm guessing? Maggie—um—Margaret Ericson?"

"Not to date."

"I'm guessing she wouldn't really..." He declined to explain. "Yes, I'd like to speak with my mom, if she can, and Emily. Even the Kiernans if they would want to. Of course I'd love if any of them came, though..."

"We'll be sure to invite them. We'll arrange some times for you to call them."

"Thank you. I..." His eyes wandered, unfocused, as if he were groping for memories. "I'll let you know if I think of any others."

"Certainly." She scribbled something on the paper and returned it to the tray.

She smiled at Tom. "Are you beginning to remember more? Lauren noted on Wednesday that you had made some progress."

Tom cut his eyes at her. "What did I tell her?"

"She didn't specify. Just that you mentioned some memories had returned."

Tom looked blankly at her for a moment. "Ah... Yeah... Well... I think you asked about Christmas? Was that you? Did you ask about Christmas?"

"I did, the day you awoke."

"Well, I remember now. A lot of December, and I'm even remembering things from Christmas."

"That's wonderful, Tom."

"I can see the tree. My son Coby was walking, so I know it's this year."
Tom's speech was still labored and choppy. "And I remember Kate—
my wife—at her parents'. I have some really clear memories of Kate on
Christmas."

Pozzi smiled. "Good. What do you remember?

"Uh…" He looked sheepish. "Well, it's kinda weird."

She waved it off. "It doesn't matter. Verbalizing it will help you
straighten it out, solidify it. Talking it out is an aid to memory."

"You sure?"

She nodded.

"Alright. Well, we were at her parents, so the kids were asleep in the
same room as us. It was dark, and they were in blankets on the floor
because Kate and I were in the bunk beds. I think Coby was in his pen
in the corner—must have been. Anyway, I remember—um—this is—
well—this sounds dumb…" His eyes swam for a moment, deciding.
"Kate climbed up into the top bunk with me because—uh—it's weird,
but—well, with the kids way down there, we thought we'd be safe, so we
kinda—you know—did stuff. And it was really funny because the bed
was sort of—um—tiny and wobbly and precarious, and the whole thing
was so risky with the kids in there. Afterwards, Kate and I just giggled
for a long time—you know how when you're supposed to keep quiet it
makes it worse."

Pozzi noticed a look on his face—not exactly a smile—rather a glimmer of happiness, the first she had seen.

"That's all," Tom added. "I don't remember anything else after that. I
suppose she must have climbed back down, but…" He shrugged. "I don't
know. That's the last I remember of her."

The glimmer vanished. He stared for a moment into Pozzi's eyes,
then he turned his face away and laid his hand on his mouth. His shoulders began to shake.

She remained stone silent, eyes downcast. She heard him fighting to
regain control. She chose to remain still as long as he needed.

"Cabbage was there," Tom said at last. He kept his gaze on the bud-
ding branches peeking up above his windowsill, bobbing in the breeze.

"Cabbage?" said Pozzi.

"That's our dog. Or..." He paused for a long moment. "Or, I guess, *was* our dog. She was there, at Christmas, in Colorado Springs. I just remembered." He turned back to her, eyes and face wet. "Before you came in, I was wondering about Cabbage, but..." Tom paused again. "...of course she would have gone with us. And certainly she must have been in the car when—when..."

"Yes, your dog also died in the accident. I'm sorry."

Instead of grief, or even sadness, he wore a look of weariness and defeat. "It never ends, does it?"

"Tom, I'm so sorry. You've had a great number..."

"You've been trying to protect me or something. It's pretty plain. You're required to tell me the truth, but nobody's making you tell it to me all at once. I guess that's okay." He shrugged and looked away. "I guess that's okay."

She remained still.

"You'll probably have to tell me the truth if I ask who was the DOA."

"Tom..."

"I guess the nurses are so accustomed to me being asleep, they forget I can also lay still. They just..." He flapped his hand about in the air. "...forget."

Dr. Pozzi looked troubled. "Tom, this has been..."

"They were trying to whisper. One of them said, 'All instant except for Ericson and the one DOA'." He looked gravely at Pozzi. "Who was the DOA?"

Her shoulders drooped and she lowered her head. "It was Jacob." Her eyes remained downcast. "His car seat was—generally effective. But extrication from the vehicle was quite time-consuming." She lifted her eyes to him. "Tom, please understand that the teams did..."

"Poor Jacob," he whispered. "I hope he was—I mean, I hope he didn't feel..." More tears began to flow. "Oh, my poor Jacob."

Tom's crying caused him to begin a wheezing cough around his plastic tubes. Each cough caused a deeper agony to sweep across his face. "Coby. My boy..." was all Pozzi made out through Tom's boilings.

She stood and pressed the call button. His coughing worsened and sent waves of pain through his abdomen. A nurse entered. While fighting to control his breathing, Tom raised a hand and jabbed a finger toward the I.V., desperation on his face.

Not long after, Tom lay wheezing but comfortable. His eyes were glassy and unfocused. Pozzi had left the room, taking her things with her. The nurse sat nearby, casually monitoring the machines.

"Is that painkiller helping, Mr. Ericson?" he asked.

"A lever lock," Tom said, his gaze wandering. "Notches. Not just friction. It's chrome. Buenas notches. Ha."

"Okay," said the nurse, eyeing Tom obliquely. "I'll take that as a 'yes'." He swiveled on the stool and began entering something on the keyboard.

Suddenly Tom lifted his head and looked at him wild-eyed. "What about Hamlet?"

"Hamlet, sir?"

"Who is taking care of Hamlet?" The nurse stared and cocked his head. Tom started to sit, but immediately fell back in pain. He spoke more urgently. "Who is taking care of Hamlet?"

"Hamlet is fine. Hamlet is just fine. You need to relax. Are the painkillers helping you?"

Tom settled back. "Unghh. I don't know."

The nurse paused for a long moment watching Tom, then he slowly turned back to the keyboard, his eyes the last thing to swivel around.

CHAPTER FORTY-TWO

Tom lay flat, his head propped a little on a thin pillow. He wore a telephone headset like the kind worn by the fake customer service reps in stock photos. Its cord stretched across to a phone on the side table. One of his nurses hung around near the door. Not once since he awoke had he been left alone, even for phone calls.

"From San Jose? Why?" Tom rasped into the microphone.

"Well, we live here now," his sister Emily said on the other end.

"What? Really?"

"Yeah. They wouldn't let me see you in Fort Collins, then when they moved you to Denver they still wouldn't, then after they moved you to Boston they *still* wouldn't let me come at first. I guess you were a mess. We had already moved to California by the time they allowed visitors. So, sure—it was far, but I didn't care. Are you kidding me? Of course I came."

"But you live in San Jose now?"

"What's that Tom? The connection's no good."

He tried to speak up, louder than his hoarse whisper. "I'm sorry. It's my voice. And lungs. And this tube."

"They still have tubes down your throat? Oh, Tom…"

"Yep. Just one now. It's fine. Should be soon they said—getting it out. You live in San Jose now? For real?"

"Yes, well, close to there. Palo Alto. I'm sorry I couldn't tell you. Well, actually I did tell you; you just weren't paying attention. Sorta like always." She giggled.

"Why, though? I mean—that's great and all. But why move? I thought Jonathan was…"

"He and Sachin sold the company. You were under when they got the offer. A fantastic offer. The new company wanted to keep them on. Sachin took his money and walked, but we agreed. So we moved out here."

"So, you're rich?"

"Well, sorta, yeah, I guess."

"Congratulations, Emily. I really mean it. That's great. Tell Jonathan congrats for me too. But I'll miss you."

"I'll come see you a lot. I would fly back out there today, but we've got all this stuff going on right now."

"It's alright. I get it."

"Oh, Tom, I was so scared last time. You looked like a sea creature or something, with all the machines plugged into you. You looked dead. I just cried mostly. And tried to think of things to tell you. I knew you'd never wake up."

"I'm sorry," Tom said. "It's weird; it doesn't feel like it's been months."

"And you don't remember anything, even before the crash?"

"December is mostly there, but not a thing since Christmas day at Kate's parents'."

Emily choked up a little. "Tom, it's been so hard on me."

"I know. I'm sorry. But thanks for coming to Boston to see me. And they told me even Kate's parents came out here too."

"Wow, that's good. They're so sweet."

"Mom hasn't been out yet I guess. We're going to call her next."

Emily paused too long. "Um, Mom's not good."

"What?"

"She's not good. And her cancer is back."

Tom was silent.

"Tom, you there?"

"Uh, yeah. Just… I'm just shocked. And sad. Cancer's back. She's… She's…"

"It's not looking good. Tom, she's bad. She's out of her head. I think she's in denial about you, about Kate, your kids, your paralysis."

"Of course she is. How are we supposed to…?"

"She's like…" Emily groped for words, sounding panicked. "It's like she refuses to be helped. We couldn't do anything. You were already pretty much dead, and we had to make a decision about the job, and we thought…"

"Emily, it's fine. You can't stop living over Mom and me. Emily? Emily, it's fine."

"She didn't even come to the funeral," she said desperately.

"What?"

"The funeral. She didn't come."

"What funeral?"

"For Kate and the kids. Tom—the funeral."

There was a long pause.

"Tom, are you there?"

Tom began sobbing. The nurse hastened to the bedside and whispered, "Tom?" He waved her off and mouthed, *I'm fine. I'm okay.* The nurse nodded and slowly backed away, eyeing him closely.

"I forgot," said Tom, weeping. "I forgot there would have been a funeral. Oh, God! Oh, dear God! I missed their funeral. Dear God, help them." Tom went silent.

Emily said, "Tom… Tom… Tom… Tom…" every few seconds.

At last he calmed a bit. "I forgot. I completely forgot. How was it? How was the service? Emily, how was it?"

"It was nice," she said in a broken voice. "It was horrible, of course. It was horrible for everyone, but it was beautiful and—and, I guess, fitting? Everything was lovely, and everyone was there. Everyone but mom. Everyone from Fort Collins, the Springs, everywhere."

"And," Tom said, "they're buried? Or…?"

"Yes. A beautiful place down by Colorado Springs. Hilly, trees and grass, simple and peaceful."

"Accessible?"

"Well, yeah, just off the road…"

"*Wheelchair* accessible?" Tom corrected.

"Oh. Oh, Tom! I'm sorry. Yes. I think. There's sidewalks and stuff. If not, we'll figure it out. Tom, I'm so sorry."

"It's fine. It's fine. We'll figure it out. So they're all together?"

"Yes. In the shadow of some trees." Emily said. "Long views. It's pretty."

"All but Coby's heart."

"I'm sorry?" Emily was confused.

"His heart. Dr. Pozzi told me his heart is in some kid in Maryland. She said, 'Jacob had a very strong heart'."

"I didn't know…"

"Yeah. Yeah, that's what they told me." He was silent a moment. "So, part of him—uh—lives. I hope for a really long time."

CHAPTER FORTY-ONE

Tom's new room had a decent view of the Rockies and a panoramic view of an array of air conditioners lining the roof of the hospital's west wing. Hanging low over the mountains, the sun threw glowing parallelograms onto the wall and floor. No nurse hovered nearby—they finally trusted Tom with a call button. On a rolling tray near the bed sat a cup and straw, a bowl and spoon, and a couple of cellophane wrappers from bland crackers. The elevated bed propped Tom to a full sitting position. No tubes crawled out of his nose or mouth, and no I.V. burrowed into his vein. Both his feet lay awkwardly pointed to the left. The cast on his right forearm was gone, revealing a road map of winding scars. And though his right hand turned under a bit unnaturally, he easily held up a local newspaper.

The headline "Poudre Football Star Declines Scholarships" caught Tom's eye, though it was buried deep in the paper in the right sidebar on page D1. He scanned the article looking for something to make sense of such a headline.

Poudre High School's record-breaking fullback Henry Carrizales has elected not to head off to college this fall, though his athletic prowess and academic promise earned him several full scholarship offers at Division 1 universities...

...not only universities here in Colorado, but schools as far away as California and Michigan...

...working class background...

…has enlisted in the U.S. Army…

"What?" Tom exclaimed. He lowered the paper and looked around, as if he would find someone who had just read the same thing. He returned to the column.

"…people save for years to send their kids to college, and I'm entitled to go for free because I can run fast?" Carrizales said…

"…my family has always worked hard, and we…"

"…wish I could transfer this to my sister; she gets really good grades too, and of course my parents can't afford…"

"…turn down these generous offers…"

"…I love my country, and I've always wanted to…"

Tom spoke aloud, "Don't do it, Man. Don't do it. Just take the money." He shook his head and chuckled, glancing toward where the nurse would normally be. He returned to the top of the article to read it fully.

CHAPTER FORTY

"Wow. It stinks."

Tom sat in his wheelchair just inside the open front door of his house. A young man behind him held the handles of the chair. His name was Robbie.

"Sure does," said Robbie. "We'll get that taken care of right away."

Suddenly, for the first time in days, Tom thought of Cabbage. *She would have been right here. In the way.*

Robbie flipped on the lights. "Electricity is on. Good." He walked around the counter and turned on the kitchen faucet. "Water's on. Good. Utilities sometimes take forever to get turned back on."

"Yep. I know."

Robbie scribbled something on his clipboard. "It's pretty dusty." He opened the refrigerator. Whatever that once was food was now entirely black and gray, creeping up the walls.

"Ack!" Robbie yelped, cringing and slamming the door shut. "I think there's your smell." He returned to his clipboard, dictating to himself, "Replace—fridge—ASAP." He turned toward Tom. "I'm sorry. They normally handle this better. Maybe standard procedure didn't apply to your situation very well."

"Yeah. Probably an edge case."

"I'll check on this. See who was assigned to maintain the place. They often arrange for a family member to do it."

"Fell to my mom, it looks like."

Tom craned his neck, trying to look around. He hadn't regained enough arm strength to maneuver his wheelchair on carpet. *Everything's the same*, he thought. *Exactly the same. So weird. Chairs not pushed in. Even the picture's crooked.* His eyes fell and went hollow for a long moment, then he shook himself and looked around some more. *Kate's sketchbook. Toys under the couch. Couldn't see those if I were standing.*

"You ready?" said Robbie.

"Yep."

Robbie grabbed the chair's handles and started him on the tour, explaining challenges he would have, customizations they would make. Cooking, eating, bathing, sleeping, getting out of bed, using the toilet—everything would seem impossible at first.

"...and your caregiver will assist with almost everything in the beginning," Robbie was saying. "I'll be around to help a lot too, and of course you'll see me often at the hospital. Please don't hesitate to..."

Tom didn't hear him. The ghosts were too strong. For many months, he hadn't spent a moment in any room that had ever been occupied by people he loved. And this was the most saturated of all possible places. He hadn't anticipated the blow.

Robbie rattled on. "...one story ranch style with no basement. It's basically an ideal..."

He wheeled Tom into the girls' room. Some toys were scattered. The Barbie. A pair of Hannah's pajamas.

"Blood's still there," Tom said quietly.

"What, here? Yeah, we'll get that cleaned for..."

"No, no!" Tom interrupted forcefully. "No, please. Please leave that." He quieted. "If you don't mind, I'd like to keep that."

Robbie cocked his head and studied Tom for a few seconds, then his eyes softened. He subtly shook his head and placed a hand on Tom's shoulder. "Yes, sir. I'll make a note."

Tom sat motionless, staring at the stains on the carpet. Tears began to form. Robbie knelt and put an arm around him. At last Tom asked, "You mind if I touch it?"

"No, sir."

Robbie helped him to the ground and positioned him comfortably where he could reach the blood stain. "I'll wait out here, Tom. Take your time."

Robbie paced the living room, the sounds of Tom's agony filling the quiet house. Robbie's eyes grew damp. At last Tom calmed and called out, "Okay. I'm done."

Robbie returned and helped him back into his chair. Tom said, "It'll probably be okay if you just get that cleaned too."

"If you're sure."

Tom nodded weakly.

Robbie began to back him toward the door. Tom's eye landed on the glass cage. "Robbie, hold on. Can I see that, there?" He wheeled him closer.

The hamster lay dead on his side near the edge of the box, paws curled under, incisors bared through his desiccated mouth. Tom noticed he lay under the spout of the bone-dry water dispenser. He lifted his eyes to the ceiling.

"They told me Hamlet was being taken care of. Nobody's even set foot in here."

CHAPTER THIRTY-NINE

God, please kill me.

I know I asked for that before. Tom chuckled grimly. *I'd say you missed your chance.*

He sat at the kitchen table in his wheelchair, a pencil and some papers spread before him. Only three dining chairs remained, opposite from where he sat. Behind those was the family picture, crooked again. Tom slumped over the table, head in his hands.

I even told you that Kate and the kids would be better off without me. That prayer worked, I guess. Though—sorta the opposite of what I was thinking.

They probably are better off. Whipped cream and puppies as far as the eye can see.

The humming of the new fridge and the ticking of a wall clock were the only sounds. Tom heard neither.

I don't care about treats, God. I just want my wife and kids back. Take me to where they are. Wherever they are, I don't care, whipped cream or not.

I mean it.

The ticking summoned Tom at last, and he glanced up at the time.

Oh, no.

"Alan?" he called out, craning his head toward the hallway. "Alan?" No response. Tom turned back toward the table.

I complained I was trapped because of them. What an idiot. They were the best thing I ever had. Ha—a trap. I had no clue what that meant. Until now.

How did I not see it? What a fool. God, I miss them.

Tom stared through his papers. A couple of scribbled notes were on one sheet, the rest blank.

God. I miss them.

Okay, maybe I didn't see clearly. Maybe I was foolish. Doesn't mean you had to take them from me. Is it because I tempted you? Because I said I wanted a little freedom? So you killed them all? It wasn't their fault; it was mine. But you had to prove to me the hard way how blind I was. I'm free of them, alright. You were willing to kill innocent children just to teach me a lesson.

Is it because I complained about it? Compared your marriage plan to a prison? So you said, 'Fine, you don't like my way—instead you can have a prison so deep, so constricting, so—so—um—so maximum security—even criminals can't comprehend it.'

Tom picked up his pencil with his crooked hand, but remained motionless.

Okay, I admit it; your plan wasn't so bad after all. The sex seemed like such a big deal, but it's all the other stuff I miss so bad. The subtle things. It's obvious now that stealing that one need from elsewhere would never satisfy any part of the million subtle needs. And I let some petty little human conflicts divert my attention. Of course those would happen along the way.

I was so ungrateful.

Tom stared at nothing a little while. Then he called out, "Alan?" a bit louder. He slowly wheeled himself back from the table, out to the living room, and down the hall. "Alan?"

Where'd he go?

Tom rolled to the bathroom door and stared in. It now looked industrial. There was a new low sink sticking way out from the wall; a low towel rack; metal handrails installed around a new toilet; a low medicine cabinet, its door half open, an entire shelf lined with little orange bottles of prescription drugs. Tom eyed the handrails; the one time he tried to lift himself onto the john, he ended up waiting for minutes for Alan to rescue him, lying on the floor wedged between the toilet and the tub, his spine on fire.

Tom's eyes went distant again.

Was it because I dreamed of Tara? Wanted it for free? Okay, I was selfish. But you created us selfish beings, then you crush me for it.

And I never even did anything with her.

And it wasn't Kate's fault; she was such a good person. You didn't have to go quite that far.

God, I miss her.

He rolled himself back to the living room.

I even tried to do the right thing with Tara. I even tried to fix it. You didn't care. I was even glad I did. You didn't care. Now I've got all this.

There's no reward for trying to do right, that's obvious. God just messes with people's heads regardless. Hurts them and hurts them and hurts them. In fact, it's worse if you try to have faith and obey. At least in a godless world nothing needs to make sense; it is what it is, and that's it. But with God, we're trapped in his vicious world, but we try to believe there's some point. He just breaks them and breaks them. God's callous world rolls along with patient, unstoppable momentum, rolls right over people, crushing them, taking their lives. Takes their lives without killing them.

It turns them into people so useless, they can't even take a dump by themselves.

"Alan, where you at?"

Where'd he go? Now that I need him, he takes off.

"Alan?"

Maybe Alan is God—just pretended to be there at first, but it was all an illusion. Yeah, it'd be nice of God to do something that made it seem like he was there.

The front door opened and Alan stepped in. "It's nice and warm out. Feels great." He was about forty, tall, glasses, jeans, running shoes, car keys in one hand, and balanced in the other, a cardboard box loaded with stuff.

"Teacher, I gotta go," Tom said.

Alan checked his watch. "You're right. Good for you. Well, roll yourself in there." Alan watched as Tom worked the wheels. "How's the sensation this time?"

"Really faint. I still can't tell if it's my body feeling it or just my brain faking it on schedule."

"I guess we'll see in time. Either way, you don't want to miss your intervals."

Tom grinned at him. "*You* don't want me to miss my intervals."

"Ha. For me, it's just another day at the office. I've got plenty of rubber gloves."

"No thanks. I'll keep whatever privacy I have left."

"Fighting for zero percent?" Alan chuckled. "I like a fighter. Alright, right there, now lock your wheels. Feet on the ground. Okay, put your left hand right there, pull with your right. You really try, Tom. Don't let me do it all."

"I do."

"I know. Keep it up; you'll get there. Okay, now lift. Lift lift lift." Alan transferred Tom from the wheelchair to the toilet. Tom grimaced and growled, then he panted with his eyes squeezed shut for a while. At last he opened his eyes and glanced toward his painkillers.

"Hurt worse?" Alan asked while he repositioned Tom's pants.

"Yeah, well, that twisting makes it worse for a minute."

"Sorry, Tom. Alright, you got yourself?"

"Yeah, I'm good."

"Don't be a hero; I'll be right here."

"Yeah."

"And don't flush it this time; you know I need to check it."

"Got it."

Alan patiently waited in the bathroom doorway while Tom concentrated on making muscles work, both hands on the rails to hold his torso up.

"I'll let you try to go without your catheter."

"If only."

"You never know. Either way, you gotta empty it. Every time. And do it right, every time."

"Yeah, I know. So fun."

"More fun than the alternative. Nobody's gonna yell 'fire in the hole' for ya, Tom. If something goes wrong down there, by the time you feel it, you'll be hating life."

"That'd be new."

"Well, you don't have to hate life, you know. The battle's up here," Alan tapped his temple. "Not down there."

"Yeah, I know," Tom said coldly.

"Okay."

Tom did his business, but needed Alan to help him with the catheter. Afterwards, Alan made him try to clean himself without falling off. Alan finished him up and got him back into his chair. Tom thanked him, washed up, and rolled himself back to the kitchen table.

"Alan?"

Alan appeared at the kitchen door.

"I think I'll be good for a while. I feel good. You can go for a bit if you like."

Alan brightened a little. "I would like to whack a racquetball around a few times. You sure?"

"Absolutely."

"Okay, then. Call me *before* you feel poorly, understand?"

"Yes, Captain."

Alan disappeared into his bedroom—Coby's old room—for a couple of minutes, then he said goodbye on his way out the front door.

Well, alone again. Tom thought. He retrieved the pencil, but he stared through the paper. *Alone again.* The feeling permeated him so completely it left a hollow in the pit of his stomach and the constant taste of metal in his mouth.

CHAPTER THIRTY-EIGHT

Tom jostled across the lawn to the graveside. Emily and Jonathan walked beside him, all in black. Alan pushed the wheelchair. James and Rosie Kiernan trailed behind them, followed by a small group of friends and family. The pastor waited patiently for the group to arrive and settle. Margaret Ericson's casket lay beside a hole which lay beside a headstone engraved with the name *Roland Ericson.*

Tom was stone-faced. In a different context, an onlooker would have thought him mildly angry.

CHAPTER THIRTY-SEVEN

"I suppose I'll never need a tall dresser like that either." Tom shrugged. "That's all Kate's stuff anyway."

"Okay, you wanna clear it next?" Alan headed toward the dresser.

"Sure."

They were in Abigail and Hannah's old bedroom, now a crowded storage room. Jacob's stuff was in there so Alan could use Jacob's bedroom, and much of the furniture had been moved there out of Tom's way. The pinkish remnant of the blood stain now lay under some boxes.

Alan started at the top drawer, drawing out clothing items and holding them up. Tom called out each item's destination: "Sell. Donate. Sell. Trash. Donate…" Alan tossed each item into one of three black trash bags, already tagged. "Donate. Donate. Donate. Gosh, I don't know, Alan. Do ladies want this type of stuff?"

"I think you could donate it all, or most of it. Let them figure it out."

"Okay."

Alan glanced at Tom as each item made its way to the Donate Bag; Tom nodded each time. At last Alan withdrew a little wooden box and opened the lid. "Jewelry."

"Oh, yeah." Tom wheeled himself closer. Alan lowered the box to Tom's eye level. "Some of that's just cheap," Tom said. "We'll try to sell that." He poked around in the box. "But a few of these are heirloom. This was my mom's; we were going to pass it to Abby. Hmm. I know these were gonna be for Hann. Kate loved this; it was her mom's. Kate only wore it once or twice. Yeah, set all this aside somewhere; I'll go through it later; probably see if Emily or Kate's mom wants some of it."

"I'll stick it in your room."

When Alan returned, they finished the top drawer and he continued to the second. It contained Kate's personals. Alan paused a moment, weighing the etiquette of rooting through a woman's underwear drawer if she were dead.

"I guess that's all trash," Tom said. "Nobody wants used underwear, right?" Alan began moving items one by one to the bag marked *Trash*. "Oh, that was pretty expensive," Tom interrupted. "It was for our anniversary." He caught Alan's eye. "People don't want used lingerie, do they?"

Alan shrugged.

Tom shrugged too and nodded toward the *Trash* bag.

They worked their way to the bottom of the drawer until Alan said, "Hey, a bathing suit. This is new. You could sell this." He held up a bikini set that was still clipped together. Retail tags hung from it.

Tom's eyes lit up. "Ha. Look at that; she still has that." He shrugged. "I don't know. It's pretty old. I guess bathing suits go out of style just like any woman-clothes. We could at least donate it."

"Old?" Alan asked.

"Yeah, it was her Cancun bikini. We were supposed to honeymoon in Cancun, but we never got to go. I never saw her in it. She would have been gorgeous in it." Tom smiled thinly at the memory, eyes distant. "Yeah—we always talked about how one day we would finally go to Cancun; she must have been saving it for that."

At last Tom's eyes came back, and he found Alan patiently holding the bikini.

"Sell?" asked Alan.

"Yeah, sure."

Alan leaned toward the bag.

"Wait, actually no. No. I'll just keep it. Here." He held out a hand and Alan passed him the bikini. Tom clutched it close to him. "Okay, next drawer."

CHAPTER THIRTY-SIX

The self-closing front door of the MacMillan Robotics building proved a hearty challenge for Tom the atrophied wheelchair newbie. Robbie stood behind him, arms crossed, watching patiently until Tom cleared it. He poked his head in. "Good luck, Tom. Break a leg."

Tom turned his face halfway back. "Funny."

"Call me if you need anything, otherwise Alan will be here at five."

"Got it. Take it easy, man."

"Later."

Tom watched through the glass door as Robbie receded.

Though Alan's duties as 24/7 caregiver had ended, he and Robbie both continued to check on Tom, do chores for him, and drive him places. Until today, Tom's excursions had only included therapy, checkups, outpatient wrist surgery, grocery shopping, and the movie theater.

Because Tom was a bit early, he wheeled unhindered to his cubicle. When he rolled up to his cube door, a man was sitting in his chair.

Tom stopped short. "Oh, sorry."

When the man turned, a brief surprise changed to a wide smile. "Hello, there. You must be Tim."

"It's Tom. Tom Ericson." He rolled in and extended his hand.

"I am sorry. They did say to me Tom." He shook his hand. "People told me about you. That you would return soon." He pointed at Tom's ride. "I knew you would be in wheelchair. I am George. George Lin."

"Hey! There he is. Welcome back, big guy." Roger heaved himself out of his chair and circled the desk to shake Tom's hand.

"It's good to be back. Doesn't feel like it's been that long."

"Shoot. Seems long to me. I was shocked when you went AWOL on us; you're hardly ever even late."

Never late, Tom thought.

"Then, of course, we found out—you know—the news, sometime in January, when HR had to—uh—check on you. But it's good to see you up and around..." Roger's eyes flitted to the wheelchair. "...so to speak. You're doing okay?"

"Never better." Tom delivered it deadpan. Roger didn't twitch. "Nothing seems to have changed much around here. Except I saw a couple new faces. New hires?"

"Yep. Year's been good so far. Lots of work."

"Who's the guy at my desk?" Tom asked.

Roger answered, "George."

"Yeah, I met him. Is he—staying—*there?*"

"Yes. Don't worry, there's a desk for you. Where Herb used to sit."

"Okay. That's fine. Is George the new—me?"

"Of course not, Tom." Roger reclined on the edge of his desk. "But sorta, you know, since he's in your spot. And he took over most of your work. But no."

"Uh—okay..."

"You weren't there to do the work, Tom—not your fault, of course—but we needed somebody to do the work. You understand."

Tom nodded. "Sure."

"Be glad you still have a job. We couldn't fire you, of course, but we needed a guy."

"What?" Tom was a bit stunned. "You 'couldn't,' as in, you *wouldn't,* or you 'couldn't,' as in, you *weren't allowed to?*"

Roger raised his hands defensively. "Of course we didn't want to, Tom. I mean, who would even... But, you know, we already had George, and we can't exactly fire a guy 'cause he's in the hospital—though we can't exactly afford another salary."

Tom stared a long moment, then put on a wooden grin. "Good thing there's lots of work."

Roger sat up straighter. "Yeah. We'll make it work. Totally. Anyway, it's great to have you back. You need a hand with anything, just let me know, okay?"

"Alright, Roger. Will do."

Tom rolled up to the door of Tara's cube. "Hey there."

She turned in her chair, then she stiffened as if a wire in her spine had been yanked. Like lightning she sized him up before looking him in the eye. "So today's the day." She generated a half smile. "You're back."

"Yep. How've you been?"

"Fine. Peachy. You know—nothing ever changes around here." She glanced around. A long, strange moment passed, her eyes stumbling around drunkenly, neither studying him nor looking away. "How are you?" she said at last.

"Peachy. Just stopped by to see Roger. He's the same."

She nodded.

"I'm at Herb's desk now. There's a guy at mine."

"Yeah. George. He's pretty good. Hard to understand his accent sometimes."

"He seems fine."

She remained silent, looking concussed.

"You still running?" Tom asked.

"Yep."

Awkward silence.

"I'm not," Tom added with a chuckle.

Tara remained expressionless. "I figured."

Tom sat for a moment. "Yeah, well, I thought I'd say hi."

"Good to see you, Tom. And—I'm sorry about—all you went through."

"Thanks." He began to wheel away.

"Yeah, see ya, Tom."

During lunch MacMillan held a little *Welcome Back* party for Tom in the break room. Cold sandwiches and punch. People got their awkward condolences over with and returned to their turkey. Except George—he bluntly asked Tom what it was like being in a coma and being paralyzed. Tom was glad. The people mostly listened in. Tara didn't come.

CHAPTER THIRTY-FIVE

"Mr.—uh—Ericson?" An unfamiliar female voice came from behind him, obviously reading it from his chart.

"Yes. Hello," Tom said robotically, eyes fixed on the world going by on the other side of the windows.

He lay in bed in a post-op room. It was his second surgery since Boston that required a hospital stay; this was for recurring gastrointestinal complications, as might be expected of anyone who ever had a steering column extracted from his abdomen.

He rolled his head on the pillow toward the voice. Though his expression remained unchanged when he saw her, his brain partly seized up. *Holy Mackerel* was the best descriptor it could come up with. She was petite, with black hair and eyes, flawless brown skin, and a radiant smile, and she looked no older than twenty-five or thirty. And she made her hideous nurse uniform look spectacular.

"I'm Maria." Her smile was radiant. "I'm subbing for Chad now that his weekend switched to Tuesday-Wednesday for a while."

"Nice to meet you."

She asked how he felt, whether he'd slept well, offered other typical cordialities between Medical Professional and Patient. He barely noticed. She was exquisite.

"I need to check your incision, blood pressure, temp, you know—the usual."

"Sure thing."

She propped his head a little and placed the thermometer under his tongue. She uncovered his abdomen, removed the taped gauze, and inspected the three-inch long stapled gash in his skin. "Looking great. You'll have another nice scar for your collection."

Tom chuckled. "Puhfect." The thermometer slurred his words as he spoke. "I'm hoping they eventually form an image of the Virgin Mary."

She smiled and flicked her eyes toward his. "La Virgen María, you mean." Her pronunciation was crisp and accurate.

"Yes," he said. "Or, Sí. That's about all the Spanish I know."

"Imagine if your Virgin showed up on a potato or something. You're blessed. You'll get to keep yours forever." Her English was also perfect.

As close to him as she hovered, as lovely as she was, images of Kate began to surface in his mind. *I prefer auburn anyway.* Something in him knotted, remembering her. The loneliness resurged, and it struck him that even if he could ever love another woman, no woman would ever want him.

He released a resigned sigh.

Maria retaped him with fresh gauze then retrieved the blood pressure cuff. He extended his arm just how she wanted it without her asking.

"How's your pain?" she said.

"Not terrible. I don't know. About a four or five."

"Cuatro o cinco." She smiled broadly but kept her attention on her work.

"Cuatro o cinco," he repeated, unable to match her inflections, especially with the thermometer.

She paused and looked in his eyes. "Your ten is pretty high, I'm guessing." She reached for his chart and scanned it again. "But let's wait a little while before we consider any more pain medicine."

"What's this?" He sounded panicked. Maria looked at him a bit stunned, then she followed his eyes up past the foot of his bed to the TV mounted near the ceiling. The footage showed smoke and fire billowing out of a skyscraper. The clip replayed from the beginning. As thick, black smoke poured from the building, a large airplane appeared from off camera and disappeared behind it. A massive ball of flame burst out the other side through the windows.

They both uttered expletives simultaneously. Maria subconsciously grabbed his hand. Tom barely noticed.

He fumbled for the remote and turned the sound up. Commentators were acting as stunned and confused as he and Maria were. "Apparently this was not an accident. Both towers have been struck by aircraft. This second one appears to be a large, passenger-style aircraft…" They cut to a different perspective showing two buildings burning side by side.

"That's New York," Tom said. "The—the Twin Towers. Dear God." The thermometer had fallen to his chest.

The impact of the second plane was replayed a few more times while the commentators tried to make sense of what they were seeing. Then footage from earlier was replayed, showing only the first tower burning. This clip appeared to have been filmed from a circling helicopter.

The cuff remained uninflated around Tom's bicep. Maria still held his hand, with her other fingertips on her mouth. "God help them," she kept whispering.

Additional clips of the second impact filmed from different vantage points began to air. The commentators began dropping the word *terrorism*.

"Are you seeing this?" Another nurse, Robin, stood in the doorway, distraught. She turned to the hall and called, "David. David," and waved him to come. "Hurry. Come." Robin and David joined them near Tom's bed. All of them were frozen, quietly remarking without really saying anything, mesmerized and horrified and incredulous.

"Is that a person?" David cried. "Oh no, that's a person. A person fell out." They stared in growing dread, then they all simultaneously recoiled in horror.

"Gotta be a jumper," Tom said. No one commented or looked from the TV. "I would," he added.

They remained transfixed, praying, crying, forgetting they should be checking on patients. Then footage cut to an inferno at the Pentagon. Then rumors of missing planes. Then additional footage of the World

Trade Center. Tom smoldered, glaring at the images. "Whoever did this… I tell you, whoever did this…" The dreadful footage grew as each new clip cycled in.

Suddenly the second tower buckled, gracefully fell straight down, and disappeared into an enormous gray cloud it was ejecting.

Shouts echoed down the hospital hallways.

CHAPTER THIRTY-FOUR

Tom wheeled himself along the polished concrete floor of a brightly-lit corridor. A woman beside him and a man just behind had to stretch their stride to keep up. Punctuating the whitewashed cinder block walls were heavy, gray metal doors with wire-reinforced slot windows, each with a different label: *Machining & Welding, Paint & Finishes, Electrical A, Electrical B, Materials Library.*

"You still keeping it a secret from everyone at MacMillan?" The woman said. Her jeans and flannel made her seem younger than what the crow's feet around her quick eyes implied.

Tom grinned up at her. "Absolutely—*especially* now that it's nearly done. I decided—like three years ago before I even started back to work—that they would learn about it when they see it with their own eyes. They can wait a little longer."

"Sure enough," she said.

"I'd like at least one more patent granted before they know. This is my project, my design, done on my time, bought with my money. I don't need them freaking out, thinking I'm going rogue. Especially Roger." Tom glanced back at the man. "Justin, you understand."

"Oh, yeah," Justin muttered. He wore old workboots, canvas farm pants, a band t-shirt, and black-framed glasses.

"No, we get it," said the woman. "Just checking."

Tom shook his head. "I've been essentially irrelevant at work since the wreck. The place is killing me. Year after year, I just go about my busy work, designing in my head the whole time, then I get home and draw stuff up."

"Well, it's great, Tom," she said. "Probably the coolest project we've had since I've been here at Verve. Way better than anything MacMillan's ever sent us." She reached for a door handle. "Just wait 'til you…"

"Carly, I moved it to *B*," Justin interrupted, gesturing down the hall. "Everybody was messing with it."

Carly led them on, turned a corner, and opened a door for Tom. He wheeled into a large room filled with worktables, tools, racks upon racks of labeled bins, work lights, and mechanical projects in various stages of completion.

"Back here." Justin led them around the tables to the rear.

When Tom rounded the corner, his eye landed on what they sought: perched on a workbench sat a wheelchair that looked like a sci-fi movie prop. "Wow." Tom glanced at Justin. "Wow, wow, wow! That looks so good. Man."

"Yeah, it's pretty sweet." Justin nodded with a twinkle in his eye.

A power cord ran from the wheelchair to one of the many outlets at the back of the workbench. The rear wheels were a little smaller than average and slightly canted in, and each had a bike disc brake mounted on the inside. The frame resembled a bike frame, with hydroformed aluminum tubing anodized a smoky blue, and a suspension like a mountain bike frame with two shocks on each side. Hinges joined the tubes in places, creating articulated sections for the seat, back, and footrests. The seat and back were mesh like an expensive office chair, in slate gray. Each frame section was connected to a small electric motor by a pair of thin cables that laced around several pulleys, eccentric like those on a compound bow.

"Look at those welds," Tom said. "Nice, Justin."

"My pleasure."

Tom stared up at it, rolling back and forth, a dumb grin all over his face. Justin and Carly glanced at each other, smiling.

At last Tom said, "Well, can I sit in it?"

"Of course." Carly hurried over. She unplugged it and pressed a button to retract the power cord, then she hoisted it easily to the ground.

"What's the final weight?" said Tom.

Carly answered, "With that new battery, only thirty-two pounds."

"Oh, man. You guys." Tom was giddy.

"The carbon helps a lot," Justin said. "And the mesh. And of course the aluminum is pretty thin-walled compared to what I'm used to. But it'll hold up as long as you don't go off any jumps." He chuckled.

Tom locked the disk brakes on the chair's wheels. He then positioned his own chair and locked its wheels, then he pulled himself over into the new chair. He let a small growl slip and took a couple deep breaths, frowning deeply.

"Still hurting, huh?" Carly put her hand on his shoulder.

Tom nodded a little. "Twisting my spine or flexing my abs are still the worst. That used both."

"But you're doing great, Tom." She flicked a doubtful glance toward Justin. "Just threw yourself right over there."

"Lots of therapy. Lots of pullups and dips." Tom unlocked the disk brakes. "Alright, let's test it." He took it for a quick spin around the room. Justin hopped up on the bench and sat with his feet dangling. Tom made his way back around and stopped. "Feels good so far."

Tom re-locked the brakes, then he strapped his shins and waist to the chair with wide belts. Carly stepped a little closer, hands at the ready, just in case. Justin didn't twitch.

Tom held down a button tucked under the armrest. The motor whirred to life, cables tightened, pulleys turned, shocks extended, and the chair smoothly lifted Tom to a nearly erect standing position. The footrests and two rear supports, both with rubber feet, had lowered until they planted firmly on the concrete. Tom remained perfectly stable, his hips positioned slightly back over the center of gravity, and the belts keeping his inert legs from buckling. He glanced between Justin and Carly, joy on his face.

"That was—what—five or six seconds? How did you…"

"Probably under seven," Carly answered, beaming. "Justin gets his gorilla body all the way up in about eight. You said you wanted full extension in fifteen seconds or less. Well, less is more, in my opinion."

Justin added, "Your skinny little carcass is no problem for this beast."

"Carly, how'd you get that tiny motor to…"

"It's you, Tom," she interrupted. "Your neutral buoyancy thing is the key."

"Ah—it's amazing. It's wonderful. Let's do it again. Let's do it again. Time it this time."

He held the *down* button, and the chair quickly lowered him to a sitting position. After Justin readied his watch, Tom depressed *up* again and rose to standing.

Justin eyed his wrist. "About—oh—six and a quarter."

Tom stared down at his standing body. He started quietly chuckling.

"Good job, man," Justin said. "You did it. It works."

"It's great," Carly added.

Tom progressed to loopy, unrestrained chuckling, glancing from the chair, to Carly, to Justin, to his legs. His eyes began to fill, then laughed outright and clapped his hands. "Ha ha! I can stand." He stretched out his arms to them. "I can stand! Yes!" A tear rolled. Justin slid off the bench and Carly stepped in. Tom pulled them in. Despite the group hug, the chair remained stable.

"Get everybody in here," Tom cried. "Vlad, Jim. Who else worked on it? A.J.? Get everybody."

CHAPTER THIRTY-THREE

When Tom first showed up at MacMillan in his new wheelchair, his friends had no doubt he would soon be leaving them. They looked up his patents, found out about his LLC, and of course, pestered him about the chair. Nobody doubted he would sell them by the truckload, especially when he mentioned the truckloads of money their insurance plan had shelled out on his behalf. Though he charged many thousands per unit, he didn't expect prices like that to much hinder the insurance industry. The articulated chair could reduce the costs they poured into disability assistance—caregivers, household alterations, and such—just by enabling the wheelchair-bound to better function in a society designed for *homo erectus*. His colleagues congratulated him. Some of them, in barely-masked mock humor, asked him to remember them when he made it big.

Even Tara complimented Tom on the work, though she still hadn't warmed to him much. Apart from desiring a non-awkward friendship, Tom had lost all desire for her. The irony, however, wasn't lost on him: now that he legally could have Tara, he physically couldn't have her, nor did he want her, and she clearly could never want him. Nevertheless, to her credit, she took him aside one day and revealed—him reading between the lines of her hesitant, stumbling *mea culpa*—that she felt guilty, even responsible, for the death of his family, in some Bad Karma sort of way.

As luck should have it—great luck for Tom, sour luck for his customers— injured veterans were returning from the Middle East. These self-reliant, mentally tough athletes loathed being waited upon. To them, grabbing the granola off the top shelf without begging for glacial supermarket help was worth several thousand in credit debt. Word-of-mouth bubbled up, and within a couple of years the VA began to fund his chairs. Word soon spread to the rest of the medical world. His *Made-in-America-by-a-Disabled-War-Veteran* marketing shtick didn't hurt much either—even after they discovered that his disability had nothing to do with his pain-less month in Kuwait and Iraq.

Sales exploded. Soon after Tom finally quit his job, he felt the need to plunge a double-edged knife into MacMillan's back: First, he took out a hefty loan and purchased Verve Fabrication, the shop where Carly and Justin worked, to ensure they could focus on his products. As a re-sult, Verve began declining MacMillan contracts, and MacMillan had to shop elsewhere for a fabricator. Nobody could match Verve's quality. Second, he poached three of the best people from MacMillan—includ-ing his replacement, George Lin—and brought them on at Verve. Tom intended for Verve Engineering to soon need good robot designers.

CHAPTER THIRTY-TWO

"We haven't seen you for awhile."

Pastor Mark from Powder River Community Church sat across the table from Tom in his dim little accessible house. Though he was smiling, Pastor Mark acted almost spooked, like a boy sent on a neighborhood errand to borrow a cup of sugar and a shotgun. Mark sat where Tom used to sit, and Tom sat where Kate used to sit: the place near the kitchen where it was easy to get up from the table—where it was easy to roll up in a wheelchair.

"Probably, yeah, quite a while," Tom said. "I think the last time was—uh—a couple years after the accident. So, it's been a while. It's really hard to drag myself anywhere. Not as hard as it was at first, but it's still a pain."

Pastor Mark nodded, pleasant still painted on. "I'm sure it is. You know, if transportation's an issue, we can arrange to get you there. We'd be happy to work something out."

"Okay, thanks," Tom said flatly. "But I get around pretty well on the bus."

Pastor Mark continued, "We also wanted to see if there's anything we could do for you."

"Thanks, but I think I'm fine. I still get lots of support when I need it." He cocked his head. "Insurance pays for all kinds of stuff. I'm sure they hate my guts." Tom chuckled. "Whatever parts I've still got."

"I'm sure it's been expensive. But it's good to have that support."

Tom paused a moment. "Yep."

"We could arrange to pick you up on Sunday. We'd be happy to."

Tom's eyes searched the air. "No, I don't think Sunday will work. You know. Super busy with work and stuff. And I'm pretty slow with everything now, as you can probably imagine."

"Of course." Mark nodded knowingly. "I hope you know we care about you, and we're praying for you."

"Sure. I would guess. I just wish it would work." He chuckled woodenly.

"What would work?"

"The prayers." Tom tried to keep it light. "You know, magical healing powers and stuff." His thin smile lingered. "I doubt I'm the only one who doesn't believe that."

"That God can heal?"

"That he *will* heal."

"Tom, I don't think people are praying for that kind of miracle."

"Then what?" His artifice vanished. "That God will kiss my boo-boo and make me feel all better? That he'll give me a lollipop for being brave?"

Pastor Mark sat back. "We pray that your faith won't waver through all of this; that God will use it in your life."

Tom hissed a dry, bitter laugh. "Yeah, he's using it in my life, all right."

Mark's brow furrowed. "What do you mean?"

Tom glanced about, as if deciding. Then his eyes hardened and he glared at Mark. "Maybe you should pray instead that God will change me so that I prefer pain and misery to health and happiness."

Mark's eyes fell. After a moment, he looked up and folded his hands onto the edge of the table. "Health and happiness isn't always what's best for us."

Tom rolled his eyes.

"If pain can help us or help others, a good God won't hesitate to use it. He just asks us to trust him through it."

"It's so easy to say."

"I know," Mark said. "I know." He took a breath and released it. "Okay, so last year, Trevor, my youngest, is racing his bike around in the empty lot down the street. Not wearing a helmet like we'd told him—of course. He rides under a dead tree, and this broken branch jabs him in the head; tears open a big piece of scalp, like a silver dollar."

Tom's fingers went to the huge scar hidden under his hair.

"You should have seen him. Horror-movie bloody, running home, wailing like a banshee. Just left his bike and ran. Tricia comes running in with him in her arms. So, I've gotta try and stop the bleeding, but hair is all inside it, so I've gotta hold it open and literally scrape the hair out of the flap so I can fold it back down and press on it. And Trevor's kicking and screaming. It was horrible; I didn't know what else to do. I figured I'd rather have him hate me for a while than let him bleed until he passed out. I figured…"

"But God can stop the bleeding whenever he wants, with a snap of his fingers. He just decides not to."

"I don't know all his reasons, Tom, but…"

"So God takes my family, takes my legs, takes every decent moment, and that's how he helps me?"

"I don't know all his reasons. But he asks us to trust him until we…"

"You know, Pastor Mark, that sounds all wonderful until you're the one sitting alone in this house, day after day, missing the hospital because people were there. Missing having strangers help me use the toilet, because at least someone was there."

Mark wilted. "Tom, I…"

"You can't understand."

"I know. But we care for you. We feel badly for…"

"Yeah, thanks. It's so heartwarming. They also feel sorry for a rabbit smashed on the road."

"Would you rather people not care about you?"

Tom leaned forward, fire in his eyes. "No, I'd rather have God care about me. But the one who's supposed to 'stick closer than a brother' has abandoned me. I beg for his help, and I get silence. Maybe all he cares about is hurting me. Or maybe there's silence for some other reason?"

Mark sighed. "Tom, I know it's hard. I can't imagine how hard."

"No, you can't." His chest heaved. He stared darkly across the table. "You and your little life—your perfect little life—getting paid to make up speeches to keep people coming back to church so they'll keep paying you. You can't possibly imagine."

Mark drooped his head. "I'm not here to say I can fix anything. I'm here for you if you want to reach out. But for now, I see I can't help you, so I guess I'll go."

"Yeah, why don't you go."

Pastor Mark rose. Without making eye contact, he made his way to the front door and closed it quietly behind him.

Tom snatched a bowl off the table and hurled it into the wall across from him. The crooked family picture fell to the floor with a shatter. Tom grimaced and clutched his abdomen, glaring toward the door.

CHAPTER THIRTY-ONE

Carly, meet me in the library. Alone.

—Tom

Carly looked up from her computer and glanced around, concerned. She started toward the materials library.

As she closed the door behind her, she said, "Tom, what's wrong?"

"You know a lot about cars." Tom's sketchbook was in his lap.

"What?"

"Cars, Carly. You're good with cars."

"Yeah, I guess. But Vlad's the real…"

"Shut up. You're a brain. I'm talking electrical. Your background's in hybrid."

She shrugged.

"Right?"

She nodded.

"So you know electrical systems, storage, generation, capacities, limits, system architecture, junk like that."

"Yes."

"Okay. I weigh about a hundred forty pounds in my chair. I could build an arm to lift me in my chair that would… Shoot. Never mind. Look." He wheeled over to a table, pushed back a bin of parts someone had left out, and slapped his sketchbook down. He flipped to the middle and began searching around. Carly saw diagrams, sketches, notes, several pages of what looked like a written letter. "Ah, here. Look." He slid the sketchbook over.

Carly pulled up a chair. It was a rough sketch of a robotic arm sticking out of the driver's door of a truck, holding a wheelchair above the ground. She raised a skeptical eyebrow at Tom. He nodded toward the book, and she turned the page. More sketches and notes. Then the next page and the next. Each successive page showed closer and closer details of different components: robot arm articulation, auxiliary batteries, slides, latches, and on and on. Page after page of drawings, revisions, cross-outs, fresh starts, cross-outs, notes, drawings.

She frowned and screwed up her mouth. "I dunno. Power's not a problem. We'll just remote start the engine to get the power; no need for auxiliary batteries."

"Of course," he groaned. "Remote start. Of course. Dang it, Carly."

"And a twelve volt probably could run it for egress, just in case, at least a couple of times. But the chair…" She turned more pages and found sketches of modifications to the articulated wheelchair. "Oh, yeah, well, never mind." Wheelchair with mounting brackets for the robot arm. Wheelchairs with seatbelts. Attachment points to latch onto the vehicle floor. Carly flipped through more pages showing the articulated chair both standing up and lowering itself into a driving position. "Mmm hmm. Yeah. I get it." She continued flipping. "We wouldn't even need large vehicles like trucks or SUVs. And they'll all be in handicapped parking spots; the door can open as wide as we like. If your arm could just wriggle the driver into a large—even a medium coupe, we might not even have to widen the door opening."

"Or with sedans, maybe we convert the two doors into one large door." Tom added. "Either way, the left rear seat would have to go away to make room for the arm, and the remainder would become storage or…"

"Which is perfect," Carly interrupted. "Tom." She looked into his eyes. "We're gonna be rich."

Tom sniggered. "We're already rich."

"I mean *rich*. If the market will support it. How many of these conversions are out there waiting for us?"

"I don't know. These vets hate the lame accessible vans they're stuck with. So to speak." He chuckled at his own unintentional pun. "They want cool vehicles: trucks and four by's and muscle cars. Mostly trucks. And they're just a fraction of the total need. Especially internationally. And because our chair doesn't break down, anybody with the best chair is stuck with the worst vehicle."

"You know how much this will cost."

"It's huge. At first. Huge. We could start with all-out customizations. Quite spendy. But suppose we partner with a couple manufacturers, have them pony up for some feel-good exposure. Get sub-wholesale discounts from them, even take delivery with half-baked interiors."

They talked and planned and sent up ideas and shot them down. At last Tom said, "Most of our people are too creative to long tolerate the piece-part work they're on now. They need a little fire."

"Yep. I've felt it. I feel it myself."

"Then let's go. Get everybody to the kitchen."

"They're gonna go crazy, Tom. Might as well just order some pizza and beer, 'cause today's shot."

By Christmas, their new robot arm lifted a mannequin in a wheelchair into the driver's side of a large SUV.

CHAPTER THIRTY

A glass wall separated the two worlds of the Verve Engineering office: the inner world with desks and lamps and muttering people, but one end of the room glowed brightly. Once the eye focused through the wall and adapted to the brightness, the second world appeared: sunlit rose bushes, tall ornamental grass waving under a light fall breeze, fluttering cottonwoods beginning to turn, and a squirrel struggling up a young blue spruce, his agility frustrated by the prickly branches.

Tom's desk sat near the windows along the back wall, but he failed to see the squirrel only a few feet away; he intently studied something on his computer.

Since acquiring Verve, Tom had overhauled the aesthetics and function of the entire building: landscaping, paint, decorations, equipment, kitchen, furniture—even a pair of vintage arcade games. Besides being fun for employees, they served to demonstrate his articulated wheelchair to customers; disabled folks could stand and play an old-school video game, broad smiles plastered across their faces.

At the moment, only a few desks were occupied; the sound of machines faintly echoed down the hallways branching off either side of the central office space. A man quickly weaved through the office toward the back and stopped at Tom's desk. "Tom, a customer is here, out front."

Without looking up, Tom robotically said, "A customer?"

The man waited.

At last Tom looked up and focused. "What? A customer? Uh, is anyone…"

"Barry is with him, but I think you'll want to meet him. Flew in from Virginia to be here."

Tom looked confused. "Virginia? Why? Doesn't he know he doesn't have to travel…"

"I don't know. Just showed up, I guess."

"Alright." Tom shrugged and wheeled toward the lobby. "Hey, Doug. See if Julie's around and send her out too."

"She's in California with a customer."

"Alright, whatever."

Tom made his way out the front doors to the courtyard. Cool air beautifully offset the heat of the sun. His employee Barry stood on the walkway, gesturing and talking to a young man in a wheelchair. Another man stood behind the chair. Tom overheard Barry's excited speech:

"…are tailored to your exact dimensions, our 'Phantom Hinges' aligning perfectly with the axis of rotation for both your knee and hip. Even to me it feels really natural, more like effortlessly rising to my feet rather than being forced to an upright position by a machine. The breathable mesh…"

"Hello, there," Tom called as he rolled toward them.

Barry paused and glanced back. "Oh, hey, Tom." He returned to his guests. "This is Tom, my boss. He's the one who invented the whole thing."

Tom extended his hand to the disabled man. "Tom Ericson. Nice to meet you."

"Hello. I'm Steve Barnes," he said with a smile.

Steve was missing both legs, one just above the knee, the other about six inches higher. He also lacked three fingers on his left hand. His red hair reminded Tom of Hannah. Steve looked to be in his early thirties, his friend a bit younger. His friend was Hispanic with a trace of something Asian, with dark hair and hazel eyes, but with a long nose and a narrow face, and he was quite tall and muscular. Both had the look of military.

Steve turned to his friend. "So, this is our guy." He looked back at Tom. "Army, right? Desert Storm vet?"

Tom paused, then admitted, "Correct." He felt odd about people's automatic correlation between *disabled* and *vet,* especially when facing the real deal.

The other man leaned down and shook Tom's hand. "Henry Carrizales."

"Good morning." Tom replied. He turned to Barry and chuckled. "I hope Steve doesn't think we intend to measure the distance between his hips and knees."

Steve laughed. "Several thousand miles, last I checked."

Barry glanced down at where Steve's knees were supposed to be. "No, I was just geeking out a bit." He grinned sheepishly at Steve. "I'm just really proud of our product."

Steve turned to Tom. "I asked him, actually. Stopped him on his way inside. I'm sorta geeking out too. I'm pretty glad about what y'all are doing. I know a bunch of guys who are interested."

Tom said, "Of course we can accommodate a variety of disabilities. We've worked with quite a few who've lost limbs. Barry here designed a rig for a gal with nothing at all below the hip on the left. IED." Tom motioned to Barry. "He's one of our engineers. We used to work together at my last job, and now he's come over to work with us here at Verve Engineering."

Barry smiled and stuck out his hand to Steve. "Anyway, great to meet you guys. Can't slack too much in front of the boss. I'm sure he'll take care of you." He shook Henry's hand. "I hope I'll see you around."

"You too."

Barry continued inside, and Tom turned back to Steve. "Anyway— you gentlemen are from Virginia, if I heard right. What brings you all the way out here? I hope you know we could've sent a sales rep out to you."

"No, just me," Steve said. "Henry's from here. I just flew out to visit him, but since I'm in town, we thought we'd drop by and check out your stuff."

"Great," Tom said. "Let's move it inside and talk. We've got samples, our demo vehicle, lots of information."

They headed toward the door with Henry walking beside Steve. Tom looked up at Henry. "So, you're from Colorado?"

"Yes, sir. I grew up here in Fort Collins."

"Okay. Me too. What school did you go to?"

"Poudre. Entered the military right out of high school."

Tom stopped short before he reached the button to open the door. "Wait, you're not that kid who played football for Poudre? That's right—Henry—uh—Henry—uh…"

"Yes, sir. Carrizales."

"And you were good?"

"Well, sir, I enjoyed it."

"Gimme a break, Hay Sauce," Steve said with a laugh. "Of course you were good." He turned to Tom. "Of course he was good, wasn't he?"

Tom was at a loss for a moment. "Well, I guess. I never saw him play, but people talked about him. I read about him in the paper and stuff."

Steve nudged Henry, chuckling. "See. You liar."

Tom said, "I think I read that you turned down scholarships to join the Army."

It was perfect bait for Steve. "What? Are you kidding me? Ha ha! What a buffoon!" He shot a look at Tom. "I don't doubt it. He's strong as an ox, and fast too. Shoot. Got that way running from Bobbies in Manchester. Ha ha!"

Henry rolled his eyes.

Tom looked confused, but before he could ask, Henry hurried around Steve to open the door. "Sir, let me."

"Turned down scholarships to join the Army…" Steve muttered as he rolled through, shaking his head.

Tom led them to the demo room. Henry sat in one of the few regular chairs among all the space granted for wheelchairs.

Tom turned to Steve. "I'm sorry, but now I'm wondering about the Manchester thing."

Henry slumped a little and mumbled, "Oh, no."

Steve brightened. "Who ever heard of a Mexican named Henry, you know? So we made a bunch of British jokes about him." He talked and chuckled at the same time. "Said he drove a lorry in Manchester; got so fast because he grew up running from Bobbies; stuff like that."

Tom glanced at Henry. "Uhhhh..."

Henry said, "Yeah, they do that, sir. It's my cross to bear, I guess."

"See," Steve added, "he don't like the British jokes, but he's the one with all the great Mexican jokes."

Tom glanced at Henry.

Henry turned up his palms. "It's true. I've heard 'em all."

Steve laughed. "Yeah, except you didn't like that civilian that kept..."

"Okay, let's not go there."

Steve turned to Tom, beaming. "I'm guessing the jerk stopped telling racist jokes when his jaw was wired shut. Ha ha! Oh, I wish I had it on video."

"Anyway..." Henry added loudly.

"I wouldn't know," Tom said. "Is the name *Henry* uncommon among Hispanics?"

"Not really. My name's actually Enrique. My parents started calling me Henry because they wanted me to be really—uh—American." He shrugged. "I guess they figured a guy named Henry couldn't get deported."

Tom nodded. "Okay. So what's *Hay Sauce*?"

Henry groaned and cut his eyes at Steve. "It's because I bailed hay as a kid..."

"See? He lies," Steve interrupted loudly, grinning. "Alright." He leaned forward. "Because he was always preaching to us, we were calling him Jesus." —this he pronounced *Hay Soose*. "But he wouldn't let us call him that. Said it was blasphemous. So we changed it to Hay Sauce. Or sometimes Hay Salsa. Or just Salsa. He walked in and somebody said, 'Hey, Salsa' and that kind of locked it in. Besides, we learned that he worked hay his whole life. We sorta liked to switch between Hay Sauce and Salsa. Or Hank Sauce."

"Hmmm, very..." Tom started.

"Or Hanky Panky."

"Steve…" Henry mumbled.

"Oh, or sometimes Crumpet."

"Crumpet?" said Tom.

"I don't think he's actually a Mexican. You know, he lies a lot. Who's ever heard of a tall Mexican?"

"It was my Uzbek grandfather. They say he was tall."

"Uzbek?" Tom said with raised brows.

"Yes, sir. Uzbek immigrant to El Salvador. He married a Mexican. They moved back to her home town."

"Oh, okay," Tom said. He wagged his finger toward them. "So you two were over there together, I take it?"

"Yes, sir."

"Afghan or Iraq?"

"Well, both, mostly," Steve said, "but actually we…"

Henry cut his eyes at Steve. "Mainly Afghan."

"And maybe some other places," Tom said slyly.

"Oh, no, no…" Steve chuckled. "We only went where the news said we went." He leaned his elbows on the table, lacing his fingers as well as he could. "Yeah. We were together. When I got hit, Salsa was right there. Tried to save my life but failed."

Tom sat back, confused.

"It's true. John, our medic, was also right there, one step behind him. He actually saved my life. He did have Salsa stick his grubby mitts inside my stump to pinch off the femoral for a few minutes. So I guess he sorta saved my life, though he was just following orders."

"It was gross," Henry said. "White man blood on my hands, my pants, my shirt…"

"Shut up."

"When was this?" Tom asked. "You look great, Steve. Must have been a while back."

"Almost four years ago. But Henry moved to D.C. a while after I got shipped back. We hung out pretty often 'til he moved back here."

"D.C.?" Tom asked.

"Yes, sir. I transferred out of the military to another government position."

"Postal Service? I.R.S.?" Tom joked.

"Mainly odd jobs." Henry shrugged.

Tom narrowed his eyes at Henry. "Okay. Sort of a gopher."

"So to speak," added Steve.

"Excuse me, Tom," Henry said abruptly, changing the subject. "How were you injured in Desert Storm?"

"No, not Desert Storm. I did it to myself. Car wreck. Just a few years ago. I wasn't even infantry. Combat Engineer. All I did in Iraq was ride in trucks across the desert. Uh—and round up surrendering Iraqis."

"Oh, okay. Yeah, it's a bit different now. It's changed a little."

Steve nodded in agreement. "No shh—um—I mean—No kidding. I forgot: Hay Sauce don't like me cussing in front of strangers. Says it ain't ladylike or whatever."

"It's fine," Tom said. "But I get it. I was raised like that. My wife too. She never cussed, I don't think, ever once."

"Are you a Christian?" Henry asked matter-of-factly.

"Hold up, Preacher, wait." Steve held up a hand toward Henry, but stared at Tom. "You said 'your wife never cussed' in past tense. You mean ex-wife, or…"

"She died in the wreck. Same wreck that did this. Kids too."

"Man, I'm sorry." Steve sat back.

"I'm sorry, Tom," Henry added. "How long ago?"

"It's been a while. In two-thousand. Wife and all three kids. It's okay, though. Thanks."

"But they were believers?" asked Henry, hopefully.

Tom shrugged and sank a little. "You could say that. I'm sure you would say that."

"I'm really sorry," Henry said. "That's tough. At least you'll see them again someday."

Steve glanced at Tom, raised his eyebrows, and rested his cheek on his fist.

Tom wore a blank face. "Yeah, if I can figure out how to see through six feet of dirt."

Henry slowly nodded his head. "Okay. Do you consider yourself a believer?"

Tom cocked his head. "Yeah, I believe. I believe I'm tired of carrying on one-sided conversations with the ceiling. So, no, the only arms I've got to lean on are these, and I'm pretty sure they're not everlasting."

Henry nodded. His face showed that he understood more than he was told. "Okay. I am sorry for your loss."

Steve added, "Yeah, Tom. Me too."

"Nah, it's fine, but thanks." Tom forced a smile and brightened. "So, why are you gentlemen here? Not just to talk about nicknames, I'm guessing."

Steve leaned forward with a glint in his eye. "I want a fancy chair, and I want a fancy truck."

CHAPTER TWENTY-NINE

Tom normally left the office last. *Workload,* he told himself. He wouldn't admit that it felt better than a house full of ghosts.

He pecked away at his keyboard, the moonlit night just out of reach beyond the glass. A wire climbed from his smartphone on his desk to the earbuds in his ears. The phone on the other end rang twice.

"Yeah, hello, Tom," came Jonathan's voice. He sounded tired.

"Hey, bro. How you doing?"

Jonathan paused. "Fine," he uttered in monotone.

"Is Emily around? She's not answering her cell."

Jonathan paused. "No." Another pause. "No, she's not."

"Okay. I guess I'll try her later. Just have some cool news for her. Anyway, how have things been? Business still good?"

Jonathan exhaled. "Then I guess you haven't heard."

Tom's shoulders drooped and his eyes drifted toward the window. "What?" It was more groan than question.

"Emily doesn't live here anymore."

"Uhhhh…"

"Yeah, she's moved in with her boyfriend."

Long silence on both ends. At last Tom said, "You're kidding me."

"At least they're not using my place anymore to do their thing."

"You're kidding me."

"No, I'm not. I figured you knew."

Long silence.

"I'm sorry, Jonathan."

"Same story you always hear. Came home early to surprise her. Not so much to be sweet, like bringing flowers and junk; basically I suspected. Walked right in on them. Let's just say it's good I didn't have a gun."

Long silence.

"I'm sorry," Tom said. "I don't know what to say."

"I'm sorry too. You don't need anything else on your shoulders. But— it is what it is." A tiny choking sound escaped him. "I don't know what I did to lose her."

"It's not you. At least not fully. She's always been—you know—selfish."

"I probably should have brought her more flowers."

"That's not it, Jonathan." Tom paused, thinking. "That's not it."

Neither of them spoke for several seconds.

"You know what's dumb?" Tom said. "I bring Kate more flowers now than I ever did. Every time I go down to the cemetery."

"That's not dumb."

"Like she cares now. But at least people know that whoever Katherine Ericson was, she was loved."

Jonathan was silent a long time. "Well, when you talk to Emily—if she can find the nerve to pick up the phone—I'm sure she'll spruce up her side of the story, make me out as horrible the way she has for the lawyers. Tell you all the names I called her after I found them."

"Lawyers, already?"

"Yes, there'll be a divorce. As soon as I can manage it. She wants it all, the house, half my income; probably wishes we'd had kids so she could draw child support too."

Tom didn't comment.

"I'm sorry, Tom. She's your sister. You don't need to be in the middle. Sorry. I'm just really mad right now."

"I get it. It's okay." A long pause. "I just… I'm mad too. Really mad."

"Yep."

More silence.

"Well, I guess I'll go. Sorry. Maybe I'll check on you in a bit."

"Okay. Whatever. Take it easy, Tom."

CHAPTER TWENTY-EIGHT

Demand for downtown parking usually far outpaced supply, especially on a Friday night. Therefore, when a tricked-out 4x4 deftly swung into a handicapped parking spot, a couple of people thought *Who's the jerk?* The truck—a hopped up 1967 International Scout wearing meaty tires, matte olive paint, and blacked-out trim—certainly didn't scream *disabled*. A few lookers paused on the crowded sidewalk near the handicapped spot. When the gullwing driver's door opened, the *Verve Custom Conversions* logo along the bottom of the doorframe proudly rose before them like a hoisted flag. When they saw the driver in a wheelchair instead of a normal seat, they finally noticed the permanent disability license plates.

The robot arm smoothly lowered Tom to the ground in his new articulated wheelchair, its frame matte olive to match his truck. As Tom rolled toward the sidewalk ramp, the arm retracted, the gullwing door lowered into place, and the engine shut itself off.

"Tom! Tom, is that you?" a voice called from the crowd. The man stepped forward. The face looked familiar, but Tom couldn't conjure a name or place. "Tom, it's Chuck. Remember me? On the freeway?"

"Chuck? Oh, Chuck! Yes. You rescued me when I broke down." Tom smiled and extended his hand. *Cleans up nicely,* thought Tom. *No wonder I didn't recognize him.* "You're still in town?"

"Of course. It's still Fort Collins, right?"

People flowed past them like a river around a rock.

Chuck gestured toward the Scout. "So your old piece of junk breaks down, and you replace it with a car that's even older?"

"Oh, the truck? Yeah, when I bought it, it was in worse shape than that junker on the freeway. But the folks I work with are great with cars. Fixed it up, did all the conversion work, all new drivetrain, suspension, everything."

"Man, it's really sweet. But—I'm sorry to see you in a wheelchair. Last I saw you, you were walking. To need a serious machine like this, I'm guessing you're in it for the long haul."

Tom smiled grimly. He was glad for Chuck's way of addressing the elephant in the room: matter-of-fact yet uncalloused. A rare trait. "Yep. The long haul. It was a car wreck." He cocked his head. "In fact, it was the same kind of car as that one you saved me from. Come to think of it…" His eyes searched the air. "Yep. Yeah, it was just a couple of weeks later. Hmm. You were one of the last people to see me walk."

Chuck shook his head. "I'm really sorry, man. That really sucks."

"Yeah, it's been tough, but I'm mostly used to it now. Things are better. Going pretty well recently."

"That's good. I'd love to hear about it sometime. But I probably won't see you for another—what's it been? Like ten years? I was in school then, right?"

"It was, uh, two-thousand, so, eleven years."

"Okay. Wow." Chuck brightened. "Hey, have you eaten? If you aren't here to meet people, I could buy you dinner. I'd love to."

"Actually, my other plans fell through, so I was just coming out to grab a bite. You're by yourself?"

Tom and Chuck found themselves tucked into a corner of the restaurant where Tom wouldn't hinder an aisle. Chuck discovered that Verve was Tom's company. He was smitten enough with Tom's wheelchair that he fell to his knees on the floor to watch the mechanism go up and down a couple of times.

Tom discovered that Chuck traveled selling medical equipment. "In fact," Chuck said, "I'm alone 'cause my wife and daughter are down in Santa Fe with the grandparents. They left yesterday, but I had meetings in Denver today, so I'll head down tomorrow." He pulled out his phone and scrolled around a bit, then he showed Tom a photo of his family.

"Christy, and the little one's Cheyenne. Just turned four."

"Nice. Beautiful ladies."

"Yep. They're the greatest. Hey, how's your family doing? You've got what? Four or five kids, right?"

"Uh, three. Had three. But they're gone. Died in the car crash. Kate, too—my wife."

Chuck was stunned. Tom awaited the condolences; he knew precisely what Chuck would say, how he would answer, the whole exchange for three or four cycles. *Maybe not 'precisely.' Chuck's a little different. More savvy. Maybe he'll be more interesting.*

Chuck said, "So, Christy and I are trying to figure…"

"Are you all finished with that, sir?" The waitress interrupted.

Chuck showed genuine pleasure. "Yes, thanks so much. It was really great."

She swept up Chuck's plate but left Tom's; most of his dinner remained on the plate.

"Anyway," Chuck continued, "Christy and I are trying to figure out how old Cheyenne should be before we bring her with us."

"It sounds pretty good," said Tom, "as long as you two are good with it. And it'd probably be kinda fun for her—except—I'd maybe worry that Africa isn't quite safe for a four-year-old, especially refugee camps and stuff." He shook his head minutely. "Then again, earth's not exactly safe for any kid."

"No doubt. That's what we think." Chuck paused as he connected the dots of Tom's implication. He gave him a crooked expression that said, *Oh, yeah. Sorry.* He continued, "Of course we want to keep her safe, but, you know, you're never too young to help people. Really, that's the reason:

not so she'll have fun—though she'll probably learn to love it like we do. We just want it to be a normal part of her life. And Christy and I don't really want to stop helping people just because we have a kid."

"Yeah." Tom picked up his fork and poked around in his cold food a moment, nodding subtly. "Yeah, makes sense."

"I'm serious, Chuck." Tom was animated, leaning forward, gesturing. "Instead of peddling to medical companies that just pencil you in fifteen minutes here or there, you would be working one-on-one with the people who will directly benefit from our stuff."

"That part is what appeals to me the most," said Chuck.

"As long you don't mind the flying, you should consider it. Of course we'll still have to go through all the normal stuff, interviews and junk, make sure it's truly a good fit for us both. But give it some thought."

"Yeah, it sounds pretty good," Chuck said. "Especially less traveling. Maybe I will. I think I will. I'll talk to Christy first, of course."

"Of course. Think it over. You've got our info. Just call or stop by."

Chuck nodded, staring distantly with a faint smile.

Tom retrieved his fork and stabbed a bite of food, but began speaking with the fork still hovering above the plate. "So when do you…"

The waitress appeared. "How was everything?"

Tom murmured his approval. Chuck smiled broadly, thanked her, complimented her service, and thanked her again.

She turned to Tom. "Can I box this up for you?"

"Yes, please." He slid his plate toward her.

After she gathered a few items and left, Chuck said, "Did you not like it? Or just not hungry?"

"I loved it—and I'm always hungry. I just never feel good when I eat. It always kinda hurts. And if I eat too much, I throw up, which hurts like getting kicked by a mule. It's my abdominal injuries."

"That's too bad."

"Yeah. Apparently my guts and good digestion aren't on speaking terms anymore. But I'm a big fan of the doggie bag; I'll pick away at this all night. Tomorrow, too."

The waitress returned, left the bill in its little black folder standing up indiscriminately between them, and gathered more plates. Tom immediately snatched up the folder.

Chuck protested, "Wait, Tom. I said I'd take care of this. Let me…"

Tom held up a hand and shot him a look. "Nuh uh. You saved my life, remember?"

CHAPTER TWENTY-SEVEN

Two minutes late already, grumbled Tom. The clock on the dashboard of his Scout read *4:47* as he sat at a T intersection in an unfamiliar neighborhood. He glanced left and right looking for clues that would lead him back to a road he recognized. For no particular reason he chose right. He moved the hand lever from brake to accelerate and eased the truck onto the cross street. A few seconds later he cleared a slight bend to find himself in a cul-de-sac. *Left. Of course.* He wheeled around and headed back.

As he cruised along scanning his surroundings, an oddity caught his attention: a wide, wooded alley between the back yards of two rows of houses. Parallel fences receded away bordering an overgrown aqueduct with a smear of water at the bottom. The instant before the second fence blocked his view, the corner of his eye caught movement: an object popped over the top of one of the fences. Something inside urged him to check it out. He backed his truck and stopped on the aqueduct's little bridge.

The object turned out to be a young boy, perhaps only five or six, now flailing and kicking, hanging from the top of the fence. Tom stared more closely, put his truck into park, and rolled down the passenger window. The faint sound of yelping came from the boy. His backpack appeared to be caught on the fence, forcing his face toward the ground.

"Hey! Hey, hang on," Tom called. "Hey, just hang on and I'll get you some help." The boy showed no sign of having heard him.

Tom glanced around for pedestrians, drivers, anyone to enlist. Nobody. He honked a few times, glancing about, checking his mirrors. The boy still hung, still kicking and struggling, now wailing. The backpack shifted and the boy slid a bit lower. Suddenly the sound of crying stopped, but the kicking and flailing intensified. The hood of the boy's heavy winter coat—not the backpack—was snagged on the top of the fence, and now all his weight hung by the neck, held by his zipped up collar.

"Oh no. Oh no. No. No. No!" Tom raced to unlatch his chair and activate his truck's robot arm. "Help! Help please! Anybody!" he began to shout. As he slowly whirred to the ground, he growled, "Come on— come on—come on! You piece of junk." As soon as he disconnected, he raced his chair around the front of the truck. The curb was too high for him. He unstrapped from the chair, threw himself onto the sidewalk, and dragged himself along toward the end of the bridge, where the wall tapered down. He waddled on his hands, legs trailing like mute cans behind a newlywed car. His torso exploded with pain.

The fences bordered either end of the bridge, forcing Tom to clamber up the inclined end of the wall so he could see down the aqueduct. The boy was pushing his feet down the face of the fence as if he were walking up it backward, but his shoes gained no purchase. He clawed at his hood and collar. His only sounds were thumping and scuffling; no wailing, no whimpering, no wheezing.

"Help! Anybody, please help me! Help!" The street showed no trace of activity. Tom threw his legs over and dropped about four feet onto the bank of the aqueduct and rolled down its slope of jagged stone blocks. Losing no time, he dragged his body through two or three inches of icy brown water toward the boy, never taking his eyes off him—not even noticing when a broken bottle under the mud skewered his palm. When he finally neared the boy, he clawed his way up the grassy bank to the bottom of the fence. The boy's face, still forced downward by the back-pack, pleaded with Tom in silent terror. His dark skin prevented Tom from seeing whether his face was purple from asphyxiation.

"Grab the top of the fence," Tom yelled. "Pull yourself up. Pull your-self up." Tom stretched as high as he could, but he barely reached the boy's shoes. Blood streamed down his bare arm, but he didn't figure it was his own; strangely, he wondered where the boy was bleeding from. "Stand on my hand. Push yourself up. Stand on my hand. Push yourself up." He struggled to press up on the boy's feet, to provide a meager platform, but Tom couldn't splay his legs: the higher he reached, the easier he toppled. He turned his tortured face to the boy's. "I can't reach you. You've got to pull yourself up. Grab the fence. Pull up. Pull up."

The boy didn't obey. Instead, his eyes softened and grew unfocused.

"No! No! Don't give up," Tom shouted.

The boy's arms fell to his sides, twitching, and his legs grew limp and hung. His unblinking eyes stared down past Tom at nothing, half open. But his chest kept heaving in quick, sporadic throes.

"Help! Help me, anybody? Please! Anybody? Help!" Tom cast his eyes about, searching the bridge, the back yards on this side, the back yards across, back to the bridge, his face wrenched with desperation.

God help. What should I do? God, don't let this child die. God, please. Oh, God, please.

Hoping perhaps to rip the hood free, Tom threw himself as high as he could and grabbed a foot, but he came away with an empty shoe, rolled onto his back, and slid headfirst down the slope into the water, submerging his neck and shoulders. The boy's chest convulsions had stopped. Tom raced—as fast as an exhausted paraplegic can race up a steep riverbank—back to the boy and tried to reach for his other foot. Tom's final desperation was to smack the foot sideways with his fingertips in hope that something might break free, so he tried that for a minute or two, occasionally shouting for help. The boy remained firmly tethered to the top of the fence. His body showed no movement.

At last Tom fell back into the long brown grass at the base of the fence, threw his hands over his face, and sobbed violently.

The sun fell behind the foothills. Fierce shuddering from the icy water and cold breeze brought Tom back to his senses. He tentatively opened his eyes and raised his head, as if he hoped the boy would be gone and it all a dream.

Tom hauled himself up and sat back against the fence, chest heaving, disbelief and anguish on his face. At long last he saw the gash in his palm. It still oozed dark blood. Feathery patches of red had crept into his soaked shirt, and large drops had grown into blurry pink spiders on his pants. The cold had become severely painful.

His eyes traveled down and found his left leg bent at a ninety-degree angle about six inches below the knee. He pulled up the pant leg. The sharp tips of both broken bones pressed against his skin, as if attempting an escape. *The fall.* He glanced toward the bridge. *Jumping from the wall did it.* He straightened his leg as well as he could manage. He looked back toward the four-foot drop; he knew he could never scale back up.

For a long time, Tom stared at the dead boy hanging on a fence. *No more.* He glanced down at his twisted leg. *No more.* Emotionless, he rolled over the edge, slid down the bank, and flopped onto his back in the thin creek. In a few moments, the pain from his hypothermia began to subside.

Finally a voice came from the bridge. "Hello, there! Hey, are you okay? Hold on, I'm coming."

Tom closed his eyes and shook his head, then began to weakly crawl out of the water.

CHAPTER TWENTY-SIX

The room was tall and gray and utilitarian and crowded with steel beams and parts on shelves and hoses and dented tanks and carts, and near its center a fiery red 4x4 truck gleamed under banks of artificial lights. Tom sat in his wheelchair, a gray and utilitarian expression on his face, his eyes loosely following Henry as he slowly circled the truck, smiling, nodding, darting in now and then to examine a detail here and there. Vlad lay inside on his back under the steering wheel as he fed wires to Ravi under the engine bay. A couple of other vehicles in various states of finish waited on the room's perimeter, but no one fussed over them at the moment.

Henry circled back around and caught Tom's eyes. "It's phenomenal. Gorgeous. Steve's gonna love it."

Tom dragged his mouth into a smile, but his eyes remained unchanged. "Thanks." His voice was flat. "I think he'll be pleased."

"What? He'll go absolutely nuts. Used to race, you know. Can't stand not driving."

"Race?"

"Yeah, rally. A little motocross too."

"He won't race this," Vlad called without looking up. "Not without legs. It'll handle rough ground, but with manual controls he'll have to go slow."

Henry nodded and shrugged. He turned back to Tom. "It looks like maybe a couple more weeks, huh?"

"At least three," Vlad quickly answered.

"More like five, probably," Tom shrugged and turned up his palms. "The lift is done last. It's the hardest part."

"Hey, what's with the bandage?" Henry pointed to Tom's hand.

Tom glanced down at the taped gauze. "Yeah. I cut it. It's no big deal."

"Hold up, Vlad. Hold it there," came Ravi's muffled voice from underneath.

Tom shook his head. "Too bad we can't take it out for a spin today."

"Tom, take your Scout," Vlad called. "It'll ride the same mostly."

"That's true," said Tom. "You wanna ride in my truck? Basically the same suspension. Just a shorter wheelbase."

"Sure, yeah," Henry grinned and nodded. "Of course."

"How much time do you have?" asked Tom.

"All day, I guess. I'm off."

"All right, then. Guys, we're heading out," Tom announced.

"This'll do." Tom steered the Scout into a barren parking lot and pulled to a stop. He lowered himself and wheeled around to the passenger side. Henry hoisted him up into the seat, noticing Tom grimace as he lifted him. "Wow, you're lighter than Steve, even with legs."

"I'm just bones now. Sad, brittle bones. And plastic."

"Plastic?"

Tom drew up his pant leg to show Henry his splint.

"What's that for?"

"Broke it," Tom said matter-of-factly.

"Whoa. Recently? That's no good." A slight bewilderment grew onto Henry's face. "Uh—how on earth did you break anything?"

Tom's eyes fell to the ground and darted about, and he showed a fraction of a grimace. "Well, it's kind of a weird…"

"If it hurts, we can go back. I don't need a test drive."

"Hurts? What?" Tom raised his brows. "If you mean the leg, I don't feel a thing. I didn't even know I'd broken it for like five minutes."

"Oh, yeah. Of course your leg wouldn't... I forgot." He turned toward Tom. "You've just seemed sorta—I don't know—*pained*—today."

Tom's shoulders drooped. "Sorry, Henry. I'm sorry. I just..." He paused. "Okay, but, how 'bout you drive first? Get in and give her a try."

Henry studied him a second before submitting. He left Tom's wheelchair on the pavement and hurried around to the driver's side, climbed in, and knelt on the floor. Tom taught him the hands-only controls, and within a couple minutes Henry was zipping around the parking lot.

"Fine vehicle, sir."

"Yep. Thanks."

After Tom switched back to the driver's side, he announced, "Let's head out to the property."

"Property?"

"Yeah, I'm having a house built. It's a ways out, in the mountains above Masonville. Dirt road's pretty rough, and there's still some snow; give you a chance to see how it handles. And I can check on their progress. And you've got time, right? You're off."

"Sounds great."

Tom pointed the Scout toward the mountains. They rode along quietly for a minute before Tom broke the silence. "No, I'm not 'pained' because of the pain. Except—that's a—kind of a lie. I always hurt. My gut and spine never stop. Especially when I strain. And there's some headaches. But if I let pain stop me I'd never do anything. So I guess..." He glanced at Henry. "Yeah. You're right; I'm sorta bummed out today. Probably mainly the funeral—uh, memorial service—I was at yesterday."

"Okay. I..."

"I didn't actually know the person, so it shouldn't—you know—be so..." Tom, looking angry, caught Henry's eyes. "But it was a kid. Cute little kid I watched die. The whole situation is so messed up, I can't stop thinking about it."

"What? Wow, Tom. Watched him die? That's too bad." He stared at Tom. "If you'd rather not, we don't have to..."

Tom cut him off. "Hey, you're off work. And I—I need to just drive a while." He stared forward in silence a moment. "And maybe talk to someone. Someone removed from the situation who can handle it." Another pause. "If that's okay."

Henry noticed Tom's eyes start to glisten. "Sure. I'm off."

"Sorry. I'm just..." Tom began, but he drove a block or two before speaking again. "I broke my leg jumping off a bridge." With an odd smirk on his face, he glanced over to read Henry's reaction. Henry nodded, no change in expression. "It's funny; it sounds like a failed suicide. But it was only a four-foot drop. Far enough to snap my leg, though. Cut my hand too, I guess."

"Why'd you jump off a bridge?"

"To save the kid. It was the only way to get to him. His jacket got hung up on a fence. Choked himself to death. He was only five."

"Gosh," Henry said. "That's not cool."

"No." Tom stared forward. "No, it wasn't. I was the only one around, so I tried to save him, but I couldn't reach him. Just laid under him and watched him die. The worst thing was the look in his eyes. He couldn't understand why I didn't just stand up and rescue him." He glanced over. "And I can't understand why the only person around to rescue the kid had to be a cripple."

"That's tough, man."

Tom glared at the road ahead as he filled out the story with more details. Henry slowly shook his head.

At last Henry said, "I'm surprised it wasn't on the news."

"It would have been if I had saved him—all over the news. But who feels like telling the real story? Besides—the parents didn't want any attention. Who would?"

Henry stared blankly ahead.

"Sudanese immigrants. Only been in the States a few years. Here, they'd escaped genocide—and it's not famine or an AK-47 that takes their son—it's a stupid puffy jacket. I'm still sick about it." Tom frowned darkly. "You'd think they'd be allowed a little peace..."

"Yep." Henry was shaking his head. "Yep." A long pause. "I'm sorry you had to see that."

"It's alright." He still looked angry. "It's just par for the course, I guess. At least *my* course. Don't be shocked if we witness some mishap out at the property today." He sighed and turned to Henry, somewhat softened. "There I go being all pathetic again. Never mind."

"It's fine. You wanna talk, then talk. You don't always have to suck it up."

Tom looked at him and broke. Tears filled his eyes and he glanced away, trying to quickly wipe his face with his sleeve.

"It's fine," Henry added. "Don't worry about it. It's fine."

Tom composed himself. "I'm sorry. It's been a while since I've felt this raw. Years." He turned his head to the front again. "I used to think I was one of the tough ones, that I could handle pain, but this is breaking me. It's all adding up."

"What? What's adding up?"

"All the dumb stuff. I don't know. Like—I'm sick of surgeries. I'm sick of the hospital. Every time something else goes wrong, I land in the hospital again. I can't even fail to rescue a kid without surgery and an overnight stay. It's like I'm made of nothing but pencil leads and soggy bread. Can't even stand in my chair now because of this stinking broken leg." He whacked his knee with the back of his hand. "And who knows how long I'll be in the splint; nothing heals on me anymore. Except the nerve endings. They're just fine, all hearty and robust and angry. It's as if they're trying to get revenge on me for killing off half their family." He paused a few moments. "And of course, you know... Ah, shoot. I don't know." Tom turned his eyes back to the road, now steep as it began its climb into the foothills. He slowed for a pair of cyclists slowly grinding uphill near the shoulder. When oncoming traffic cleared, he veered around them.

"What?" Henry said.

"Huh?"

"You were going to say something."

"Oh. Just—you know. I miss my family. I miss Kate." He glanced over. "My wife. I know I told you they died, because I remember feeling like a jerk; I kinda blew you off 'cause you were talking spiritual talk and stuff."

"I presumed. I guess I shouldn't have. I'm not very, uh, you know—diplomatic."

"Nah, it wasn't you. Anyway, I miss them. All the time. It's gotten a little better over the years, but it still eats at me when I'm alone. And I spend a lot of time alone. Probably because *Paraplegic Guy* is all work and no play." He showed a faint little smile. "Not much fun to hang out with a dude who can't do anything." It faded after a moment. "And now the little boy chokes himself out. I don't know why that affected me so much." He stared ahead blankly. "But all this garbage feels like it's adding up, breaking me." He glanced over, shook his head, and looked back toward the road.

"You're not gonna break," said Henry. "You'll see."

"Maybe I will. It just feels…"

"Maybe. But I've watched people go through far more than they ever thought they could bear. I've seen some messed up things myself. Too many times I've seen it. But people adapt and survive. Lots of people quit if they're allowed to quit—if they have an 'out'—but if they're not allowed, those same people just keep going."

"Ah, yeah, I guess so." Tom inhaled deeply and let it out. "Sorry. I feel like a little—a little crybaby—blabbering like this to—to someone like you. I don't know why I feel like unloading on you." He shook his head a little, eyes still fixed on the road. "You know…" He chuckled wryly. "I used to think I was—um—'tough.' I used to think I could've handled hard stuff—stuff like special ops training; that I never would've quit. I'm not so sure anymore. I'm guessing you have some clue about the training I'm talking about."

"Sure, yeah, I've had some tough training. Who knows whether you would have made it? Only one way to know. But when I was a kid, I thought being a Green Beret or a Seal or something meant being physically superior—an athlete. It's not that; not really, though of course that's a part. Later I realized it's something else; something inside. It's as if there's a switch in your head you learn how to turn off: like a Pansy Mode switch. It controls not just the desire to quit, but your whole outlook. You even learn to enjoy certain kinds of hardship. But I learned that if things get crazy enough, Pansy Mode can switch back on, sometimes like that." He snapped his fingers.

Tom raised his eyebrows a bit.

"That's the point of interrogations: Make 'em turn Pansy Mode back on."

Morbid realization dawned on Tom, and he glanced over with a grimace.

Henry continued. "That's why having good buddies—a solid team—is so important. If you start to lose it, they bring you back. They get it. And they cover your butt until your mind game is back. For our guys, those moments were always very short—even when their legs were missing. Don't tell him I told you, but even Steve—maybe the toughest guy I ever met—spazzed for a bit when his body was all over the place. Who can blame him? I felt it too for a few seconds, but I knew I had to be there for him. And when he saw me being strong, he came back and sucked it up; even helped us save his life."

"I don't really think anybody can be considered a pansy for losing it when his legs are blown off…"

"Exactly my point," Henry interrupted. "But learning how to switch off Pansy Mode saved his life. He was all practiced up." He quietly added, "Steve seems like a goofball when you meet him, but he's tougher than snot."

Tom drove in silence a moment. "Wow. I feel like a sham hanging around guys who've been in real combat; not like the cakewalk I was in."

"Everybody goes through stuff; it doesn't have to be declared a war to feel like a war."

"Yeah, I guess. But at Verve, we meet a lot of vets who've been through serious stuff. Makes me feel more like a kid playing G.I. Joe than a war vet."

"Doesn't matter. A Purple Heart doesn't make a wheelchair comfier."

Tom stared blankly. "True."

"Main difference I've found between people is not how hard their experiences were, but how hard they try to use their experiences as an excuse to live how they want." A little fire grew in Henry's eyes. "I can't tell you how sick I am of seeing these losers standing there begging for money, holding up cardboard signs that say *War Vet.*" He rapped on the side of Tom's wheelchair. *"Especially* if they've got two legs. If they really are former military, they ought to have the intestinal fortitude to get off their butts and solve their own problems."

"Probably so."

"People usually just feel like being drunks, or perverts, or acting entitled, or playing the victim card, or whatever. So they do. But they use their experiences to justify it; as if it somehow merits them forgiveness for selfishly messing their lives up. It's a rare man who just admits that he's rotten."

Tom laughed. "It's pretty true. Dang. Makes me feel sorry for feeling sorry for myself."

"I wasn't meaning you."

"Regardless—probably be good if I stop whining now. Really." Tom glanced over. "So what's your story? All I know is you're good at football and you're probably some kind of Hardcore."

"Ha. My story?" Henry shifted in his seat to face Tom. "Okay. Well, I was raised right here. North end of town. My parents were farm workers, so once I was old enough, I was a farm worker too. Later on, I actually did toss a lot of hay bails, like Steve said. Probably helped me do well in sports, I guess."

"How old was 'old enough'?"

"Ha. That's kinda part of the story." He raised his brows. "Poor folk don't pay much heed to child labor laws, you know, so, I guess, eight or nine's probably when I started working outside the house. We weren't exactly always 'legal' people. Same reason I left D.C. last year and headed back home."

"Huh?"

"Yeah. It caught up with me." Henry chuckled. "You see, I had gotten pretty far in the Army, uh, special ops-wise. You guessed right."

"Like Ranger, S.F., or what?"

"Yeah. Basically that kind of stuff. After a couple tours with the Ranger battalion, I was invited to try out for another, um, let's say, more heavily-bearded unit."

"Ah…" Tom cut his eyes over.

"This new unit—which will remain nameless, okay?—requires a pretty high clearance level, which worked out for me at first. Then after more years and more tours, I was invited to try out for a different government position in Washington. Non-military."

"You mentioned that, first time we met. Said it was 'odd jobs'."

"Yep," Henry chuckled. "Anyway, my T.S. clearance transferred with me, and I…"

"You needed a Top Secret clearance for 'odd jobs'?"

"I never said they weren't important. And they definitely were odd." He gave Tom a crooked smile and a nod. "Anyway, my clearance transferred, and I passed the qualification process, but as soon as I was in chest-deep, it was discovered that—um—don't hate me…" Henry put on a grimace and a fake cower. "…I'm not actually a U.S. citizen."

Tom's shoulders sank. "Uh oh. So you…"

"Yep. Whoosh. I was out of D.C. They were gracious, though; got me a permanent work visa lickety-split. But rules is rules, I guess. Clearance was revoked, and I had to go. At least they hooked me up with some Fed work back here in Colorado, and they're trying to expedite my citizenship. So now I work for a department that works for another department that works with Homeland Security. I mainly push papers. From soggy bread to pencil lead, as you might say."

"Seriously? Ow, that hurts. So you were ousted for lying to them?"

"Well, no—my whole life I believed I was a U.S. citizen. My parents always told me I was born here. But truth is, I was born in Mexico. Right in our nation's capitol I found out that it's not *my* capitol. We had immigrated before I was one, so I never had any clue. My parents came clean with me after I showed up on their step with bags in hand and a bit of a scowl on my face."

"Man, that is raw. I'm sorry."

"My parents got their citizenship years ago. They just tried to sweep my real story under the rug—thought I was covered. But certain folks in Washington know how to dig deep. Probably some twerp sitting behind a computer in some basement, whose only boast is his ability to collar people he'll never meet."

"Hmmph," was Tom's response. That moment he turned off the highway onto a dirt road marked *Private Property. No Trespassing. Residents and Guests Only.* "Hey, here's my new neighborhood, if you can call it that. A lot of the houses can't even see other houses. Pretty rural."

"Beautiful terrain."

"Wait 'til you see my plot. It's pretty sweet."

Tom drove along as Henry took in the valley rising around them. Barbed wire fences lined the road, with occasional gates granting access to dirt driveways winding through sand-colored grasses. The land rose steeply behind the ranches, ponderosas thick on the higher slopes. A remnant of the last snowfall looked indigo in the shadow of the pines.

At last Tom said, "You married?"

"Nope. Not yet. So far God hasn't led me to the right girl. In fact, I was the only single guy on my team. Funny thing is, they prefer married guys; they're more stable." He laughed. "Maybe someday I'll marry—though not many girls want an ugly dude like me."

"I'd trade bodies with you in a second."

"Listen, sir, don't go feeling sorry for yourself again."

"Right."

The Scout jostled along as the dirt road climbed, for it became rockier and a bit rutted. The hillside grew steep on their left, and the valley dropped away below them on their right. A glint from the sun appeared here and there on the opposing mountainside, revealing a few homes perched on its reddish knees and tucked back in wooded draws.

"Wow, this is great," Henry muttered.

The trees along the road grew taller and denser, beginning to obscure their views. Along the way, a few dirt driveways snaked back into the woods, and the peak of a roof occasionally showed through.

"Okay, we're on my property now," Tom announced, turning onto one of the spur roads. A sign at its mouth read *TBR Design + Build / Ericson Project*. The drive immediately led them up a couple of steep switchbacks before resuming a gently climbing traverse. "The cement trucks loved those hairpins," Tom said. "Good thing all that heavy work was completed before winter." The trees thickened as they climbed.

"So, what else you wanna know?" Henry asked. "I'm single. I worked jobs I can't talk about. Apparently I'm a Mexican. I played sports; you know that. I'm a Christian; I suppose you figured that out." He chuckled. "I always seem to take the long way round to things; I was raised by a Muslim mother and a Catholic father."

Tom raised an eyebrow. "Really?"

"Mom's dad was Uzbek. Did I mention that? She tried to be both Muslim and Catholic; didn't really work out too well—except she heard from both sides that if she was good enough, God would let her into heaven. I used to think that too until…" He laughed. "Believe it or not, I did have a girlfriend or two—a girl I dated got me thinking deeply about Christ. I guess you could say she's the one who helped me learn to trust him instead of myself."

Tom continued to stare straight ahead.

"So I'm back in town now these few months: hanging around, pushing papers, not shooting people, checking out the ladies, checking up on Steve's truck, trying to find a good church. That's about it."

Henry eyed Tom. He drove along expressionless, rocking back and forth as the Scout bumped over the crowns of exposed boulders.

Henry asked, "So you're not going to church anymore, I take it?"

A tiny but weighty delay. "Nope."

"I'd be interested in hearing…"

"Here's some mud and snow," Tom interrupted, as he slowed to a stop. "Not too steep here. You wanna try the truck out in this?"

Henry watched Tom until he looked over.

"It'll climb right through it," Tom said.

"Naw, I don't trust using just my hands in terrain like this. You go ahead."

Tom eased forward and aimed for the muckiest, slushiest holes. As he powered through the rough patches, with mud slinging up along the length of the Scout, he explained how Steve's truck would have many of the same upgrades. Henry listened politely and made appropriate comments. Finally Tom eased back onto smoother road.

"Listen, Tom, I…"

"Okay, house is just around this bend."

A clearing opened up before them. At the lower edge of a gentle slope lay the house, seeming to hang over the edge of an abyss. Beyond it the hill dropped off, with nothing but miles of blue air between them and the massive ridge across the valley. Atop the ridge, the back side of Horsetooth Rock jutted up above the horizon. Beyond the ridge lay the town. Further back, the prairie stretched away to where it met the sky.

CHAPTER TWENTY-FIVE

Tom skirted the yard and stopped the Scout beyond the side of the house near the dropoff, the passenger window facing the view.

"Are you kidding me?" Henry whispered involuntarily, gawking. He began to chuckle. "Man, Tom, this is something."

Tom grinned from ear to ear. "Nice, huh? There's money in the medical industry, that's for sure."

Three or four trucks were parked near the house, and construction equipment dotted the yard. Men bustled in and out. Some snow remained where it had not been flattened by tires or boots, with a thicker coat back under the trees.

The house seemed nearly finished. Rectangles of glass, granite, cedar, and iron defined the exterior. Expansive windows provided a view all the way through a couple of interior spaces to the valley beyond. Massive polished gray stones buttressed square beams pinned by heavy iron fittings, all crowned by dark metal roofs sloping in unexpected directions. A quartet of stone chimneys rose above the ridgeline. A secondary structure sat about thirty yards from the main house, connected by a glass-enclosed elevated walkway that overlooked the vista.

"Dang," Henry mumbled. "Stunning." He kept craning his neck to take it in. "When do you think you'll move in?"

"Not until it warms up and the sidewalks are in, of course. Landscaping won't go in 'til spring."

Henry opened his door and dropped to the ground.

"Hey, Henry," Tom called. "After I'm down, you'll have to push me. Ground's still too rough."

As Tom descended from the Scout, a worker approached, his breath trailing off in the cold air. "Can I help you?"

"I'm the owner. Tom Ericson. Just dropped by to check out the place." He extended his hand. "How's it coming? What's your crew do?"

"Stonework. Our part's looking pretty good. We're close to wrapping it up. It's still a big mess in there, so you'll have to be careful. Let us know if we need to move some stuff for you."

"No, you guys just work. We'll poke around where we can."

The worker left, and Henry muscled Tom's chair through the rutted dirt toward the house. "Swing around back," Tom said. "We'll start out on the deck." The massive deck cantilevered several yards out over the steep hillside into open air. Because the bridge from the deck to the soon-to-come sidewalk was incomplete, Henry had to hoist Tom in his chair, then he hopped up himself.

"Okay, watch that edge there," Henry grasped a wheelchair handle.

"Yep, I got it. That'd be a fun little tumble, eh?"

Most of the deck was a clean dropoff along the edge, with nothing but the topmost fringes of a few ponderosas between them and the horizon. Only on the far end had deck railing been installed, and a few men were attaching another section of the barrier, made of nothing but hefty panes of thick glass.

They gazed at the view a while. Henry walked near the edge, stopping now and then to look down or turn about. "Tom, are you kidding me? This is spectacular."

"Thanks. Thought you'd like it."

Tom gave him a couple minutes to explore, then called, "Hey, let's look inside." He wheeled toward the back of the house, at the moment completely open to the panorama. "This here's where an all-glass wall goes. Right now it's retracted into those walls—right there—and over there. See it tucked in there? All motorized." He swept his hand toward the house. "Handicapped-accessible everything. Of course the whole house is all on one level. That's why it's so wide; it contours the edge of the dropoff here and makes for killer views all the way along the house."

Tom called inside. "Hey, we're coming in, okay?" A man appeared from around a wall and showed a thumbs up. Tom rolled over the tracks for the glass wall. The ceiling vaulted far overhead.

"So, great room there. Kitchen, of course. Dining's going there." He led him to a passage blocked by construction tools. "A couple bedrooms back there. You can't see it from here, but that little house at the other end of the glass passageway is a complete guest quarters. I'll be hiring some full-time help; they'll use that."

"Oh, man," Henry interrupted. "They'll be fighting for that job."

"We'll see." He rolled back toward the other end. "My office and master suite are through there, though—sounds like they're working. Maybe you can see it when it's done. Both have access to the deck, big views. 'Course you saw the garages on the other side. Utility and storage all connected back there."

They returned to the kitchen area. "Once I'm dead, no disabled person will want a place way up here, so I'm making everything as normal as possible. My standing wheelchair helps with that."

"What made you want to live way out here anyway?" Henry motioned toward the panorama. "Besides the obvious, of course. Seems kinda logistically complicated for you."

"Good question." Tom showed a hint of disgust. "Here—come out here." They returned to the deck. The workers wrestled with a pane of glass. "Down there," Tom pointed back toward the valley mouth, "is where I grew up. We had a few acres, a fine little ranch house. I ran around in this valley for years. After my dad died, my mom sold off the place. Practically gave it away. Ticked me off. I wanted it—bad. Mom said she couldn't bear the reminders of Dad every minute. So I gave up hope of ever moving back out here. Then along came the car wreck, so it sorta didn't matter. Can't run or hike anymore anyway. But when Verve took off, suddenly I have a standing wheelchair, an accessible four-wheel-drive, lots of money. So, there you go. Why not?"

"Well, it's great." Henry turned about, taking in the views and the architecture. "I'm glad for you." He looked across to the distant ridge. "Wow."

Tom rolled over to the railing installers and spoke with them a moment. When he returned, Henry said, "Wow, Tom. I'm proud of you. It's insane."

"Thanks."

"And just *look* at that. God sure made a beautiful place for you to enjoy." He cast a heartbeat's glance toward Tom.

Tom remained silent and stared out over the valley.

Henry turned to him. "Soon as I mention God, you clam up."

Tom shrugged without moving his eyes.

Henry spoke with deliberate, quiet intensity. "Listen, sir, you've been bursting at the seams all day, wanting to unload on me. And I'm glad. I'm glad to listen if you want to uncork your suffering. Good grief, it's only so long a guy can suffer alone and put on a tough shell day after day. But now we get to the bottom of what's really paining you and you want to bottle it up some more. Talk about the truck, the house, anything except God giving those Sudanese immigrants such a raw deal. Or God giving you a raw deal."

"Huh?" Tom attempted a shocked expression. "What makes you so sure?"

"Come on. I know you know what I'm talking about. You might as well wear a hat with it sewn on there. Who else makes bitter comments about 'Leaning on the Everlasting Arms'?" Henry showed no anger or impatience, only mild resolve. "It's not like I mind; it's between you and God as far as I'm concerned."

Tom shrugged again, looking as disinterested as he could manage.

"So unload on me all you want. Whatever you say stops right here; trust me on that—not that there's anyone I know to tell anyway. Maybe I'm your guy, since you've got no one else to unload on. With people who depend on you for their income, of course you can't look weak or vulnerable in front of them; I get that. Who else you got?"

Tom parted his lips, but no words came. His eyes dropped for a second before meeting Henry's again. They were starting to harden.

Henry continued calmly. "If you're bitter at God right now, don't worry that if you speak your mind, I'll hold it against you. I'll not even try to change your mind, really. But I will try to talk sense as I see it. You've at least got to allow for that, 'cause anyone who can't tolerate that—it means they prefer hiding behind some wall they've made—some wall they don't have a lot of confidence in."

Tom looked away toward the trees below, glaring. "Henry," he began, but paused.

Henry waited.

"Henry."

Henry sat down cross-legged near the edge of the deck and looked up at Tom.

Tom flicked his eyes toward him and looked away. At last he spoke. "Yeah, I've got church in my past. I've got God in my past. But past is past. You want me to 'let it out,' but there's nothing I would say that you won't disagree with, so why should I bother?"

"Nothing?"

"Nothing about any of that stuff, at least."

"Not even something like: *In the beginning, God created…*"

Tom gave him a stony, sideways stare. "Look—you want me to unload?" he started, his voice a bit hotter. "Okay. I don't need you trying to evangelize me or convert me or save me, or whatever your crowd calls it. Trust me, I know that drill."

"That's not my intention. But if I mention God, I expect you won't get mad at me or something, as if I've said something repugnant."

"So what if it is repugnant?" Tom spoke louder. "Being sick and tired of the circus isn't the same as hiding behind a wall."

"Okay. But then I would wonder: why is it repugnant?"

"And that's none of your business. I don't need you prying into my head, or accusing me of being bitter against God."

Henry calmly nodded.

"And no, I'm not bitter against God; there's no God to be bitter against."

"Okay," Henry said. "Then who are you bitter against?"

"Who said I'm bitter?"

"Come on, Tom…"

Tom glared at him as long as he could then turned away with a huff.

"Okay," Henry began. "So, you're bitter about the Sudanese immigrants' string of horrible luck. You're mad that some folks seem to have nothing but bad luck, and you want to blame Fate, because Fate should intervene before people roll too many snake eyes in a row—you know— for fairness' sake. But Fate chooses not to intervene. But—if that's the case—Fate would have to have a mind and a will and ability…"

"Hey, I don't have to…"

"You're bitter," Henry said a bit louder, "because you crave to see justice and fairness in the universe, although the whole thing's just an accident. You want the universe to somehow choose to do 'right' by people, instead of doing them 'wrong'."

Tom opened his mouth as if to speak, stared a moment, closed it, and shook his head minutely. At last he spoke. "Look, see? You're egging me on. Why can't you leave well enough alone?"

Henry remained unruffled. "'Well enough,' huh? So—everything's good in your life?"

"I'm just sick and tired, man. Can't a guy be upset that his whole life is screwed? But there's nothing you need to fix. Nothing can be."

Henry sighed. "Listen, Tom, I understand being upset. Good grief, nobody can fault you. I've seen some messed up situations, and you're right, yours is one of them. But, problem is, you don't sound 'well enough' to me. Maybe I'm just trying to help reset your Pansy Mode switch; your situation would at least *seem* less awful."

"Seriously, now you're calling me a pansy?"

Henry raised his voice. "Oh no. You're not gonna turn this around on me, as if you actually *believe* I'm attacking you. You know what I meant. But you prefer to wallow, even though it's killing you."

Tom glared at Henry, his mouth opening and closing as if it wanted to speak before his brain found the words. At last he sat back. "Sure—the universe can't choose to do right, but you could—instead of being some kind of self-righteous wannabe savior."

Henry paused a moment, nodding. The hint of a smile began to play at the corners of his mouth. "Whatever I am, it's only because I'm part of the universe; part of the big accident. How could I *choose* to do right? I'm just a product of genetics and environment."

"Don't pull that on me. You know you ought to at least treat a fellow human with some respect."

"*Ought* to? A fellow bag of atoms? To what end? So that bag of atoms will experience a brief chemical reaction it interprets as—non-unhappiness?"

Tom stared hard and cold at him. Henry's serene, unwavering gaze won out at last, muscling Tom's eyes away toward the valley. "Anyway," Tom started, "I don't have to come up with every reason to explain why I don't get all dreamy-eyed and lift holy hands just because a mountain's pretty. That's all."

"Okay. Good. But listen, I'm not going to act weird like I need to walk on eggs around you if I talk about what I believe. Just don't clam up if I say 'God' or 'Jesus' or 'Bible.' Believe me, I can handle it if you wanna call B.S. on all of it. But I might ask you why you think so. That's all."

"Alright. Fair enough. You feel free to talk about what you want, and I'll feel free not to talk about what I don't want."

"But you do want to. You've been simmering all day."

Tom slowly turned toward him. "If I ever wanna unload that deluge of acrimony, you'll know."

"What deluge of acrimony?"

"No…" Tom shook his head. "Now you're just trying to suck me in again. I get it. It's not gonna work."

Henry lifted his palms, as in surrender. "Alright."

Tom remained still and silent except for fingers that worked busily twisting at each other. Henry stayed seated, his head and eyes turned toward the sunlit ridge opposite. Suddenly Tom wheeled himself back a foot or so. "I'm sorry, I'm freezing now, even in this coat. And my legs might be frostbitten for all I can tell. We'd better head back."

Henry rose to his feet. "Too warm for that. But you're right—let's head on."

Henry effortlessly lowered Tom, chair and all, down from the deck and wheeled him back to the Scout, with Tom jiggling and rocking as he bumped along across the dried mud.

As Tom drove back to Verve Engineering, Henry never mentioned God or Jesus or the Bible. His three or four attempts at small talk were met with silence. At last he said, "Thanks for showing me the house, it's really amazing."

Tom answered robotically, "You're welcome."

CHAPTER TWENTY-FOUR

"Oh, yes. Yes. Yes. Yes! This thing is sweet." Steve again pressed the *up* button on his new articulated wheelchair. "Whoever wants to ride it next, go ahead and form a line. Not promising I'll get off any time soon." Henry, Tom, and a few Verve employees watched Steve as he glanced gleefully from face to face.

Henry leaned close to Tom's ear. "Just wait 'til he drives the truck."

"Yeah." Tom lost all expression and kept his eyes on Steve. "But he can't be happy about having to wait three more weeks. And no way he'll like the whole hassle of testing and certification and all that before he can even take it home."

"He'll be fine. He's waited this long." Henry watched for a glimmer of change in Tom. "How've you been, by the way?"

Tom kept his eyes forward. "Never better," he said flatly.

Henry nodded and stood.

Julie knelt by Steve to point out more of the chair's features.

Tom's fingers fidgeted with a few little round pills in a tiny plastic bag in his pocket.

CHAPTER TWENTY-THREE

Tom leaned over the Verve conference table, pen in hand, a laptop and a few papers spread before him. Across from him, Chuck wore a tie and folded his hands neatly on the table, trying to look as pleasant and sharp and capable as he thought he ought to look without looking like he was trying to look pleasant and sharp and capable.

Tom spoke. "And I can say that the folks who interviewed you were pleased. Julie, in particular, said you were great. But of course—she may have an ulterior motive; she's itching to split her traveling load. And I'll be honest, I'm pretty happy with what I'm seeing. No promises, but if you're interested, I could talk to the team about making you an offer."

"Yes, I'm very interested. I like everything I've seen. The people seem really great too."

"Yeah, they are." Tom shuffled a paper or two. "Now, this is noted in your application as—uh—let's see—'flexible schedule requested'." He looked up. "Is this for your trips to Africa and stuff?"

"Yes, primarily." Chuck sat up straighter. "Yes, I'd need that. There'd be plenty of notice, of course, and I'd be willing…"

Tom waved him off. "Yeah, sure. It's no problem. As long as you're not gone too long or too often. You could apply some of your paid leave to that. Or all, if you want. Or take unpaid leave. Whatever. It'd be up to you. Of course you'd have to work around Julie's needs, our needs…"

"Of course. Yes, of course. Understood."

Tom set down his pen and folded his hands. "So, did you guys take that trip? To Africa? When was that?"

"Nope, haven't gone yet. Haven't even purchased tickets. Nothing's arranged." Chuck leaned forward a little. "In fact, I've been waiting to see how this job would play out before we lock in dates. But that's why I'd like a flexible work schedule. These things are really high priority for us."

Tom paused a long moment, looking squarely at Chuck. "So why do you do it?"

"Do what? Go to Africa?"

"Help people."

Chuck sat dumbfounded. "Uh..."

Tom smiled. "I mean it. Really."

"Because it helps people."

Tom chuckled. "Yeah, I know. But why? What's your motive? That's a real question, by the way."

Chuck did a slow-motion shrug. He looked at Tom obliquely with a strange little grin. "Because it's good to help people. Isn't helping people why you started this business?"

"Sure, maybe—or maybe I'm just a greedy pig getting rich off of cripples. But that's not the point. *Why* do you? Why do I? Why do any of us help others? That's what I'm wondering." He glanced down and intertwined his fingers, then he lifted his face to Chuck. "I've been wondering it a lot, I guess."

Chuck remained still a moment, then he straightened up and looked gravely at Tom. "I think helping people is important because, well, number one, it betters..."

"No, don't worry," Tom interrupted with a wave of the hand. "It's not part of the interview. I'm being serious." He looked distant. "Maybe I've just had too much time to think. You're a smart guy; I figure maybe you've figured this stuff out. Since you want to help people, maybe you can help me, too."

Chuck glanced at his wheelchair. "Well, I don't know that I can do much for you in particular. I'm only good with..."

"No, not like that. Um, more like—maybe—like this: Why does

everybody feel so sorry for me and want to help me? Why do I deserve anyone's help?"

"Who would deserve help more than a disabled person?"

"But *why*, Chuck? All I do is balloon their insurance rates, take the best parking spots and movie theater seats, make them pay for special bathrooms and kneeling buses. I'm a drain on society."

Chuck's brow furrowed with concern. "But you're not a drain; you're a—you're—you've invented things that help people."

"Only *my* people. Only the inefficient nuisances."

"Aww, don't say that. I don't feel that way. Only a real jerk would feel that way."

"Exactly my point. What makes him a 'jerk'? Shouldn't he be a hero for suggesting we eliminate anyone who hinders our progress? That's the way of nature. Survival of the fittest. Kill off the weak so there can be advancement, progress, you know. Even a mother bird feeds the strongest first, and abandons her young if they won't learn to fly."

Chuck started slowly. "Surely you don't…"

Tom became a bit more animated. "I mean, we're all just animals on our way to the grave. So, you're heading off to Africa—risking your own daughter—to feed a bunch of strangers. Why? So they won't die? Do we think we're preventing their deaths? Or are we just extending their years of misery before they die? Maybe we're *not* helping them. I don't know. That's why I'm asking."

"Oh, okay. Deep stuff." Chuck laughed. "I think I get what you're driving at."

Tom leaned onto his elbows. "For example, why'd you risk your life on the side of the road in a snowstorm, just to help me?"

"It was the right thing to do."

Tom stiffened and flung his head. "But *why?* What makes it 'right'? It's just a computer program—a herd instinct programmed into us by mistake. Sure, the species that evolved altruism outlasted their self-centered counterparts. It makes for good herd instinct, but it doesn't make it *moral*. It's like Pavlov's dogs telling each other it's 'right' to drool when a bell rings."

"Weren't you glad that I pulled over and helped you?"

"Of course I was glad—it benefited me. But now that we've evolved the ability to reason—if we dare to trust our reasoning: just another string of code that got stuck in our heads—how do we still get away with calling a demonstration of instinct 'doing right'?"

Chuck lifted his hands. "Okay, so our ignorant forefathers used words like that to describe a feeling we evolved. It's no crime to still refer to the instinct in those terms."

"Yeah, but it's now a crime *not* to demonstrate the herd instinct. Think about it—we make laws that require people to help others. If people don't possess that instinct, we call them 'bad'—or pick whatever term you like: *selfish, unethical, greedy, immoral.* Doesn't it seem we would have instead evolved an instinct that considers it 'moral' to snuff out people like me who slow the pack down?"

Chuck stared in silence, lips parted.

Tom heard himself speaking, and his eyes widened. "Gosh, I sound like a Nazi here. But you get my point right? Am I completely nuts? I'm not saying we actually *ought* to think like that. I'm just wondering why we don't." Tom heard himself again. "Yikes! And there's that word *ought.*" He shook his head. "I just can't escape the moral aspect of all of this."

Chuck said, "I don't think you're nuts. And of course there's a moral aspect. It's obvious we shouldn't go around hurting others."

Tom cocked his head. "Is it obvious because we all agree? Or because it's *true?*"

Chuck remained silent, working out how to answer.

Tom folded up Chuck's paperwork and slid it aside down the table. He set his pen on the folder and leaned forward. "Okay, we all despise people who go around hurting others. Like that rich guy who scammed millions of people out of just a few bucks apiece. Even though the pain felt by each victim was pretty minor, we can't help but think of that greedy pig—that *jerk*—as so 'evil.' But why? Maybe he just ended up with a different instinct. Not really his fault."

Chuck shrugged and opened his mouth to speak.

Tom cut in. "And what is 'pain' anyway? It's also just a meaningless, programmed response—like compassion. *So what* if the jerk causes others pain? They'll all be dead soon anyway. And we never congratulated him for becoming 'the fittest'."

"Well, geez, Tom…"

"Or what if I cure cancer? Who have I helped? All the people who will never die? Everybody dies. Why does it matter when or how? Because on a cosmic scale, nobody's important." Tom shook his head. "We try so hard to make ourselves feel so important, but we're not. Nothing we do matters at all in the long run, because—because—" He stared through the table. "—because the only way anything could possibly matter is if it could outlast the long run." He lifted his face, looking stunned.

Chuck slowly shook his head. "What question do you want me to answer first? I hope you pick the easiest one, 'cause, man…" He chuckled.

Tom shrugged. "I don't know. I don't think there's even a real question in there. I think I'm just—venting."

"There's a ton of real questions in there, seems to me. Good questions, too. But I guess I've never really thought too much about it. But man—I've never had to lay in a hospital bed for months either."

"I hope you don't have to." Tom remained still a few moments, then he grinned and caught Chuck's eye. "Though—I can't explain *why* I hope that."

"Dude, you're messed up," Chuck joked. "If you're trying to convince me that I'd be doing important work here at Verve Engineering, I guess…"

"I know." Tom laughed. "I know, I know. Ignore me. Consider it a philosophy discussion. I can ponder this theory all day long, but even I can't come close to believing it myself. I don't even know why I unloaded on you. Thanks for listening."

"Happy to help," Chuck grinned. "At least I think I am. Suddenly I'm not so sure…"

"Okay, okay. I deserve that."

CHAPTER TWENTY-TWO

A piece of Tom's eyes, and a smaller part of his mind, were on the TV. A game show gesticulated for Tom's attention, but it already had three strikes against it: the sound was off; Tom would just as soon watch a carcass decompose as watch a game show; and the I.V. drooping down to his arm had the tail end of a dose of opiates wriggling through it.

This hospital room was essentially the same as the last one he was in: lifeless and sterile, punctuated by kitschy attempts at pep and warmth. The framed art on the wall was probably a picture of something nice, in case anyone thought to look at it. The water jug on the little cart was a friendly color. The curtain hanging from the U-shaped track was also a color of some sort, but whenever it was drawn it sounded like a roll of razor wire sliding around in the bed of a truck.

Tom's roommate was hidden at the moment because his curtain was at half a U. He suffered from something that made him groan from time to time, and he sounded old. At least Tom had the window seat; one of the perks of his frequent flyer program.

A man's voice sounded from the door. "Hello? Tom?" His head appeared around the end of Groaner's curtain.

"Henry! Come in, come in." Tom lifted his I.V. arm and waved him over, smiling weakly.

"I heard you were back in the big house, so I thought I'd see what's up."

"Antibodies are up." Tom's speech was slurred. "Something in there going bad again." He patted his abdomen. "And this busted leg. They're trying a different thing, I guess. The other thing didn't…" Tom's eyes drifted off.

Henry waited for him to finish. At last he decided to speak. "That's too bad."

"Yeah. I'm sorry too."

Henry studied him a moment. "So, when did they say…"

"Hey, how'd you find out I'm in here?" Tom interrupted.

"Yeah. I called Verve to schedule a time for Steve and me to pick up his…"

"Pick up his pickup. That's what you'll do. You'll pick it right up. And they said next Thursday, is what they said."

"Yes, Thursday."

"That's what they'd say, because it makes perfect sense. You probably could pick it up, toss it right on the back of a hay truck."

"No. No, that's way too…"

"You know, they might of gave me too much of that analgesic this time. Pain's all gone."

"Well, that's good, I sup…"

"No, wait. No, it's still there. Never mind. I just forgot, is all." Tom chuckled.

Henry watched him a few seconds, then he walked over to the chair near the bed and motioned to the seat. "Do you mind?"

"Of course not. Thursday makes perfect sense. I just said that."

Henry paused a moment then sat. "I hope you're able to…"

"Well," Tom said loudly, "it was nice of you to stop by. Very nice. You're a nice man. I like you."

"Uh…" Henry stood. "I like you too, Tom. I really hope you're able…"

"I like having visitors. Nobody visits me much. Except sometimes someone from work. They have to, 'cause I'm their boss, and I pay them." Tom chuckled.

"They like you a lot, Tom. They visit because…"

"I like you a lot," Tom slurred. "I was mad, but now—but now…"

"It's okay. I completely…"

"I hope you'll visit again. Soon. I mean it."

Henry took a step toward the door, but paused. "Thank you for letting me stop by and…"

"You're welcome." Tom's eyes were toward the TV.

Henry turned and silently left the room.

Tom's roommate groaned.

Tom's groaning roommate had been moved, or got sent home, or died—Tom couldn't tell—but he had the room to himself again. He lay on his back holding his smartphone above his face. The earphone cord trailed down to his ears. He punched in a number and anxiously waited.

"Yeah, hi Henry," Tom said. "Yep, I'm fine. Feeling okay. A little better. How are you?"

He listened a bit and then spoke. "Good, good. Hey, um, thanks for stopping by yesterday. I really appreciate it."

His face grew sheepish. "Uh, sadly, yeah, I remember it. I remember everything. At least I think I do."

He chuckled. "Yeah, I know. Sorry if it was weird. I—you know—stuff happens. So, hey, you wanna grab lunch or something once I get out? I'll pay. I gotta make up for my behavior yesterday."

"Ha ha. Yeah, well, I want you to know more of me than just me crying all over the inside of my truck and me talking out of my head."

"Oh, yeah. I guess there's also the first time we met. At the office. I may have seemed almost normal then."

A slight smile formed. "Yeah, great. Okay then."

"I'm not exactly sure when. Depends on how fast I heal, and whether these meds kick in. Yep. Sure, I'll call you when I know a time."

"Thanks. Yeah, just wanted to make sure you'd have time, and be okay with it."

"Good. Then I'll let you know."

"Yeah, bye."

Henry appeared in the door to Tom's hospital room. Tom looked over. "Hey, what's up?"

"Just checking in," Henry said. "Just got off, so I figured you might prefer some company now rather than waiting 'til you're off the hook."

Tom showed a genuine, almost relieved, smile. "Fantastic. Thanks." He motioned to the chair near the bed. "Please."

CHAPTER TWENTY-ONE

"I honestly don't know why I…" Tom started, but he paused to lift a tiny paper cup to his mouth and jiggle a clod of ice out of it. He crunched for a couple of seconds and swallowed. "You said nothing wrong, not officially; you just gave it to me straight." He glanced over at Henry sitting by the hospital bed, his elbows on his knees. "In fact, it's a relief to have someone—anyone—not treat me like some weak powderpuff who needs sympathy all the time. You treat me like I've still got a backbone. Even if it is made of crumbs." He smiled grimly. "I appreciate it."

Henry shrugged.

"You're one of the few who…" As Tom reached to set the cup back on the tray, he suddenly inhaled through clenched teeth. Henry calmly watched as Tom gradually relaxed his brow and fists. Tom blew out and glanced at him sheepishly, then he took a couple of cautious breaths. "You're one of the few who doesn't act as if you feel sorry for me. I probably need it. So, anyway…" Tom grimaced again, but less severely. He retrieved the cup of ice. His hand tremored as he held it.

Henry allowed Tom another moment to settle before he spoke. "I don't see you as weak at all. Because you're not. I've spent a lot of time around both: the fragile and the tough."

"I feel weak." Tom didn't move for several seconds, except his eyes. "Weaker all the time."

"It's just a feeling."

Henry stood before the picture on the hospital room wall, perfunctorily gazing at it. "So, you're an atheist?"

Tom lay motionless on his back, his eyes toward the unchanging ceiling. "Sure, why not?"

"What evidence led you to this?

Tom paused. "The absence of God." His voice was toneless.

"What does that look like?"

"It looks like…" Tom rolled his head on the pillow toward Henry. "It looks like decades of waiting on God to do anything that looks like there's a God, and nothing ever happens. Praying for God to help us, and of course, nothing. Praying for him to show himself to my kids, and nothing. Trying to be Mister Good Church Guy, only to be punished. Dozens of people praying for old Saint So-and-So's bruised pinky, and her arm gets amputated." He returned his eyes to the ceiling. "The ratio of *answers to prayer* to *dead silence* is no different from what every random Joe on earth experiences—except out there it's called 'luck'."

"Yep," Henry said.

"So I figured, why bother with church and God and the Bible if there's no benefit? Only after I stopped caring about that stuff did I start having some success. I had never directed any attention to the real because my mind was so burdened with the fake."

"The fake?" Henry wandered over to the window and searched for a latch. He turned to Tom. "Do they let you open these?"

Tom shook his head.

Henry turned back to the view outside. Trees showed the first signs of green. "So, apathy about church and God is what brought you happiness?"

"I didn't say happiness; I said success."

"You mean, *business* success?"

"Correct."

"Then apathy about that stuff is what brought you business success?"

"No, not apathy. Focus. Putting my energy into real things."

"Okay. So, success is what made you happy?"

"I'm not hap…." Tom caught himself. "Well, some, I guess. I'm happier than I was. But you really can't expect me to be happy when every good thing has been taken from me."

Henry turned around. "Taken by whom?"

"Taken by…" Tom stopped dead. Half a smirk crawled onto his face, and he eyed Henry narrowly and shook his head.

"Whoa." Henry took a seat. "Mad at someone who doesn't exist. Sounds exhausting." He looked at his hands and tapped the fingertips together, then he lifted his eyes to Tom. "So, your evidence for the non-existence of God is that he did things you didn't like, and didn't do the things you would have liked."

"No, no…" Tom returned his eyes to the ceiling. "Not evidence for non-existence. Just no evidence for existence."

"None?"

"Hardly any. Whatever is there is anecdotal at best."

Henry paused. "So, if you don't see it with your own eyes, you don't believe it?

"Exactly."

"You don't just swallow whatever you're told. You demand proof."

"Right."

"And that's why you believe in evolution?"

Tom paused. "Uh, yeah."

"What proofs for evolution have you seen?"

"I look around me. It's everywhere."

"Doesn't that qualify as 'anecdotal evidence'?"

"I mean all the evidence. Discoveries."

"Where'd you see those?"

"You know. Books and documentaries and stuff."

"I've seen aliens abductions in books and documentaries."

Tom was silent a moment, then he frowned. "That's different. Those people aren't scientists."

Henry sat back and set his ankle on his knee. "Ah, the infallibility and unimpeachable integrity of the scientist!" He chuckled.

"What are you saying?"

"Don't dare question the supreme authority of the scientist, or you'll soon find your proletarian intelligence belittled, and be classified alongside the obstinate, scripturally inept, arrogant church officials who denied Galileo's findings centuries ago."

"What?" Tom screwed up his face. "It's not their authority they appeal to, it's their method."

"You mean, verification through personal observation and testing."

"Exactly."

"Okay. So, they've seen animals change from one species to another? They've seen life come from non-life?"

"Geez, Henry. Of course not. But the facts all line up."

"Which facts?"

Tom was becoming exasperated. "The evidence for evolution."

"Right. But which facts are you talking about?"

"Listen, I'm not going to sit here and list them for you. But scientists are convinced it's true."

"Which scientists?"

"All of them. Or most of them, anyway."

"How do you know?"

Tom waved his hand in the air. "You know, I don't know. I read it. Or heard it. I didn't..." He trailed off.

"Hmmm." Henry paused. "You haven't carried out the science yourself. You haven't spoken to scientists. You haven't even studied their scientific papers and journals. But you're willing to believe the testimony of media that claims that the majority of 'qualified individuals' agree that evolution is true. Not to mention that to be qualified, they have to personally observe and test empirical evidence, or at least objectively analyze the findings of a great number of scientists who do. Otherwise they're merely casting a naive vote for the consensus."

Tom remained silent.

"This further disregards the immense likelihood that scientists may have an emotional stake in the outcome that could sway their interpretation of the evidence."

"So, you're saying they're biased."

"I'm not asserting that," Henry said. "Just allowing it as a psychological likelihood. They are human, after all." He leaned forward and caught Tom's eye. "What have you seen? Do you generally find that discoveries bring about new evolutionary theories, or that preexisting theories are suddenly backed by newfound evidence?"

"I haven't really researched it."

"But you're staking your life on it as if you have."

Tom sank into his pillow and his eyes found the ceiling again.

"So it's possible some are biased." Henry said. "For example, despite their claims of open-mindedness, they disallow that a mind could exist outside of matter, and that it may possess the ability to sometimes override normal processes. They start with a philosophical predisposition against it, and just because their instruments haven't detected it, they label it 'supernatural' and throw it out."

"But science should only concern itself with the natural."

"If God is why everything else exists, and preceded it all, how does that make him 'unnatural'? Of course scientists should never just 'chalk it up to God' and stop seeking why nature does what it does. But if their job is to get to the bottom of things, and he's truly at the bottom of things, then he certainly should be named among the theories. But they don't. Won't. *Can't.*"

Tom frowned. "But the creation story sounds only a tiny bit more plausible than all those myths: 'Randy the god barfed the universe onto the back of a giant flying raccoon'."

Henry laughed. "Right." He chuckled a bit more, then he sat back and searched the air for words. "Okay, think of it this way: Suppose you were to go back a thousand years and try to explain the internet. You couldn't use any words like *computer* or *data* or *electricity*. You couldn't even say *type* or *wire* or *photo*. You'd have to dumb it down with so many analogies, just to convey the vaguest idea of the concept, to them it would sound like a crazy fairy tale. Imagine trying to explain the creation of matter, electromagnetism, gravity, spacetime—all of it—to a bunch of slaves in ancient Egypt."

"I wouldn't bother," Tom said.

"It would take a lot more than a couple of pages, for sure." Henry shrugged. "My point isn't necessarily that evolution is false; it's that you claim to require proof, but instead you've proven that you're filled with faith. But your faith isn't in science; you've never done it. Your faith isn't even in scientists. Your faith is in the testimony of people you've never met who create documentaries claiming that 'science' has proven evolution." Henry sighed. "That requires several layers of faith."

Tom shrugged. "So does believing in God."

"Of course it does," Henry said. "Nobody denies that. But the difference is, you're willing to believe a theory which requires—*requires*—a vast body of evidence, which you've never personally seen and cannot see. That's faith."

Tom kept his eyes on the ceiling.

"So don't wave the banner of skepticism unless you're genuinely skeptical."

Tom glanced at him darkly.

Henry quietly spoke. "You could instead allow that a different theory could be true. Or better still: honestly pour yourself into researching every option, seeking truth everywhere it can be found, striking down your personal bias each time it rears its ugly head."

Tom grimaced and held his breath as a wave of pain coursed through him. Henry watched him silently. At last, when his breathing was settled, Tom said, "Henry, look, you really don't need to keep…"

"You're not an atheist."

Tom turned his gaze outside. A train of wispy clouds was turning pink. "I don't know. Maybe."

CHAPTER TWENTY

A teen boy hoisted bags from a grocery cart into the back of the Scout. Tom watched from his wheelchair, resting on the pattern of blue diagonal stripes bordering his immense parking spot. He had retrieved his groceries by himself because he could stand again—though his splint would remain for *two to four more weeks, Mr. Ericson, just to be sure.* Even with a standing wheelchair, shopping was slow and complicated, but it helped him feel human.

"Tom?" a voice called behind him. "Tom! That *is* you." A female voice. A familiar voice.

He spun his chair around the same instant the voice and the long ago face found each other in his brain. "Tara. Hello." He landed somewhere between shell-shocked and bewildered, but he did his best to simulate the appropriate facial expression. "How 'bout that? Been awhile, huh?" She still looked about the same, though he was taken aback by how uninspiring she seemed. She almost looked haggard. *Oh man, Kate was sure prettier. Is it the years? Or was I just blinded by covetousness?*

"Wow, Tom. Yeah. So long," she said.

Affair Goggles, he thought.

"There you are. Wow. Yeah." She seemed embarrassed, almost confused, glancing about. "So, um, this is a Verve vehicle, I guess? I've heard really good things about you guys. Ran into Barry—I don't know—a year ago? He was telling me how well you guys are doing. Doing some manufacturing in China now too, huh?"

"Yeah. Strictly contract stuff," Tom said. "Components only. Design and assembly's all still right here. But yeah, it's going really well. Yeah. How are things with you?"

"Still at MacMillan. Maybe you knew that." She slumped a bit. "Tom, you left at the right time."

You got that right. He pictured his flight down her stairs.

"It's always sorta—deranged—now. Roger finally got fired, but now we just tread water all the time."

"That's too bad," Tom said.

"Hey, uh, that's it," The boy interrupted. "Anything else I can do for you?"

"Thanks. No, I'm good."

The boy reached down to lift the tailgate.

"No, I got that," Tom said quickly. "It's motorized." He pressed the button on his remote. The tailgate, rear window, and spare tire on its swing arm rotated into place and latched.

"Nice," Tara said.

"Have a good rest of your day." The boy dragged the cart toward the storefront.

Tom waited a moment and turned to Tara. "What's with everyone saying 'have a good rest of your day' all of a sudden? It's like saying, 'Can I eat a rest of your waffle?' Sounds dumb."

She laughed, probably a bit too loudly. "Tom, you're funny."

Uh, not really.

She gazed at him a moment. "Wow, Tom. It's so crazy to run into you. You look good."

Liar. "Thanks."

"Hey, um…" she began sheepishly. "What do you think about, um…" She glanced at the ground and pushed a strand behind her ear. "Maybe we could meet for lunch sometime." A tentative smile. "And catch up."

"What?" He looked at her as if she'd suddenly grown a beard. "Why? I'm paraplegic. I got nothing to offer."

"No!" She was stunned. "No, I was just thinking…"

"Or are you interested in the money?"

She faded back a step. "I was thinking just to talk, you know, like old friends who've…"

"Ah—you're after a job." He smirked. "Look Tara, we aren't hiring. And we don't…"

"Tom, no!" She nearly yelled. "I thought maybe we could just sit and talk. I thought I wanted to talk with you, maybe even—" Her eyes flamed. "—maybe even apologize for—for before, but—I guess maybe I disgust you. So never mind. Go enjoy your life. See ya, Tom."

As she stormed away, her head and shoulders wilted and her hand covered her mouth.

Tom's eyes widened and his mouth dropped open. He clapped both hands onto his head.

Warm sun glowed on fresh landscaping surrounding Tom's mountain home. Bordering the curved driveway and paved walks snaking through the grounds, newly planted shrubs exploded with blossoms, young aspens quivered their delicate leaves, and short spruces showed pale new growth on the tips of their blue branches.

As Tom approached in his Scout, he spooked off a magpie that had been poking around in his planters, and it glided onto the lawn to wait for him to get out of its way. Tom rolled the truck into the garage, then he tapped some buttons on his phone and held it to his ear.

"Oh, good—you're here. I'm back. With groceries. You mind unloading for me?" A pause. "Thanks, Tatiana."

Tatiana appeared at the door as Tom detached his chair from his lift arm. She was tall and strong, with stormy dark eyes, pouty lips, and salon blonde hair. Tom didn't glance up.

"Good trip to the store?" This she pronounced *gude treep to ze stoor* in her heavy accent, her voice and her face monotone.

"Yeah, fine." He opened the tailgate with the remote. "I won't need dinner tonight; you can just put the stuff away." As he reached down to roll his chair forward, he winced.

"Have your pain returned?" She studied him sternly.

He looked up at her. "Just a little. I'm not really hungry, that's all."

She narrowed her eyes. "Okay, if you say."

"In fact, take the rest of the day off. Go into town if you like. I'll be fine."

"Tom…"

"I promise, I'm good."

"Okay." She headed for the back of the car. "You want to lie down?"

"I can do it," Tom called as he rolled inside. "Just go have fun. Take some money from the drawer and treat yourself, okay?"

She poked her head around the back of the truck and frowned at him.

"Okay, Tatiana?"

"Okay, Tom. Hard boss."

Tom waited until he heard her car reach the gravel before he rushed to the cabinet where his bottles of pills were kept.

CHAPTER NINETEEN

"Well, turns out I'm a horrible person." Tom glanced up from his food, grinning strangely.

"So, what's new?" Henry chuckled, his attention still on the third of his four tacos.

"I mean it."

"Of course you're horrible. Everyone is." Henry frowned at his taco. "Holy cow, these are good. Even for white man tacos."

"Yeah, this place is great." Tom took in the restaurant's lunch crowd.

Henry eyed Tom's taco lying alone in the basket, barely touched. "What's the matter?"

"I've gotta eat slow. I get sick if I get full."

"But it's good?"

"Yeah, it's great."

"You're just not hungry?"

"I'm always hungry. I just can't let myself get full."

"Alright." Henry took a bite and organized it in his mouth before speaking. "So what brought this on?"

"The accident. I could always eat before that."

"I mean being a horrible person."

Tom rolled his eyes. "Oh, yeah." He picked up his taco and replaced it without taking a bite. "It's sorta embarrassing, but you already know I'm a blockhead, so…" He shrugged. "I ran into an old friend the other day. A girl I used to work with. Made her cry."

"Did she deserve it?" Henry asked, munching.

"Maybe a few years ago, yes. Now, I don't think so. I didn't give her a chance."

Henry looked up, wiping his mouth with a napkin. "Yeah, and…?"

"She was just trying to say hello. Being nice. Offered to meet for lunch. She was super nervous and shy, and I just shot her down."

"Sounds like little Tommy missed his chance at a hookup." Henry cocked his head. "Why would she be nervous?" He watched him from the corner of his eye as he worked on his food.

"Well, she—um—we—um—there was…" Tom groaned, and sloppily whirled his head around. "We once had a major crush on each other."

"While you were married…"

"Yes." Tom slumped. "And she knew I was."

"Hmmm."

"We never actually did anything," Tom added quickly. "Just came real close. That close." He held up a thumb and index finger. "I opted out at the last second."

Henry turned his taco about, seeking his next bite. "Always hungry, but can't let yourself get full…"

"My wife died a couple weeks later." He grunted. "My reward for trying to do the right thing."

Henry froze and stared at him. He swallowed. "The girl was nervous because she still feels guilt."

"Exactly. Even told me she meant to apologize, but it was too late. I'd already treated her like trash."

"Do you still feel guilt?"

"Over Kate?" Tom paused. "I don't know. I never actually cheated on her." His eyes wandered. "At least not all the way." He shrugged. "Maybe."

"But you feel guilt for disrespecting this girl who clearly deserved it, at least at some point in her past."

"Apparently so."

"I guess that's good. It means you're still human." Henry turned his attention to the basket of chips. "Doesn't make much sense, does it? We're just animals, but we feel guilt over following our instincts."

Tom at last took another bite of his taco. He carefully chewed and swallowed, and looked up. "You're right. I'm not an atheist."

"So, what's new?" Henry chuckled.

"I want to be one, but I can't."

"I guess that's—good?" Henry sat back. "Why do you want to?"

Tom shrugged. His eyes drifted over toward the floor.

Henry said, "You can't honestly claim to have ample evidence that we came into being without a God."

Tom nodded.

"But you're not convinced you have ample evidence that there is a God."

Tom nodded.

"Nevertheless, the evidence you've got points to a God you wish wasn't there."

"Right. That's what I can't escape." Tom frowned. "I just wish that whatever was out there would be—I don't know—a better God."

"A God like you want, rather than the God you ended up with."

"That's a funny way to put it, but yeah."

"Makes it sound like we were here first and then God came along and spoiled it all."

"And of course—I hate even admitting this—disliking a possibility doesn't exclude it. That's the part I can't escape."

Henry tilted the salsa bowl to make a puddle to scoop from. "Yep." He popped a chip into his mouth.

Tom continued. "And no religion can solve the problem, because we're still only talking about the evidence we've got rather than the theories behind the evidence."

Henry held up the little bowl and glanced around the restaurant for a waiter.

Tom said, "Isn't it your turn to tell me how your religion solves the problem?"

"Oh, are we taking turns?"

Tom shot him an annoyed look.

Henry shrugged. "I doubt you want me to spout the same stuff you've always heard."

"I don't."

"Okay then. So we're stuck with the classic problem: we can't escape that God seems to be there, and by looking around with our brains on we assume he's got power, but the evidence shows that he's not good."

Tom sighed heavily.

"But you've always been told how good he is," Henry added.

Tom grunted. "Sung songs about it. Heard endless sermons on it. Listened to people drool over their answers to stupid prayers like, 'We prayed for traveling mercies to the mall and back, and praise God, here we are'." Tom prodded at his food. "And I always expected to see his goodness for myself, but..."

Henry nodded thoughtfully. "Okay. Therefore, unless there's some religious theory that can satisfy the discrepancy, or unless you've misinterpreted the religious teaching you've heard, there's no good God out there."

"Believe me, I didn't misinterpret the religious teaching."

"You might have, at least in part. In fact, it's quite likely, given that you're just a human—a broken machine receiving complex information from biased, flawed humans who barely understand it themselves. There's no way it was always presented perfectly; I don't care how great the church is. But just because a theory is presented with a screwy explanation doesn't make it false."

Henry signaled a waitress who didn't see and walked past them. He turned back to Tom. "And of course you understand what 'good' is. It's how you know it wasn't 'good' to make that dirtbag girl cry. God can't possibly mean that suffering or pain, in and of themselves, are good."

"But we see it everywhere."

"Yep." Henry pinched up some shards of chips. "But what if making that girl cry actually helped her in the long run? Not that you ought to have done it, but God might have used it anyway to do her a good. It might have been part of a sequence of events that added up to change her for the better. Forever—since that's the only change that matters."

Tom held up his hands. "Which is the garbage I've heard all my life. You know: 'the doctor may have to hurt you to fix you'."

"You're saying you never had to let one of your kids suffer for their own good? Made them drink the medicine? Crammed your fist into the wound and pinched off the artery?"

Tom stared at him blankly. A blood-stained carpet swam before him, and inside his head his voice echoed *Trust me, okay Kate?* He flinched a little. "But I never created the suffering so that I could pop popcorn and sit and watch them squirm."

"But that's what God does?"

"Clearly."

"That," Henry said, "may be misinterpreting the evidence."

Tom raised his voice. "But where's the 'good' that's supposed to happen? 'Cause it isn't."

"Listen, Tom. You can't expect God to be a slave to your timeline. Expecting that the eternal…"

"Yeah, yeah." Tom cut him off. "Whatever."

Now Henry raised his voice. "What? You gonna plug your ears and run away? Oh, that's right: you can't. Maybe that's why God stuck you in that chair. Maybe it wasn't him punishing you for almost having an affair."

A couple at the next table glanced over.

Tom was too stunned to show much anger. "What?"

"And maybe your business success didn't come from ignoring God."

"Hey, you can't sit there and…"

"No—listen, Tom. You can't keep seeking evidence to fit the theory you want to believe. As if proving that God's a bad God makes him not exist. Or if Christians do dumb things it makes God not exist."

Tom lost his fire. He blinked a few times, almost dazed.

Henry spoke quietly. "And of course Christians do some dumb things. But it's a convenient bandwagon to jump on: 'Christians, right? Those hypocritical, backward, old-fashioned, closed-minded, racist,

pea-brained, redneck, flat-earthers? You don't want to be one of them…'
As if being Latino isn't enough, I've gotta face even more broad general-
izations and prejudice for being a Christian. But it's fair game for bigots
to wage a smear campaign against Christians and spew every smug insult they want."

Tom sat stone-still.

Henry softened a bit. "Isn't the whole point of Christianity that we're
wrecked, corrupted, broken beings? But somehow the un-Christlike behavior of Christians automatically invalidates all arguments for Christ.
As if smear tactics against fellow humans somehow make God vanish.
And people jump on board, forgetting that the ugly picture that's painted doesn't represent the people they actually know. You've seen this kind
of thing, right? But certainly when you look at, say, your dad, you don't
think *shallow-minded hypocrite,* do you? Your dad's a Christian, right?"

"My dad is dead."

Henry hesitated, sobered. "Really? I'm sorry. How long ago?"

"Early nineties. On my wedding day, by the way."

"Yikes…"

"I know."

"Your mom still alive?"

"Nope. Died a few years ago."

"Holy cow, Tom. You're bad luck."

Tom sat back with mouth open. "Wow. Such a gentleman."

"Come on, Tom, it's a joke. Listen, you're tired of being handled with
kid gloves, so I'm not gonna. Trust me, you're man enough. You're no
snowflake."

"Okay," Tom said. "Okay, I get it."

"And your circumstances are tough, I admit that. But just because I
can't know God's reasons, or whether he even has reasons—maybe he
just lets bad luck happen sometimes—it doesn't make me run into the
arms of atheism. Yet, of course I can't know what it feels like from inside
your circumstances. Maybe it would break me. Maybe that's why God
picked you to face it."

Tom's head wavered. "That's not really comforting."

"I know."

Tom remained silent.

Henry continued. "So, my point is, we all gravitate toward evidence that aligns with what we want to believe. Both atheists and religious people. It's called confirmation bias. We all do it."

"Yeah, I suppose."

"And God lets us do it if we insist."

Tom shrugged.

"And of course Christianity looks messed up when we're looking at the humans. But that doesn't mean we throw out the baby with the bath-water. People will say, 'Yeah, I've been to church, and it was all a big show' or 'they only beg for money' or whatever. And they're probably right. But they've been to—what—two different churches? Never been to a church in China or Iran. Never been to a little underground church in the 1300's. But still it's enough to invalidate the claims of Christ. Or they say, 'But that book is thousands of years old,' as if they would jump on board some brand-new religion started by Hay Sauce the Hallucinator. Or they say, 'You wanna base your life on the words of men?' as if they can prove they were just making stuff up. Either way, for some, it's plenty enough proof that it's all a farce. Makes it easy."

The waitress appeared at the edge of the table. "More chips and salsa?"

"Yes," Henry answered. "Yes, please."

She cleared the empty basket.

Henry continued. "So we're still stuck: either God's not there, or he's a bad God—which wouldn't matter, 'cause there's no point in trying to suck up to a capricious ogre—or it's possible that he's actually good like he said, though it's not always easy to see."

"That's a big problem for me."

"Yeah, me too sometimes. Believe me."

Tom eyed him suspiciously.

Henry added, "I guess it's a matter of either trusting what he said and waiting to find out, or saying, 'screw it, I'm gonna do whatever I want, and I don't care whether I contribute to the problem of evil'." Henry was still a moment, then he shrugged. "Or I guess a person could be an atheist and also try to live a 'good' life, as if their millisecond of cosmic time easing an atom's worth of misery matters in the least."

Tom stared absently, nodding. "Yep, that's a big problem for me."

The waitress returned and, having assumed that Tom would eat his share, laid a heaping basket of chips and a new bowl of salsa before them.

"I think I'd better stop there," Henry pushed the basket of chip crumbs away.

"You sure you're not gonna pop?" Tom said. "I would be dying, probably literally."

"I could finish it. I just—" Henry eyed the basket. "—I shouldn't."

Tom shook his head, jealous and disgusted. "Anyway," he continued, "I've got this nurse. Sort of nurse. Live-in help. Never quite finished her nursing degree. *Tatiana.* You should meet her." His eyebrows bounced a couple of times.

"Tatiana, huh? You order her online?"

"No, she's legit. Really."

"But you handpicked her, right?"

"Well, yeah; she met the criteria." He sloppily bobbed his head, not quite making eye contact. "But you should meet her. Honestly. She's fine. Come up to the house."

"Nah, I don't care for foreign chicks."

"All done here?" The waitress had materialized again.

Henry nodded. Tom said, "Yes, but I'll need something to put this in." He motioned to his half taco. "I'll finish it later."

"Okay then." She smiled graciously and carried off some things.

CHAPTER EIGHTEEN

The Verve office lay dark and quiet. A lone, dim lamp hovered over a single desk near the now black windows. On top of a scatter of papers, a framed photo of a toddler lay within the circle of lamplight. The boy's brilliant blue eyes were lifted to something off camera, his face aglow with delight. A twinkling Christmas tree was his background. A pane of glass separated him from his father.

Before the desk, Tom slumped motionless in his wheelchair, his unblinking eyes staring somewhere past a computer screen that glowed cold and indifferent. His face was blue. His desk drawer was open. Inside the drawer, a sandwich bag was open. Inside the bag remained three round, white, chalky pills.

And across town, under the browning lawn of Tom's house, the house where he had once lived with Katherine and Abigail and Hannah and Jacob, Hamlet lay still.

CHAPTER SEVENTEEN

Henry knocked on the massive cedar door and waited. When his subconscious egg-timer finally sounded, he pressed the doorbell. He glanced at his watch and waited a bit more. He knocked again and turned his back to the door, looking about.

Tom's lavish new mountain house now had smooth paved walkways winding through verdant grounds, tended and lush and serene. Cloud shadows slid over the pine-clad hillside rising beyond.

Still no sound came from within the house. Henry turned and knocked again, peering through the leaded glass bordering the door, but he saw no movement. He looked around again. A small SUV sat in the drive down by the guest quarters. Henry headed that way, eyeing the distant ridge through the glass passageway that connected the two houses.

"Yes?" an attractive young woman, tall and sturdily built, answered to his knock. Though she had spoken but one word, her accent was evident.

"You're Tatiana, I suppose? I'm Henry."

"Yes. You are Tom's friend?"

"I am. I'm here to see him, but he's not answering the door. I thought maybe you'd…"

Her face paled. "Oh." She stared a moment. "Okay." At last she forced a smile. "You wait here, please?" Her smile vanished as she spun and hurried toward the passageway.

Henry turned from the open door and laid his hand on his head, worried.

At last Tatiana's footsteps sounded from the wood floors inside. He spun around. "Yes, you may come." She looked at ease. "Tom did not hear you knock."

Henry followed her in and through the passage.

"Why are you asking me?" Henry said. "I'm no pastor or scholar."

"You think I trust any pastors?" Tom frowned. "It's you I trust. A little." He chuckled. "Not too much."

Henry and Tom faced each other at a table out on Tom's huge, cantilevered deck, the valley yawning beyond their profile. From the opening where the retractable glass wall normally stood came sounds of Tatiana inside, busy in the kitchen.

"Good grief, I don't know," Henry said. "I mean—I've always looked at it like one of those tracks. But it's stupid."

"You mean railroad tracks? I think I've heard this one."

"No, you haven't. It's not railroad tracks." Henry's eyes drifted around as if he sought a clue whether to talk about it. "Okay. You know those tracks they build that they roll those ball bearings down? A couple of parallel metal rails on some kind of support?"

"Like a railroad track," Tom inserted.

"Well, yeah, a bit. But small. A toy. A novelty. Like a track for toy cars, but they roll steel balls down them, and it's got jumps and spirals and gates and levers and stuff. The balls do tricks and try to stay on the track without falling off. Except of course the balls don't try, they just roll, and the designer has to angle the track just right so the ball stays on."

"Oh, okay, yeah, I think I've seen one of those."

"Anyway," Henry said, "imagine that people are the ball bearings, and the tracks are the course of people's lives. Each person is placed on a track at a certain point: birth; and stops rolling at the end of the line: death."

Tom nodded. "Okay. People are balls rolling down the tracks of their lives."

"Yes, now imagine that every track needed for every person who ever lived is built into the same massive structure. Billions of tracks, weaving in and out of each other, looping and spiraling, running parallel for a time and diverging. And because God is omnipresent through space and time, he sees the entire structure all at once, billions of balls on billions of tracks with all their twists and turns and obstacles. Not only that, all at once he sees each ball at every point it will ever be on the track; to him, the path each ball follows could look like a long metal snake—like a composite photo with billions of frames."

"Got it," Tom said.

Henry continued, "For you and me it would be impossible to process all that information, but for God, it's as if the whole thing is frozen to him because he's everywhere over all of time at once. Maybe that's why he's omniscient: if he wants to know what's going to happen or what once happened, he just looks at it at that particular spot in space and time and just watches it happen. If he thinks it, he knows it. So, if he wants to know where you'll be in five years, he just looks at you at that moment on the track because he's there already; he encompasses it all. That's undoubtedly an oversimplification, but take it for what it's worth."

Henry paused to take a breath and blow it out. "Now, to take a stab at answering your question: *Sovereignty* means he can adjust any track to have any angle he wants it to have. If a ball rolls off its track at a certain point, it's not like he watches the ball fall off and then tilts the track to the right angle afterwards; he sees it as a snake half on and half off, and he just reaches out and tilts the track a little at the right spots until the snake shape is corrected, lying entirely on the track. He does this at what we might call the 'beginning of time'—though that's probably not accurate; it's probably more like the one moment of 'God time' that overlays all of history past and future. But from our perspective the track was laid before our birth. Regardless, he adjusts the track and the ball stays on." Henry paused. "Okay? You with me?"

"I think so." Tom looked doubtful.

"Okay. So, here's the *Free Will* part. The difference here is that the balls are not inanimate metal balls; they're balls with minds. Let's say they can freely change their moment of inertia."

Tom said, "Ooh, I love it when you talk geek."

"Don't be gross," Henry shot back, chuckling. "Anyway, though a ball must maintain the correct moment of inertia (within some acceptable range) to stay on the right track, God allows it to change its mass or size at will because he's already compensated for it during 'God time' by providing a perfectly prepared track. In part, the ball's decisions helped dictate what shape the track would be down the line."

Tom nodded.

"You know where the word 'providence' comes from, right?" Henry said.

Tom shook his head.

"It's from 'provide,' which means 'foresee.' Like 'pre' and 'video.' Ants foresee winter so they provide food."

Tom raised his hand and held it there.

Henry watched him a couple seconds. "Yes, you in the back?"

"Um, teacher, why'd you act like you'd barely heard of *Sovereignty versus Free Will* when I asked about it?"

"Sheesh, I don't know. I mean—I've thought about it a little, but it's just me guessing mostly. I'm no scholar."

Tom stared blankly, then he twirled his hand and said, "Proceed."

"You sure?" Henry eyed him suspiciously. "Okay. That's why each ball has so much latitude to vary its moment of inertia: the God-designed track keeps the snake on it."

"This is getting spooky," Tom whispered, smirking.

"Listen, sir, next time you interrupt me when I'm trying to answer a question you asked me, I throw you off this stinking deck."

"Sorry, teacher."

"So, anyway," Henry announced loudly, "*Sovereignty* and *Free Will*, not at war, but in harmony. I figure maybe *Chance* is in there too, for God can even weave the structure around weather, germs, avalanches, tire blowouts, you name it, and use them as well."

Tom raised his hand. "What if a ball wants to be on a different track?"

"A track different from the track God designed for it? Sure. It can't really see the other tracks as well as it thinks it can, but God allows it to exceed its weight limit if it wants and throw itself off the right track—to derail itself—hoping to land on a track it assumes is better. And all the balls do that now and then. God calls this 'sin.' He won't adjust his perfect track to force an errant ball to stay on it. He allows the derailment. That's Free Will. Nevertheless, because God sees all, he can set an alternate track in place beforehand to catch the ball and keep it from falling to its death. A 'rerailment.' That's Sovereignty."

"Really spooky."

"And because balls exceed their boundaries all the time, God has provided an endless amount of alternate tracks. Even when bad, selfish balls ram into other balls and knock them off, he can get them both on alternate tracks. Some of the alternate tracks can even be quite enjoyable."

Tom said, "And some of the right tracks can be quite painful."

Henry raised his brows and nodded. "Of course. The balls all need some work. He knocks off the rough edges. He desires well-tempered steel, not bad-tempered steel."

"Now you're cheating."

"I'm painting a picture, Tom. Bear with me." He cleared his throat. "So, Free Will and Sovereignty can peacefully coexist because God always sees all our choices, even wrong ones, and he simply tweaks the system at that one weird moment in 'God time' so that all choices combine with all the designed twists and turns to add up to some final good at the end of the line. But here's the rub…"

"Uh oh," Tom murmured.

"I mean, here's the good news…"

"The gospel."

"Precisely." Henry smiled. "God won't let all the bad balls keep hurting each other forever. Eventually he's gotta put a stop to it. He also wants to stop smoothing and tempering the balls once they're suitable, because pain isn't a good in and of itself. So he offers to fix the problem with their warped moment of inertia. For those that accept, he promises to fix it at the end of the line, before they are moved to the eternal track."

"The eternal track in the sky," Tom offered.

Henry pointed a finger toward him. "Yes. And until then, they'll still make some bad decisions, which he'll use to further polish them, but he promises that they'll land safe at the end, to be fixed once and for all, and thereafter they'll always stay on the right track."

"Those who don't accept the offer?"

"He gives them plenty of chances to accept, plenty of rerailments, but even he's got his limits. He'll let them throw themselves off the track one last time."

"And he melts them down into a homogeneous mass of misery."

Henry shrugged. "Maybe. Or maybe he vaporizes them. Or maybe both. Or neither. Whatever it is, it'll be just. Either way, he's not letting them on the eternal track in the sky to ruin it for everybody else, and after all, it was their choice that made them miss the safe landing."

"But each of them was set on the track with an inclination toward bad choices built into them. At their first 'railment.' Not their fault."

"That's why he doesn't demand that they make perfect choices—just to submit to being fixed in the end. He'll take care of all the rerailments for those that ask." Henry folded his hands and looked at Tom with a funny little expression, as if he had just popped his head out of the curtain at the end of the puppet show.

Tom sat back and gave a slow, thoughtful nod. "Okay, Mr. Engineer. You and your 'moment of inertia.' Pretty interesting stuff." He nodded again. "Though…" He patted the arms of his wheelchair. "…at the moment I feel pretty inert, trapped in this thing. Regrettably, it's not just a moment for me, it's a whole life. I wish it were just a moment."

Henry's eyes gleamed. "But how long is a moment? Though it's undefined, it's short, right? Perhaps one day you'll look back on your whole life and wonder why it felt like it took so long. You'll realize it was just a moment. After all, life is but a…"

"But a vapor. Yeah, I know."

"Okay, guys," Tatiana called from the house as she approached with a tray.

Henry turned. "All right!"

She laid down the tray and began setting a meal before each of them. Tom's plate contained only a quarter portion. She turned to Henry. "He eats all day a tiny, tiny meal many times." Henry nodded. She rose to leave. "Say to me when you want any more, okay?"

"Thank you, Tatiana," Henry said.

"No problems." She carried the empty tray inside.

After she passed out of sight, Tom looked slyly at Henry. "So, what do you think, huh? About Tatiana?"

"All business, huh?"

"Yeah, but you two could make some serious football players together."

Henry shrugged weakly. "Sure, she's decent."

"Oh, whatever, you dweeb. Never mind."

Once they started eating, Tom noticed Henry wearing a blank expression and chewing slowly. Tom said, "It's horrible, isn't it?"

"Uh, well," Henry said. "It's not great."

"No, she's the worst cook," Tom chuckled. "I don't have the heart to tell her."

"So, what exactly are the criteria for live-in help," he glanced toward the house, "since taste buds clearly aren't on there? Besides looking adequate, of course."

"She's a trained nurse. Like three years in Lithuania or Latvia or someplace. She does enemas and stuff."

Henry froze. His eyes fell to his plate.

Tom threw his head back and laughed. "She washes up afterwards." He glanced at his food. "I mean, I think she does."

"She gives you enemas? Seriously?" He eyed Tom, apprehensive.

"It happens. Look, I got no shame left. I'd let you give me an enema right now if you wanted."

"Nah, I'm good."

"…so there's this woman, all burka'd up," Henry chuckled, "screaming her head off at Steve, saying she was gonna feed his heart to the dogs and stuff—like somehow she's scarier than her husband and sons we had just disarmed and hog-tied—so he…"

"She spoke English?" Tom said.

"No, it was Pashto. So he…"

"You speak Pashto?"

"You know—a little. So Steve starts…"

Tom grimaced and laid his hand on his abdomen.

Henry watched him a moment. "Hope it's not that, uh, prison food." He jabbed a thumb back toward the kitchen.

Tom shook his head. "No. It does this. It's normal."

"Alright. You good? Anyway, Steve starts screaming back, super loud, right up in her face; except he's screaming the words to *Jingle Bells*." Henry mimicked a screaming voice, "Dashing through the snow on a one horse open sleigh…" He laughed. "And of course the poor lady's got no clue…"

CHAPTER SIXTEEN

Tom and Henry reclined in cushioned lounge chairs out by the glass rail of Tom's immense deck. Rather than allowing Tatiana, capable as she was, to muscle Tom into the chair, Henry had transferred him as easily as if he were a stuffed bear. The shadow of the lowering sun had crept over them as they gazed lazily across the valley toward the glowing, yellowed western slope of Horsetooth Mountain.

Tom suddenly broke the reverie. "How do you know the Bible is true?"

Henry answered nonchalantly. "I don't."

Henry felt Tom's head turn toward him. "What?"

"I don't."

"Then why do you listen to it?"

"Because I believe it's true."

"Pffft." Tom scrunched up his mouth. "Know. Believe." He flapped his hand around. "So *why* do you believe? Because it claims to be true?"

Henry looked over. "Any liar can *claim* to be telling the truth. In fact, he'd better, or he won't get very far as a liar. But the person I learn to trust is the person who consistently tells the truth."

Tom silently looked over the valley, a subtle tension starting to grow on his face. His breaths gradually became fast and shallow, and his eyes glazed and turned to the sky. Henry turned from Tom to the panorama, waiting for the wave of pain to pass.

"Sorry about that," Tom said at last.

"Mmm hmm," Henry answered.

"You were saying?"

"Um, reliability, I guess. Reliability is why I believe the Bible. What it says aligns with what I've experienced and learned. That's why I don't think men just made stuff up."

Tom nodded, but remained silent. They watched the shadow creep up Horsetooth.

After a while, Tom said quietly, "What you've experienced and learned." It was directed more toward the sky than toward anyone.

"Yeah." Henry's eyes remained distant. "Experience and learning seem to be all we've got to work with."

Tom turned. "Work with for what?"

"To know truth." Henry shrugged. "If 'know' is even the right word."

"So you say 'believe' instead of 'know'."

"Not really. Sometimes. I only said that because we can't really 'know' much."

"Can't know much?"

"Yeah. For the most part, all we can *know* is that something exists, and that whatever exists is what it is, since our beliefs about it can't make it not itself."

Tom stared silently. "I think, therefore I am," he mumbled.

Henry chuckled. "Yeah, like that, I guess." He reclined further into his chair. "I'm not saying there's no such thing as real fact, or that truth is relative. After all, *fact* is just a description of what actually exists."

Tom added, "Or what did exist or will exist."

"Right." Henry said. "And I'm not suggesting that we can't actually know things, considering that knowledge is nothing more than facts inside of heads. If there's a real fact in your head, then you know something, whether you know it or not." He snorted, amused.

"Yeah, but..." Tom scratched his head, frowning. "But to know something, you can't just have a fact rolling around in there; you've also gotta believe it's true. Otherwise you'll mark B when the right answer was C."

"Good point. I suppose you don't know the right answer if you don't believe it's the right answer. Otherwise you're deceived."

They remained silent awhile before the vista. At last Henry said, "Kinda crazy, huh?"

"What?"

"That knowledge is so slippery. To know fact, first we've got to personally observe a thing, then we must trust that our senses weren't tricked, then we've gotta trust our memory of it, and lastly our conclusions about it. It takes a load of faith in ourselves to think we *know* something."

"Wait…" Tom shook his head. "Why do we have to personally observe it?"

"If we don't, then we're trusting the testimony of the people who did. Trusting their senses and conclusions—and honesty. And like the telephone game, stuff undoubtedly gets lost in translation. That takes even greater faith."

"Okay. I see." He sighed and glanced down. "And unfortunately, what we can't personally experience is almost everything in the universe." He smirked. "Experience and learning, kicked to the curb."

"No, not quite." Henry shook his head. "Not quite. Since the only knowledge we get comes from experience or learning, we have to trust them if we expect to function. And it works: we generally believe we're right, and our confidence is reinforced by successful living day to day. Nothing wrong with that. Furthermore, we draw conclusions from patterns so we don't have to experience every single thing: 'Since banging that hammer on my thumb sucked, I'll bet banging that rock on my finger would also suck'."

"Yeah," Tom chuckled.

"It'd be a truly crippled person afraid to trust that the sky won't fall on him if he goes outside."

"Of course the sky won't fall on him."

"Both of us believe that, and we're probably right. But regardless of what goes on in our heads, the sky's gonna do what it's gonna do. There's the fact. We just believe the fact is what we think it is." He caught Tom's eye. "But I guess that's the point: in order to function, everyone relies on belief. Or trust. Or—can we use that dirty word—*faith?*"

Tom said, "So you're saying that knowledge requires faith. In everyone. All the time. Faith in themselves at least, and faith that their experience and learning provided truth."

"Yep. For both the atheist and the religious. Even for scientists—especially for scientists—nothing can be known to be 'true'; things can only be proven false. Only if it hasn't been refuted and the evidence deems it likely can it be *believed* to be true." He shrugged. "But of course, many people believe what they believe because they want to believe it, regardless of evidence. Both the atheist and the religious."

Henry set his glass on the deck beside him. "The problem arises when people refuse to be 'wrong.' They cling to physics because they fear to allow for metaphysics. Or they reject legitimate science because they're comfortable with their dogma. People are just too proud or afraid to risk watching their house of cards tumble. Just because people claim to be open-minded doesn't mean they are."

Tom silently chuckled and subtly shook his head. "Yep."

"Those who think they're infallible are certainly further from truth than those who admit they're probably wrong about some stuff."

Tom turned to him. "So be wary of your beliefs."

"Uh," Henry paused. "Maybe not as much 'wary of your beliefs,' but wary of your bias that corroborates those beliefs."

"Okay," Tom said. "But that includes you too, you know."

"Of course." Henry laughed. "Sheesh. Especially me. But all of us should be willing to say, 'As a human, I tend to believe things convenient to my intentions. As a human, I might be wrong. But best I can tell I'm not, so I'll act accordingly until further notice'."

"Sure," Tom grunted. "But who does that?"

"Oh, I don't know. You and I can try, at least. Continue to trust in what we think we know, but temper it with genuine open-mindedness—not as an end in itself; not for the consolation of wearing the title 'Open-Minded'—but for the purpose of finding truth, of allowing ourselves to be straightened out."

"Yep. I suppose…" Tom began, then another wave of pain began to creep up on him. He quietly endured it for a few moments.

"Your gut?" asked Henry.

"No, my back," he gasped. "Along the spine."

Henry gave him a little longer.

At last Tom relaxed a bit. "Okay, I'm good," he whispered. His brow was damp. "You were saying?"

"Yeah. I don't know." Henry shrugged. "I think I'm done. Don't want to bore you to death."

Tom looked at him weakly. "I wouldn't mind."

As Henry turned his car out of Tom's driveway to make his way down the mountain, his headlights fell on a figure quickly moving to intercept him. He stopped where the gravel road entered the woods. Tatiana approached, but she passed by and waved for him to follow her deeper into the dark. She walked several yards down the road then turned and peered through the trees toward the house. Henry pulled alongside and killed the vehicle lights.

She leaned down and placed her hands on the open window. "You are a very good friend of Tom?" She breathed heavily.

"Yeah, I think so."

"I want that you help him." She shook her head and glanced down. "He is not very good. I mean not his body; his body is—" she gritted her teeth and gestured *small* with her thumb and finger "—is okay. It is his mind, his…" She tapped the side of her forehead. "He swallows narcotics as if they are candy. Right now, after you walked outside, he went fast to his room, and I heard him open a medicine bottle."

"I know he's in severe pain a lot."

"Yes, severe. But many nights, he sits on his chair and stares hours. I must stay awake and make him move often. He sits outside, but he does not see the hills or sky. He looks down to the deck or wall or corner of the house."

"All the time?"

"A lot of times. That is when he is home. One time he never come home at all, the whole night. I went in his work for check up on him, and he talk very mad to me. But most the time he is just sad."

"He seems like he's managing. I know he's frustrated, but he's doing his best."

"No. With people, he is pretending to be happy, but every time he is alone, he is very sad. I worry."

"Oh, Tom." Henry sighed. "Tom, Tom, Tom." He looked at Tatiana. "What do you think?"

"I want to phone to the hospital, but they will take him maybe, or he will get mad and take job from me maybe. I need this job. If Tom kills himself with narcotics, then I will have no job." Her eyes flitted away, then she looked back at Henry. "I feel myself very afraid. You must help him."

He patted her hand on the doorframe. "Don't worry. I'll figure something out. I'll come up with something. Don't worry."

She typed his number into her phone, and he instructed her to call day or night. Then Tatiana sneaked back to her quarters, and Henry resumed his dark, quiet drive down to town, praying all the way.

"…and so the eccentric pulleys are what hold the chair in both standing and sitting positions," Tom said, zooming in on a CAD drawing on his monitor. "The latches are merely a failsafe."

Henry leaned over Tom's desk, watching. "Yeah, I get it. Wow, Tom, you're sort of a brain."

"Ha. Thanks, I guess."

Henry glanced up to see Justin hurrying toward him. When Justin met his eyes, he slowed his pace, nodded at Henry, and gave him a covert thumbs up.

"Yeah, that's super cool," Henry announced. "Steve'll definitely want to see that, since he's a bit of a gearhead."

"For sure, next time he's out."

"So you ready?"

"I guess." Tom shrugged. "Can't really be sure since I have no clue where we're going."

"Don't worry; you'll love it."

Tom closed his laptop and wheeled himself back. As they headed for the entrance, Tom stopped by the front desk. "Hey, I'm taking off."

"Alright, Tom," the receptionist answered. "Have a good rest of your day." Her eyes lit up as she lifted them to Henry. "See you later."

"Take care, Eileen," he returned politely.

Tom was already halfway through the courtyard by the time Henry exited. "This way Tom. I'm parked on the side." Tom wheeled about and followed him toward the employee lot.

Henry hoisted Tom into the passenger side of his big old sedan. As he positioned him onto the seat, Tom growled through bared teeth, eyes squeezed tight. Henry drew back his hands and froze. "Oops! Sorry. Sorry. Was that me?"

"Not your fault," Tom hissed between rapid breaths. "When it twists just right, it does that." He inhaled and steeled his eyes, then he pushed the seat down and squirmed until his spine found a better position. He paused and waited, as if listening.

"You good to go?" Henry asked cautiously. Tom nodded, forcing half a smile, chest heaving. Henry watched him another moment before he began coercing the wheelchair into the back seat.

Tom turned his head. "We really could take my truck. I don't mind driving."

"Nah, I got this." Henry finished, hopped in the driver's seat, and headed out to the road.

Henry studied the sky as he drove west across town. A few friendly white clouds hung above the foothills, with nothing but blue over the high peaks beyond. Though the day was hot, the shade would be ideal. A pleased look played on his face, and he cut his eyes over. Tom stared absently through the dashboard. With a little grimace and a tiny shake of the head, Henry returned his attention to the road.

After a while, Henry turned onto the county road that wound and climbed toward Tom's mountain home.

"We going up to the house?" Tom wondered.

"No. You'll see."

Tom continued to stare ahead. After a long silence he announced, "How do you know it's all true?"

"What?" Henry looked over.

"Creation. Incarnation. Resurrection. Afterlife. That stuff."

Henry chuckled. "Oh, so *stuff* is what's bothering you? I thought you were hurting."

"What?"

"You've been quiet. I thought I hurt you. Physically."

"No. Well, yeah. But I'm fine. I'm just sorta—thinking. Wondering how you know it's all true."

"God doesn't ask you to know; he only asks you to believe."

"Oh yeah, that's right." Tom nodded slowly. "Just believe," he muttered. "Yeah, well, I already did that."

"Uh, did what?"

"Trusted Christ."

Henry looked surprised. "You *did* that?"

"Yeah."

"What's that mean?"

"You know—I got saved."

"You *got* saved…" Henry shook his head. "Sounds odd. Is *saved* a noun?"

"What?"

"You know—I got root beer; I got diphtheria. A direct object."

"You've never heard that?" Tom asked.

"I've heard 'I *was* saved.' As in: 'Though the fire blocked the stairs, I was saved by a fireman'."

"All I mean is I asked Jesus into my heart."

Henry turned toward him, bewildered. "Into your heart? Why?"

Tom returned a bewildered look. "To get saved." He stared a moment. "Why do you think?"

"Is that in the Bible?"

"Is what in the Bible?"

"Asking Jesus into your heart."

Tom stared through the windshield a moment. "I don't know." His eyes drifted out the passenger window toward the landscape.

"When did you stop?" Henry asked.

"Stop what?"

"Trusting Christ? You said you 'trusted' him. In the past tense."

"That's not what that means."

"You made it sound like trusting Christ is a task you complete."

"It means I prayed to trust Christ."

Henry looked at him sheepishly. "I'm sorry. I don't know what that means either. You asked him to help you trust him?"

"No, I asked him into my heart."

"Okay, I'm confused."

Tom raised his voice a little. "About what?"

"What your faith is in, I guess." Henry shrugged. "It sounds as if your faith is in yourself—in some task you did or some prayer you said. Or it was, at least."

"Gosh, I was just a little kid. Can God really expect a deep, philosophically rich understanding of theology from a kid?"

"Well, I don't think so. I suppose he expects childlike faith from a kid. But what he wants from you is to trust in him—not to trust in some prayer you said that you didn't even understand. You can't live your life in enmity with God and expect that he's required to forgive you because of some meaningless act you did decades ago."

Tom looked halfway between insulted and enlightened.

Henry continued, "He's not a genie in a lamp obligated to perform for you because you discover the right gesture: praying the rosary, or kneeling the right direction, or refusing to eat pork, or parroting a bunch of words your Sunday School teacher told you to say—especially if your heart's far from him. Man, I would be terrified to face the afterlife resting on some gesture I did as a child." Henry looked sincerely at Tom. "Do you understand? It's not about what you did, it's about what Christ did. What is your faith in?"

"Well, that's the thing I can't understand." Tom spoke gruffly. "Why would God choose faith as his—his Big Important Thing. How is that the thing that qualifies a person for heaven?"

"Whoa. Okay. So, *faith*… You never make it easy on me, do you? Okay. Well…"

Tom grunted. "You don't have to answer if you don't want."

"No, I just..." He turned into the parking lot of the Horsetooth Mountain recreation area. "We're here."

Tom looked up and recognized the place. "Hey—we going for a hike?"

"Yes, sir."

"Ha. You're funny," Tom said deadpan. "You know there's no accessible trails up here, right?"

"Yes, sir." Henry pulled into a parking spot and killed the engine. "You'll see."

Tom waited impatiently while Henry hopped out, opened the trunk, and banged around for a moment. He then retrieved Tom's wheelchair from the back seat, moved Tom into it, and rolled him behind the car. On the asphalt behind the open trunk sat another wheelchair—the most bizarre one Tom had ever seen.

"Ta da," Henry said.

Tom wheeled himself around the machine. It was essentially a harness strung between a trio of mountain bike wheels on a metal frame. A pair of footrests straddled the front wheel, and a pair of handles extended off the back.

"What the heck is it?"

"It's for you. From me and the folks at Verve. Mainly from them, since they built it. Justin got it done a couple of days ago. He snuck it into my trunk earlier while I distracted you."

"Okay. What is it?"

"I told you—we're going on a hike."

Tom saw that Henry was serious. "Really? A hike?" He looked uphill toward the mountain, a smile starting to form. "No..."

Henry nodded.

"What? Really?"

"Happy Birthday. Ish."

"You're off by five months, but I'll take it." Tom's eyes were soft.

After Henry showed off the chair's features, Tom said, "But I'm in my work clothes."

"Not to worry." Henry pulled a bag out of his trunk. "Since Tatiana does your laundry, I didn't think you'd mind if she went through your stuff."

"She's in on it too?"

"Yep."

Tom slowly shook his head, dumbfounded, staring at his new off-road wheelchair.

Henry helped Tom change in the cramped trailhead bathroom, then he strapped him into the chair. He grabbed his backpack from the trunk and put Tom's work clothes and regular wheelchair inside. "Alright, we're locked and loaded," Henry said, and he wheeled him toward the trail.

Because Tom's seat was low-slung between the rear wheels, his knees stuck up on either side of the front fender. A couple of hikers stared as they passed them coming down. "I look like an overgrown baby in a stroller made by hillbillies," said Tom.

"Yes, sir." Henry grinned from ear to ear as he muscled him up the trail.

In order to clear ledges, rocks, and roots, Henry would tilt the chair back and float the front wheel over the obstacle, then he would lift the back wheels and roll Tom like a wheelbarrow. To get past rough spots and steep places, Henry just carried the chair—Tom and all—by hooking a tab on the back of the frame onto his pack's belt. Strapped into his little sling, Tom bounced along happily, craning his neck to look around, staring up into the pines, noting all the landmarks he had memorized long ago.

"This switchback was my ten-minute mark. Wow. I was so slow at first. I think I got that down to eight-forty."

"What was your fastest time, round trip?"

"This route? Ah..." Tom thought. "Thirty-something. I wanna say thirty-eight and a half or so."

"Wow. Not bad."

Parked in the shade at a trailside overlook, Henry took a well-deserved rest while Tom took in the panorama of the town and prairie below. Henry mopped his brow with a bandana, and swigged from his bottle. "Sorry," Tom grunted. "You're killing yourself heaving me up a mountain."

"No biggie." Henry wet his bandana and wiped his face. "You're not heavy."

"I'm enjoying feeling warm for once while you bake to death."

"It's fine. I love this. I'm enjoying you enjoying it." He guzzled another drink. "Besides, I need the workout."

Tom glared at the marble statue beside him. "Yeah, right."

Henry turned to him, twisting the cap onto his bottle. "If you're ready, let's keep moving. You're okay? Not in too much pain? The jostling isn't aggravating anything?"

"Yeah, I'm good." His face didn't quite match his words, but he smiled anyway. "Let's go." He took a sip of his water and handed the bottle to Henry.

Henry packed up and rolled Tom back to the trail. A couple of hikers appeared from down around the bend. "Afternoon. Nice day, huh?" Henry said.

"Sure is," one answered breathlessly. They paused to let Henry go first, studying Tom and his alien wheelchair.

"No, you go ahead," Henry said. "We move kinda slow."

A couple of minutes later, the hikers had to stand aside as Henry passed them.

"Alright, we'd better leave the chair here," Henry said. "I'll be carrying you the rest anyway."

"You intending to summit?" Tom looked worried.

"Of course." He didn't glance up. "The climbing's barely class three."

Tom hesitated. "Ohh…kay."

Henry turned his pack around and wore it on his chest so he could carry Tom piggyback. He knelt, and Tom clasped hands around his shoulders.

"Hang on." Henry slowly hoisted him. "Alright, you got it?"

"Yeah."

"Let me secure your legs." Leaning forward with Tom laying on his back, he tied Tom's legs to either side of his pack. He then gripped Tom's wrists with one hand and lifted his hips with the other so Tom's arms would bear less of his weight. "You good to go?"

"Yeah."

As they ascended the last quarter mile, a couple other hikers stopped to gawk and offer help. Henry politely declined. When he reached the final rocky ascent, he used one hand for handholds and kept the other firmly on Tom's wrists. At last it leveled off and he set foot on the highest point. He turned about to take in the grandeur.

The ground fell away dizzyingly on all sides. The drop to the east was nearly vertical, revealing the slopes they had just ascended, the lake beyond, finally giving way to an arrow-straight horizon. A parade of mountains extended southward all the way to Pikes Peak—a faint, mountain-shaped shadow on the sky, and northward to the rusty hills of Wyoming. And to the west, the green valley thousands of feet below them was draped with lethargic cloud shadows following the land like great herds of buffalo.

"Wow," Tom said. "Wow. Thank you man. I mean it."

"No problem, sir."

"There's my house." Tom looked west across the valley.

"Just you wait. Let me find a spot you can sit." Henry found a rock Tom could lean against, and he gingerly sat in front of it and loosed him.

Tom scooted himself back. "Ow. Ow," he growled.

Henry eyed him. "Your back?"

Tom nodded, frowning.

"You good?"

"That one hurt." Tom adjusted his posture a little, wincing. "Yeah, I'm fine." He slowly relaxed.

Henry lowered his pack and opened it. He extracted a thick pad for Tom to sit on and positioned it under him, then he returned to the pack and rooted around in it a moment. "Look what I brought." He grinned and held up a spotting scope.

"Gosh, how much stuff you got in there?"

He ignored him. "Okay, which one's your house?"

Tom pointed.

Henry sat next to him and scanned across the valley to locate the house. "Yep, there it is. Oh, look, there's Tatiana out on the deck. Uh, sunbathing." He paused a second. "Dude, is she naked?"

"What, really?" Tom blurted.

"Have a look." He passed him the scope.

Tom grabbed it up and scanned a few moments. Finally he said, "You jerk," chuckling. "It's just Jorge watering the plants."

Henry guffawed. At last he said, "Tatiana knows we're headed up here. You should call her. Have her come out and wave."

A few moments later, while looking through the scope, Tom spoke into the phone. "Yep, there you are. Henry, stand and wave at her. Tatiana, do you see us? Right on top against the sky, on the left side next to the big crack." A pause. "She can't see us."

"Have her use your telescope."

In a couple minutes Tom said, "Yeah, that's us. Wave, Henry. Ha ha! She sees us."

Henry noticed the look on Tom's face. A wide smile: genuine, innocent, and untinged by the slightest trace of his burden.

CHAPTER FOURTEEN

Supplemented by his cast-iron physique, Henry's unremarkable face was
no hindrance to the pair of college girls who had sidled up to nonchalantly discuss with him whatever they could think of: Horsetooth Rock,
hiking, the weather. As Henry talked and gestured, his eye fell on Tom,
who sat motionless with his head hung. Henry excused himself from
the ladies and went and sat on a hump of rock near Tom. "You hurting?"

Tom glanced up with a half-hearted smile. "Nah. Well, yeah of course,
a little. But I'm fine."

Henry paused for a few seconds. "Okay. Good." He looked out over
the valley a while and began working on a bag of granola.

"So, what were you asking about in the car?" Henry added at last.

"Huh?"

"About faith or whatever."

"Oh, yeah." Tom waved his hand in the air and put on the most disinterested face he could muster. "I—I don't know." He shrugged a time
or two. "It just doesn't make a lot of sense that faith is the one thing that
suddenly makes God stop being ticked off at people." His facade began
to fade. "They go from being these monsters he wants to smash with
flaming meteors to these precious children he longs to fill with joy, and
all they've gotta do is 'have faith.' Doesn't matter if they're good or bad,
they've just gotta believe a thing that doesn't seem true. If they don't,
they're doomed; if they do, they qualify for a big eternal pat on the back."

"Alright." Henry paused thoughtfully, nodding his head. "If God wanted to smash people, why would he continually plead with them for their lives? It'd be like a swindler cautioning you not to buy his snake oil. So let's not assume our philosophy is sound because our straw men are so easy to knock down."

Tom gave half a reluctant nod.

"Likewise, we can't assume that when God says to have faith, all he means is: 'You just gotta believe!' —like some lame slogan on a motivational poster." Henry tossed back a little more granola and spoke with his mouth full. "People do this all the time: paint an inaccurate picture and then criticize that. They say, 'I don't want to go to heaven if all we're gonna do is sit around on clouds and play harps.' We've been so bombarded with cartoonish imagery, we envision idols rather than just listen to the words." He frowned and shook his head. "People hear the phrase 'go to heaven' and picture some fairyland filled with fat little flying babies. No, instead, I think we're in for it. Maybe the reason God has to toughen us up first is so we won't fall to pieces on our first glimpse of the real place."

Tom paused, brows raised. "Okay," he said. "But I'm not asking about heaven; I'm asking about faith."

"Right. For the same reason, we should beware our cliché ideas about faith. You see, every discussion depends on semantics. When we imagine *faith*, you may picture butterflies and pink clouds, while I might picture, I don't know, steel I-beams and concrete. But it doesn't matter what we think, it matters what God means."

"Of course," Tom said. "So what does he mean?"

"To start, I'm certain God doesn't want us forcing ourselves to believe a bunch of ridiculous fairytales. You said that people gotta believe a thing that 'doesn't seem true.' Well, God must think it does seem true and that he's presented ample evidence for it. Only an unreasonable God would expect you to believe an unreasonable thing."

Tom frowned doubtfully.

"But," Henry added, "this is where it gets tough. Trying to articulate something as controversial as faith…"

"Controversial?"

"Yeah, you know—not just ordinary faith, like, 'I believe it's gonna rain'—but like you said, the kind that qualifies a person for heaven. Yeah it's controversial."

"And frustrating," Tom grunted. "Somebody really tries to be a good person, but they're doomed anyway because they don't happen to believe a specific batch of information."

"Exactly."

Tom raised his voice. "As if all somebody's gotta do is wander up to the right bridge and mosey on over, and they make it safely across the chasm—doesn't matter if they're Mother Theresa or an axe murderer."

"Exactly." Henry nodded. "Trust me, with my background, I can empathize. No one can come away from an honest reading of the Bible thinking that God doesn't mind if we sin. So let's not assume—at least for the moment—that our efforts play no part in our final outcome."

Tom paused, looking unsure. "Right. Okay." Henry offered him the open end of the bag of granola. He waved it away. "No, thanks."

"Okay, then," Henry said. "Regarding what God means by *faith*, we know at least this much: you can't simply claim to believe something you don't actually believe. It's gotta be real. No one's gonna swindle God."

"Well, yeah, that."

"Also, even real belief is clearly not enough."

Tom frowned and sat back. "Wait. Hold on. 'Real belief' is not enough?"

"Yeah. *Faith* can't mean that all you gotta do is believe he exists or believe he died on the cross. Devils believe that much."

"Okay, I see. So, not a mere acknowledgment of facts."

"Right. Also, *faith* can't mean 'calling on Jesus' name'."

"What?" Tom looked confused. "But that's in the Bible."

"Yes, of course." Henry waved his hand. "You know—just saying words. Like your parents forcing you to tell your sister 'I'm sorry'."

Tom nodded. "Okay."

"Also, I guess…" Henry began with a shrug. "I also mean that God wouldn't require 'calling on Jesus' name' as some kind of formal regulation.

He wouldn't say, 'Sorry, you're out of luck; you never said the word *Jesus*.' —as if he's just a clerk reading the rules off a clipboard."

Tom looked at him sideways. "But what about: 'there's no other name by which people can be saved'?"

"Absolutely. Of course the man named Jesus is the only way— because he's the only one who did the necessary work. But does God require that the name cross everyone's lips? Abraham never said the name Jesus, yet his faith was enough. He never even had the law. He just responded to whatever little light he was given." Henry caught Tom's eye. "We can't assume God makes a bunch of arbitrary rules and then holds everyone accountable to them, as if souls are a game to him. Rules like: 'Believe in a guy you've never heard of.' I don't buy that a just God would condemn someone over that. If nothing else, he's certainly wise, so his expectations must be reasonable."

Tom stared absently a few moments.

Henry continued, "Sure, Jesus said, 'I am the way; no man comes to the Father but by me.' But do you need to know the name of a bridge in order to cross it? You just need to cross it. For example, I have no idea how God reached the hearts of Native Americans a thousand years ago, but I won't assume he was powerless to do so and never did. But if he saved any of them, it's certainly by the same bridge. If they're forgiven, it's through the work of Jesus." He cocked his head. "Undoubtedly, once anyone who had been forgiven was educated about Christ, they wouldn't point to any other name as their savior."

Tom said, "That's contrary to everything I've been taught my whole life. How can anyone come to saving faith without hearing the gospel?"

"I don't know. But however God treats people who never heard, I'm sure he does it justly and mercifully. And I'm certainly not one to restrict the wideness of his mercy or speak against his justice."

Henry stared at the ground between his feet a moment, then he looked at Tom. "All I know is you and I aren't in the same boat as them; no way *we* can claim he never told us. I can't speak for them, but at least for you and me, he appears to hold us accountable if we won't believe."

Tom rolled his eyes and cried, "This is what's so..." He threw his hands up.

"I know," Henry said, then more quietly, "I know. And unless he's unjust, then it's for a good reason we're accountable. We won't be able to shake a finger in his face and say he didn't play fair."

Tom's expression grew darker. "He hides from us, then he condemns us for not believing he's there. How can that be just?"

"And therein lies your original question: How is it sensible that God considers faith the thing that 'qualifies' us for heaven?" Henry sat forward. "That's what we're trying to figure out: what grants access to the bridge? Or better yet: what prevents it?"

Tom muttered, "And you say it's unbelief."

"Not me."

"Okay then. God. But why?"

"You mean, how can he hold men accountable for not believing?"

"Exactly," Tom snapped. "That's what's so stupid."

"Okay." Henry spoke quietly. "Okay. Hold on." He interlaced his fingers and sat back. "Justice can't condemn someone for a thing that was inevitable. And if disbelief is condemned, then the kind of disbelief that condemns must be by choice."

"Huh?" Tom looked puzzled.

"Um..." Henry searched the air for words. "Let's say a tornado blew a man's roof onto his neighbor's head, and a judge condemned him for murder. We'd call the judge 'unjust' and throw him into the street. The man couldn't help it." He looked earnestly at Tom. "You see? A person condemned for disbelief must have chosen it, because justice can't hold someone accountable for a thing that was inevitable."

Tom looked across the valley a while, slowly nodding. Finally he said, "Alright, maybe." He huffed and shook his head. "But why should people have to qualify for heaven at all?" It was a complaint more than a real question, though when he heard himself, he indeed began to wonder it.

"In other words, why can't everyone just be herded across the bridge?"

Tom nodded and looked away. Henry held his peace. For a long while they both stared out through blue air toward the ponderosa-clad slopes around Tom's house.

At last Tom said, "It's sure pretty."

"Sure is."

They remained silent another minute before Henry spoke. "Knowing that a forest is infested with bark beetles, even if it looks perfect, is perhaps sadder than seeing a long-dead forest. It's a tainted version of what 'ought' to be."

Tom gave him a puzzled look.

"It hurts because deep down we know beetle kill isn't *right*. It's *unrighteous*. Beetles should be mutualistic, not parasitic."

Tom shrugged.

Henry paused a moment. "Perhaps we desire heaven because deep down we long for restoration to the right, natural order. We crave a just, equitable society."

"What are you saying?"

Henry turned to him. "If you were to live forever, would you want it to be with people who will mess up the place and do you harm, or would you rather it be perfect?"

"Well, of course…"

"Me too." He caught Tom's eye. "That's why the demand of God is not 'try to be good'—but 'be holy.' Be thoroughly and permanently sinless. You let one selfish person into eternity, he will try to gain at others' expense. One parasite would taint it for everybody."

"But God could stop him."

"Except he wants it to be a place of perfect freedom, not restrictions. Would God be a good God if he allowed anything but perpetual righteousness into a perpetual society?"

"Well…" Tom began, but paused to sort it out. "Well, no. No, I guess."

"That's why people must qualify for heaven. But it's not faith that qualifies, it's perfection. Only the holy get in."

"But nobody's holy. Nobody's ever been."

"Precisely," Henry said. "Hence the need for a bridge. Even the remote tribe knew right from wrong, and their conscience rebuked them. But to live forever, we must do more than happen across the right bridge—we must somehow become holy."

Tom rolled his eyes. "And now you'll say that all we've gotta do is believe in Jesus, and he'll make us holy." He scowled. "Which makes no sense."

"No. My point..." Henry started.

"Even if it were true," Tom said, "people are born proud and selfish, so they're naturally inclined to *not* want to believe that stuff. It's not their fault they're like that. But still God smashes them for not wanting to be different from how he made them. How is that just? It's like smashing somebody for being born in New Jersey rather than Texas. Though some people would do that."

"People do that sort of thing all the time—but people are unjust by nature. As we said, justice can't hold you accountable for the inevitable. That's why the mere presence of a sinful nature isn't what condemns. It's why a baby that dies isn't condemned—only a devil would want that. On the other hand, only the holy can enter the eternal kingdom."

Tom huffed. "But God condemns people for being sinners."

"Are you sure?" Henry leaned forward to catch Tom's eye. "Are you sure? Because all are sinners, but some are forgiven. The holy live forever, though all are sinners. You know this. It's as if you're hiding from the answer. God knows we can't be good, that's why he was good in our place. He knows we deserve smashing, but he took the smashing on himself in our place. It's why he became one of us. Justice called for a solution to the predicament we inherited, and mercy provided it."

Tom stared, open mouthed, then he shook himself. "I don't... I just don't..." He looked at the ground.

Henry thought a few moments. "So, to be permitted into eternal perfection, we must become eternally perfect—otherwise heaven is tainted. But Jesus can do the thing we cannot: make us perfect. No matter how hard we try, we can't. He promised he will. We were born incapable of holiness; he can't blame us for that, but he can blame us for choosing to remain unholy while he offers holiness for free."

"You're saying that not believing means we've chosen to remain unholy?"

"Because men become accountable when they won't believe, it appears that faith is what permits him to clean us up and straighten us out and make us eternally perfect. But he doesn't just look for simple belief. He demands faith, but only a *particular* faith, a faith that enables his perfecting work."

Tom was glaring, shaking his head, glancing between Henry and nothing. "Why can't he just make everyone holy anyway? He doesn't need our permission to do the right thing."

"Because it's voluntary. He doesn't force it on anyone. He can't perfect a person without forgiving him, and he won't forgive a person who rejects his forgiveness. They've gotta want it. If someone chooses to remain unholy, God allows it."

Tom groaned and looked away.

Henry ate and drank a little more and rested back on his elbows for a bit. Finally he spoke. "So, we're back to the original question: what does God mean by 'faith'?" He sat up. "Of course it means *belief,* but does it include belief and *something?* Clearly it's not enough to merely acknowledge facts like a devil does. So, what's the *something* that accompanies belief?"

Tom picked up a pebble and tossed it toward a tiny puddle in a dimple in the rock. He missed by nearly a foot. "I don't know. I have no idea."

"There's all kinds of stuff people say we should do. Good works perhaps?" Henry paused. "But—how many works? And of what kind? And how strict would God's standard be?"

"If it's works, I'm sunk." Tom tossed another pebble and missed again.

"Same here. And furthermore, would God be just to require good works from people like us: born—with no choice in the matter— inclined to selfishness, hardly capable of ever doing good without being filled with pride over it?"

Tom shook his head.

"But faith appears to include belief and *something*. What about other stuff? You know—virtues? Could the *something* be trust? Like the kind you showed by climbing on my back and letting me haul you up here. You might have died, after all. But here you are; you proved your faith in me real, and I proved it reasonable."

Tom said, "Okay, sure, but why would *trust* be the thing that qualifies us for heaven? Childlike trust isn't a virtue in and of itself—especially if the 'ice cream man' drives up wanting something besides money."

Henry nodded knowingly. "Of course God doesn't want us gullible; he expects reasonable faith. So, what's the *something?*"

"Maybe it's asking for forgiveness? I don't know."

"Perhaps. But it's gotta be honest: not vague and insincere. So maybe it's confession? People certainly need forgiveness, and surely no one will ever ask forgiveness for a thing they refuse to admit." Henry glanced at Tom. "A criminal record can never be expunged without admission of guilt. People need to say to God, 'I'm a sinner. Be merciful'."

"So all we gotta do is say, 'I'm a sinner'?"

"No, no—not merely. *Mere* confession can't be satisfactory. Flippantly saying 'Yeah, I did it. So what?' is confession, but without remorse or humility. God's no fool."

"Then the *something* is remorse?"

"Surely it's involved. God's not bound to the fool who says 'forgive me for this' right before he mugs an old lady. To be sure, God won't forgive a man proud of his sin." Henry cocked his head. "So, humility, maybe? But how much is enough? I doubt I've got enough humility to fill a thimble. And certainly no one can say to God, 'If anyone's good enough for heaven, it's me'."

Tom shrugged.

Henry stared blankly, deep in thought. "Only the humble, the contrite. An honest recognition of one's true state. So—is the *something* contrition? Or trust? Confession? Honesty?"

"Maybe it's fear of God," Tom said. "Though—why God likes us afraid of him..."

Henry screwed up his mouth. "Perhaps not 'afraid' of him. At least he wants us wise enough to care that he could vaporize us without lifting a finger. I may not be afraid of a beehive, as long as I'm wise enough not to start whacking it with a branch."

Tom nodded. "Makes sense."

"Or is the *something* repentance?" Henry shrugged. "At least feeling remorse and deciding to change—or at least trying to. I mean—a person who doesn't at least give it a try must not have truly repented."

Tom opened his mouth but remained silent. At last he said, "So what's your point? You're just toying with me, dangling me in front of this 'something.'"

"No," Henry said. "No, I'm trying to sort it out, put it into words." He stood and began pacing on the tiny patch of available rock between Tom and the cliff edge, staring down blankly, tapping the joint of his index finger against his mouth. Tom grimaced as he watched Henry's feet on the edge of the precipice.

"All these things—" Henry started, "honesty, humility, fear of God, contrition, confession, calling out for forgiveness, trust, repentance, doing good—all parts of the same thing. Almost all one big thing, really. But they're probably not the *something*. Maybe they're side effects—stimuli, consequences, evidences—of the *something*. The *something* is a change of state—a change inside a person that requires or produces these things."

"Uh, I…" Tom started.

Henry unwittingly interrupted. "God seeks in us something that enables us to be perfected by him and given eternal life. It's a state, a spirit, some appropriate spirit—but not inherited or merely granted, because it's a choice. It's not mere belief, and certainly not external actions." He glanced at Tom. "External actions would mean that we buy eternal life from God and he owes us. But the *something* is a state—or attitude—acquired by choice. Maybe—maybe—the change of state cannot even be attained by the person; they just choose it and allow God to perform it. It's a willingness to be conformed to—to—the *spirit* of heaven: the spirit of flawless love."

Henry stopped pacing.

"I don't know," Tom said. "I don't think I can know."

Henry didn't hear him. "There's never a real conversion accompanied by stubbornness, pride, rebellion. That's for sure. The *something* is… The *something* is…" He resumed pacing, absently gesturing. "It's all through the Bible, every page. Confession. Contrition. Humility. Repentance. No one can sincerely ask for forgiveness or desire holiness while hostile to God, while nourishing rebellion and unbelief."

Henry sat down, but he paused and stared through the ground, as if he were seeing some treasure under the surface. "It's a white flag." He caught Tom's eye and began to grin. "The *something*. It's a white flag of surrender—not to an enemy that's overpowered us—but because we realize we've been fighting for the wrong side. Not a traitor, but a defector from evil to good." Henry was energized as if electricity surged through him, a joyful smile spreading across his face. "It's submission."

"I'm sorry, Henry." Tom looked distressed. "But you're gonna have to get me moving. My legs are turning blue."

CHAPTER THIRTEEN

Tom's legs were back to their normal unsightly selves as he jostled down the trail in his mountain wheelchair. Henry worked to keep Tom's jostling to a minimum—though his primary task was to prevent him from careening down the trail and launching into an abyss. Every other hiker took note of the big guy and the disabled guy rambling down the mountain rambling about religion.

"…and God can finally reveal the place of perfect freedom," Henry was saying, "once he's done gathering those fit for such a place."

"Once the wheat is separated from the weeds," Tom added wryly.

"Yeah, so to speak." Henry stopped at the top of a steep, rocky slope. "Here, hold on." He hoisted Tom in the chair and began to carry him down.

Tom bobbled back and forth as he spoke. "An exclusive club with stringent membership requirements."

"Ha, right. Extraordinarily stringent." Henry set Tom down and resumed rolling him. "Perfect freedom can only be granted to the perfectly trustworthy. So we've gotta be tamed—shaped to fit in there without spoiling it. But God promises he'll get us squared away."

"Except not everyone."

"Of course ," Henry said. "He won't compel anyone. He wants friends, not slaves. Voluntary love, not automata."

Tom thought for a few moments. "Yeah, okay."

"And we shouldn't act as if the club excludes the 'bad people.' It's clear nobody's good enough. It's why God meets the club's stringent requirements on behalf of the members; they've just gotta surrender to it."

"What about at least trying to be good?" Tom said. "Why can't God view that as surrender enough?"

"Good works without genuine surrender can't be enough. That's a Pharisee." Henry slowed down to navigate a rocky patch. "On the other hand, can anybody put sincere, persistent effort into obeying God and not come to faith? Like Martin Luther: he tried to be perfect, and he found all his trying grossly inadequate. It led him to faith in Christ's work rather than his own. After all, it's why the law was given: as a schoolmaster to lead us to faith."

Tom opened his mouth to speak, then he closed it and shrugged.

"Which reminds me," Henry added, "I said earlier that we shouldn't assume our efforts play no part in our outcome. I meant it in this way: not because they qualify us for heaven, but because they can lead us to the humility that produces submissive faith. Like Luther."

"Sure, I get that."

"And no doubt anyone who ridicules obedience is still far from forgiveness."

Tom remained silent, subtly nodding.

"Furthermore, a refusal to wave the white flag will certainly produce disbelief."

Tom thought for a moment, frowning. "*Produce* disbelief? How's that?"

"Because disbelief is the easy way out. It feels better to say, 'I don't believe all that bunk about a creator or miracles or a god that died,' than it is to say, 'Although I do bad things and need God to forgive me, I just don't care.' It's not that people don't 'happen' to believe, it's that they refuse to believe."

"Because you think if someone didn't choose a thing, it isn't just to condemn them over it."

"Exactly," Henry said. "Nobody likes to believe they're guilty—at least guilty enough to deserve condemnation—so they stubbornly hide behind unbelief, regardless of the evidence. Really, they want a cloak, because light was shined on their true inner selves. 'This is the condemnation: light has come into the world, but men loved darkness rather than light, because their deeds were evil.' These people don't just ignore the evidence; they decide the evidence isn't even true. With persistence, they eventually believe themselves. Therefore, in willful disbelief is sin imputed."

Henry paused near the edge of the trail to allow some hikers to pass, who greeted them and stared at Tom's wheelchair. After Henry resumed rolling, Tom muttered to himself, "In willful disbelief is sin imputed."

"Right," said Henry. "But for anyone who approaches sufficient evidence with an honest, humble spirit, belief is the logical outcome. That's true for any subject, by the way. Therefore, a person who doesn't choose to defy God will have less trouble believing the evidence, and will come to 'faith.' Not that it requires complete understanding of all the facts, or nobody would go to heaven."

"Alright." Tom craned his neck to look back. "Hey, Henry, can you hold up a sec?" Tom squirmed his hips into a new position, then he showed a thumbs up. "Okay, I'm good."

Henry continued downhill. "Alternately, true belief produces submission. For example, if you really believe you can't win the war, and that fighting on will only create more grief, and that you're fighting for the wrong side, you *will* surrender."

"So you're saying that no one will surrender to God unless they believe, and all who truly believe will surrender."

"Yeah, I think so." Henry maneuvered Tom down a little rock step. "So in a sense, faith 'qualifies' a person for heaven. But God requires this submissive kind of faith so he can complete the 'qualifying' he began by taking the punishment for crimes upon himself. He can now transfer to us a state of innocence, and will later transform us into permanently righteous people living in a permanently perfect place."

Tom bounced along for a few moments in silence, deep in thought.

Henry said, "And eternal life in a perfect place is why God made us in the first place."

They passed from the trees onto a smooth, wide section of trail under the sun, then shortly came to a branching side trail that Henry carried Tom down a few yards. They continued down a couple more switchbacks before Tom spoke. "You know, I was always taught that it's faith *alone* that saves, not faith and *something*."

"I would cautiously agree. But 'faith' appears to entail *belief* and *surrender*. I'm sure 'faith alone' is only meant to imply that God doesn't demand certain works before he'll forgive us."

"But wouldn't 'waving a white flag' be a 'work'?"

"Surrender isn't some external action like baptism or feeding the poor or laying off beating your wife. When God warns against works, he's warning against thinking that he's bound to forgive our bad deeds just because we do some good deeds or perform vain religious gestures, even though our heart is far from him." Henry paused a few seconds. "The sacrifice God wants is a broken and contrite heart."

Tom said, "I've heard some people make 'faith alone' so important, they even say that people can't be forgiven if they think that God expects submission in addition to faith."

"I don't know," Henry said. "I have a hard time trusting anyone vehemently opposed to the idea of submission to God."

"I imagine you do."

"In fact, having to pray a particular prayer sounds more like a work—a religious gesture—and resting on that kinda scares me. We mustn't mistake that for a genuine cry to God for forgiveness. Really, surrender is just a choice, and isn't meant to imply that the person is suddenly perfect, nor even discernibly better—nor even that they always feel submissive ever after."

Tom unconsciously nodded his head.

"Though of course," Henry added, "genuine faith will indeed alter external actions. For example, if I told you this granola in my pack would heal your paralysis, and you didn't take it, I'd know you didn't believe me."

"I don't believe you."

"Right. An action proves that you genuinely believe something. That's why faith without works is inert—or 'dead,' as James put it. It must be living faith: that submissive breed of faith that results in good works. Can anybody sincerely believe what God says and not give obedience a shot?"

Tom shrugged.

"So, it's certainly not our works that save; it's Jesus and his work that saves, and we just need to believe it and submit to it."

Tom rode along silently a moment, then he strangely said, "Yeah, I know," as if he were speaking to someone Henry couldn't see.

At that moment they left the trail and rolled into the parking lot.

Tom sat in a tiny plastic chair with tubular metal legs on an avocado carpet in a tiny windowless room with wood-paneled walls. Ten other children sat by him in two arc-shaped rows of chairs just like his, except his was aqua blue, and theirs were persimmon or citron or avocado. The other aqua blue chair lay on its side on a desk in the corner with a stray bolt taped to its seat with masking tape. A dark stairwell in the opposite corner led up to a place where friendly cool light filtered onto the walls.

Standing before them at the focus of the pair of arcs was a lovely young woman with long brown pants that flared at the bottom and long brown hair that wouldn't hang as straight as she wanted. "…so if you want to go to heaven when you die, why don't you come up here, and we'll pray to Jesus together?"

Tom scooted forward a bit on his seat, but paused to look left and right at the other children. Two boys were making dumb faces at each other. A girl rose and started forward. Tom tensed. A second girl watched the first, then she too went forward. Tom stood and followed.

"Mommy, I asked Jesus into my heart today."

"You got saved?" Maggie Ericson cried, beaming. "Oh, that's wonder-ful." She drew him up into her lap. "In Sunday School?"

"Yes. Miss Carrie prayed with me and Lisa and Jenny. After Bible story."

"Oh, I'm so proud of you. That's so wonderful. Good for you."

Tom smiled shyly and put his hand inside hers.

"What did you pray?"

Tom thought a moment. "We said, 'I'm sorry for doing bad things.' Um... We said, 'Thank you for dying on the cross.' Um... We said, um... We said..."

"Did you ask Jesus to come into your heart and life and be your Savior?"

"What?"

"Did you ask Jesus to come into your heart and life and be your Savior?"

"Um..." Tom's eyes searched the ceiling. "Yes." He suddenly giggled. "Jenny had ketchup on her butt."

Maggie frowned. "Tommy, don't say 'butt'."

"...her bottom."

She pursed her lips and glared at him.

"I'm sorry, Mommy."

"Thank you." Maggie smiled and pulled him closer. "Now, tell me more—wait: we have to go tell Daddy. He'll be so happy. Come on."

Tom slid down and started toward the other room. As she followed him, he turned back toward her and showed a beaming smile. "Now I can have the cracker and the juice in big church."

CHAPTER TWELVE

Henry's phone buzzed in his pocket. He drew it out and held it up. It
was Tom.

"Hey, what's up?"

"Nothing," Tom said. "You got plans?"

"Like right now?"

"Yeah."

"No. Well, I mean—I need to wrap up a couple things; I could be
outta here in like fifteen. What do you need?"

"You wanna come up to the house?"

"Is Tatiana cooking?" Henry said tentatively.

"Of course—but I think she's making those meatballs."

"Oh, nice. Yeah, alright."

Henry approached the deck from the kitchen, where nearly the entire
side of Tom's house had been opened up to the evening. Over near the
deck rail, Tom peered through the telescope at Horsetooth Rock as the
last few minutes of sun washed it with gold. Beyond Horsetooth, the full
moon lay fat on the horizon like an enormous dollop of molten glass.

"She says she doesn't need anything." Henry plopped down next
to him.

"I told you," Tom answered, keeping his eye on the telescope.

"Oh, wow. You see the moon?"

When Tom lifted his head a little gasp escaped, then he remained noiselessly still. The moon grew paler as it rose. Rounder too, like slow-motion footage of a rebounding ball. Neither man spoke for a long time.

At last, Tom broke the silence. "I want you to stop praying for me."

Henry swung around and stared at him for a moment. "I can't promise you that."

"At least stop praying that I'll come to Christ."

Henry cocked his head. "I never told you I did that."

Tom gave him a look. "Oh, don't play dumb with me. I know you." He turned back to the east. "It just won't do you any good."

Henry shook his head. "I don't understand, Tom. What's the deal?"

"It's because I don't need it." Tom turned to him again, showing the trace of a smile. "You were right. I gave up. I'm done fighting."

Henry slowly sat up straighter, a light appearing in his eye.

Tom added, "I asked him to fix me. Not my legs. Not my loneliness. Me."

CHAPTER ELEVEN

"I'm so sorry, Henry," Tom cried. "I just—I don't know—I've been so good for so long. But recently…"

"It's no problem. Don't worry about it." Henry lowered Tom's naked body onto his special plastic seat in the master bathtub. Tom scowled in pain. The faucet ran down the tub drain while the water warmed. "Believe me, I've dealt with a lot worse than that."

"But it's just so nasty. You shouldn't have to…"

"Listen, sir." Henry cut him off. "Just shut up about it. I've been up to my elbows in other people's crap before. At least this time it came out the right place, instead of a crater in your gut."

"Oh, gosh," Tom gasped, then remained quiet.

"Okay, you squared away?"

Tom nodded.

Henry checked the water temperature. "That should be good." He passed Tom the handheld showerhead hose and rerouted the water. "You work on the rest of that while I go take care of that carpet. I'll be back in a sec to finish you up. Holler if you need me."

"Alright."

Henry disappeared, and Tom sprayed down his smeared legs and body as well as he could, then he worked on rinsing down the tub.

"The floor's all good in there," Henry announced as he returned. "And I hosed your clothes off outside and tossed them in the wash."

"Thanks, man. You get the spigot covered back up so it won't freeze?"

"Yes, sir. Hey, is there any dirty laundry I could toss in there?"

"Don't worry about it. Tatiana never even lets the basket get half full."

"Alright." Henry found a washcloth and took over the sprayer from Tom. "You've got yourself some scars, don't you?"

"Nice, huh?"

"You know, you've never really said much about the accident. You've mentioned your Sleeping Beauty episode, of course, but…."

"I don't remember anything about it, that's all." Tom shrugged. "Nothing to say, really."

A few minutes later, Henry poked around in the refrigerator while Tom rested in his chair by the panoramic windows in the great room. An ashen sky lay close overhead, looking like a film of gossamer bearing a sea of leaden snow.

Tom spoke. "I was just busted up real good—scrambled a couple hunks of intestine, steering column punched out a piece of spine, legs broken to bits, broken ribs, arm too—here—you've seen that. Oh, my scalp. Have I ever shown you the scar? Check it out."

Henry came around and helped Tom dig through his hair to find the scar. "Wow. It's the whole head."

"Uh huh. With the staples in it, it looked like a baseball. But the scalping probably saved my life. Helped whatever it was to deflect off my skull. At least it wasn't my face, otherwise I wouldn't be nearly so handsome." He grinned.

"Yeah okay," Henry mumbled and returned to the fridge. "And you hurt a lot while you were recovering? Of course you still hurt a lot, but…"

"I can hardly describe it. But probably the worst thing wasn't so much the pain as how nonstop it was. I almost went insane. But then again, even that wasn't as bad as later."

"How's that?"

"You know," Tom sighed and shook his head. "When the pain began to subside, I felt Kate and the kids more and more. As if the pain had been a distraction. Their absence was a dark cloud, of course, but when I could finally sit still and not really hurt, all my head could do was go back

to them. I couldn't go *do* anything, so I just sat and—and—remembered."
He looked vacant. "The nurses would leave their grave faces in the room
and go in the hall and giggle about their blind dates, while I ached like
I'd swallowed a weather balloon. I'd cry until my abdominal injuries hurt
so bad I had to will myself to stop. Then I'd stare. I'd stare at nothing.
Even if it was the TV, I'd be staring through it at nothing. Then I'd finally
sleep and dream about them."

Henry stood at the fridge with the door open, transfixed, watching Tom.

"I still dream about them. All the time." Tom's eyes were adrift. "All
the time." He glanced up at Henry and forced a half smile.

"I'm sorry." Henry remembered himself, grabbed something off a
shelf, and came to a chair by Tom.

Tom continued. "Getting back to work really helped because I started
forgetting—you know—*them.*" He gave Henry a sheepish grin. "Sounds
bad. But I'd go an hour or two and forget to hurt. I'd forget to feel sorry
for myself. But now and then a memory would rush in, and suddenly
it was like someone crammed a wet vac down my throat and sucked
my insides out. Even after I'd stopped bawling altogether, I'd remember
something and I'd suddenly go blank, as if somebody had cut my cord to
the outside world. Middle of a phone call and the other end would be
saying, 'Hey, can you hear me?' It was—you know—a pretty tough time."

Henry remained silent, but showed him a sympathetic little crooked smile.

"The worst thing…" Tom glanced at Henry and recoiled a little. "The
worst thing was—usually it was a memory of me being a jerk of a dad or
husband." A grim sigh escaped him and he looked up toward the ceiling.
"I became a real jerk. I even yelled at God. One time I accused God that
marriage was no different from prostitution." He looked soberly back
at Henry. "But *that* prostitution wasn't so bad after all. Boy, did I learn
that lesson the hard way. It's a mutual contract of giving and receiving, and not just the one pleasure, you know. Every possible need." His
eyes dropped for a moment. "God's arrangement wasn't a sham. It wasn't
some sordid echo trying to steal a portion of the real thing. It was the

model. It provided for a whole interconnected set of needs: the obvious ones and the more subtle."

Henry slowly nodded.

"Hey, look." Tom pointed toward the window. An army of fat snow-flakes spiraled down under deteriorating light. He motioned to Henry. "You know—just sleep here tonight."

Henry studied the sky a moment. "Yeah. Alright."

They watched the show for a couple minutes in silence.

"Even when business started going great," Tom said, his gaze still outside, "I'd still just come home and sit." He shrugged. "And those hours were the worst. They were so long. So long. I was trapped in a chair with nothing but memories. And all my life's aspirations forever stolen." He glanced over. "No, not stolen—murdered."

"By God."

Tom held his eye a long moment. "Yep."

Henry slowly nodded.

"I still do that sometimes, I guess. Sit and mope. Even still, home is a prison. Even here—in this place." He swept his hand toward the massive windows.

Henry cocked his head with a little smirk. "Why then, 'tis none to you, for there's nothing either good or bad, but thinking makes it so. To me Denmark is a prison."

Tom sat back and frowned. "What on earth are you talking about?"

"Nothing." Henry laughed. "Sorry. It's from Shakespeare. You know—'though trapped in a nutshell I'd count myself king if it weren't for these bad dreams'."

"Uh, no." Tom looked at him sideways. "Hamlet, I suppose?"

"Yeah."

"Of course." He rolled his eyes.

"Sorry," Henry chuckled. "I just…"

"And of course you read Shakespeare."

"Well, not really…"

"And you never told Steve you read Shakespeare."

Henry's eyes widened. "Of course not."

"Whatever." Tom shook his head. "Either way, I think I'm okay now. I think. It's easier. And I see why God chose to take them. Save them from me." He chuckled. "And probably save me from myself. Apparently I'm a hard nut to crack." He shrugged. "And now—I hate saying it; it sounds callous—but I'm really starting to forget them. Mostly what I remember of them is how they look in photographs."

Tom had no trouble landing a great parking spot each week near the sanctuary of the Powder River Community Church; today his Scout was parked in the second closest spot. As he rolled out of the sanctuary doors to head home, a voice called out behind him, "Hey, Tom!"

Tom stopped and spun his chair. Pastor Mark quickly approached drawing his coat around him. "Oh, hey Pastor. What's up?"

"You got a second?"

"Sure."

Mark hurried up and stopped before him. "So, how's it going?"

"Good. For sure. Good enough for me, anyway. Ha ha."

"Excellent. Verve keeping you busy?"

"Of course. No shortage of disabled folks, you know."

"Yeah, I suppose. Anyway, uh, we were thinking, you know the F.H.L. Class?"

Tom nodded, then added, "Never been to it."

"Yeah, Clint's being transferred to Seattle. His job. So F.H.L. will be without a teacher in a couple of weeks."

"Okay," Tom muttered suspiciously.

"We were wondering if you'd be interested in teaching, maybe just a few sessions to start. Give it a try."

Tom acted like he'd bitten a lime. "Oh, no. You got the wrong guy there. There's no way I could teach."

Mark smiled and cocked his head. "You sure? I think you'd be really good. A couple other guys—independently—both came to me and said the same thing."

"Well, that's nice and all, but—there's just no way. I could never teach. At this point I'm just trying to figure out why God made me in the first place."

"Alright, Tom. But don't sell God short. I'll keep praying, and you at least think about it. Deal?"

"Okay, but pray all you want. I'll never be a teacher."

Because Henry's third-floor apartment had no elevator, and Tom's new house was a half-hour beyond the other end of town, and Tom's old house had no food, they often found themselves hanging out in restaurants. They currently awaited their entrée at a pasta joint.

"…so I've abandoned hope that I'll ever remarry," Tom was saying. "I'm half a man and a full-time headache; only a gold digger would want me. Besides, I wouldn't wish myself on an enemy, let alone a woman I loved."

"You never know," said Henry. "Don't limit God. There might be *one* woman on earth who could love you for who you are." He chuckled.

Tom rolled his eyes. "Yeah, whatever." He shrugged. "But it's okay. My husbanding earned me this loneliness."

Henry frowned. "Don't be a jackass, Tom. God's not like that."

"No, I'm sure of it. It's not like I'm glad he took my family, but at least he spared them from me. And all that pain must have been good for me too. It's clear I needed it; he finally got my attention. Now that I'm done fighting him, he doesn't have to keep breaking me over the anvil. I'm glad it's over."

Henry raised his brows suspiciously. He opened his mouth to speak.

Tom didn't notice. "I may never have a wife, but I'm sure he's got some other happiness in the works for me. I'm actually looking forward to whatever he's cooking up. And I truly hope he'll figure out how to use a grumpy old cripple to do some good in this world."

Henry studied Tom thoughtfully until it was almost awkward. "You know that day it was so warm a couple of weeks ago? I went for a hike up in Poudre Canyon. Came across this pile of big rocks. They were squared off and sharp like they were freshly broken, and arranged in an obvious pattern. It was clear they had fallen off the face of the giant boulder just behind them."

Tom raised an eyebrow. "Okay?"

"You know what made them break off? A cottonwood. It had grown from a small crack in the boulder. Slowly, patiently, it got taller, its roots dug deeper, and it grew thicker. Year after year, it pressed on that crack until one by one each of those rocks broke off and fell where it now lies. That little twig tore a giant boulder to pieces. And not once over all those decades did it worry because it was trapped in a rock. It was never hasty. And no one ever gave it credit for what it would do."

Tom turned up his palms and showed a weak smile. "And...?"

Henry leaned forward and looked squarely at him. "God's objective is not for you to understand what he's up to; his objective is to transform you into something spectacular—though it often hurts and makes no sense."

"Uh... What's your point?"

"It seems you've often had skewed expectations of God. If he wasn't giving you what you wanted, he must have been punishing you. But our focus shouldn't be on how pleasant or fulfilling this life ought to be; we should simply trust him and to cling to hope for the next life. That's where his promises are all fulfilled."

Tom sat up, fixed on Henry.

Henry said, "He's in no rush to prove his will is best, because one day it'll be crystal clear. One day, you'll look back and see all the dead stuff he smashed apart and discarded to make way for the glorious living thing he always intended you to be. And because his plan will be obvious that day, he feels no need to make it explicit today. So we live in hope, even though misery will undoubtedly return." He held Tom's eye. "For our suffering is light and fleeting, but it's preparing for us an incomparable weight of glory that lasts forever."

CHAPTER TEN

As Carly hurried past the Verve conference room, Tom's voice brought her to a halt.

"…and naturally survival of the fittest favors those who dominate their competition."

She nonchalantly peeked and found Chuck the new sales guy leaning on the table, patiently listening as Tom blissfully blathered and gestured.

"But instead, we help the weak simply because it's 'right.' When we do that instead of callously exhibiting brutal animal instinct, it looks more like the divine in me bowing to the divine in you. It's evidence that genuine goodness was inserted into the animal from outside the animal—into the material body from…"

Carly rolled her eyes and moved along to where she was headed.

A few minutes later, as she returned, she turned an ear toward the conference room.

Tom still blathered. "…just because an explanation is plausible doesn't mean it's the only possible explanation. And for it to be real science, we can't merely dream up plausible explanations; we must also provide empirical evidence—otherwise the claim *must* be presented as theory and not as…"

Carly headed back her desk, shaking her head. She mumbled, "Come on, Tom. Give it a rest."

CHAPTER NINE

When the nurse entered, her eye fell on Henry seated next to Tom's bed. "Oh…hello. I'm sorry, sir, but visiting hours have ended."

"Amanda, he's a family member," Tom interrupted loudly. "Can't you tell he's my twin brother?" He chuckled.

"Tom…" she said.

"He's family. He can stay."

She smiled at Henry. "Of course." She proceeded to check Tom's chart, make small talk, take his temperature, and inspect his latest abdominal incision. "Alright, well. You know where to find me, Tom." She thanked them and left.

"Anyway." Henry turned back to Tom. "It's been weird. I'm feeling—ah—weird."

Tom shook his head a little on his pillow. "Okay?"

"Alright, here's the deal." Henry scooted forward on his chair, leaned on his knees, and laced his fingers. "I've been having dreams. Almost every night. I keep seeing their faces." He glanced down at his hands, then back up at Tom. "I don't know if it's God showing me something—or if it's just some side effect of PTSD. But if it is, I feel strangely calm about the idea of going back there. In fact, thinking about staying here stresses me more."

"What are you saying?"

"Well, I never told you, but for a while now I've been brushing up on my Farsi and Pashto. I'm progressing faster than I thought I would. Getting kinda fluent."

"Wait—you know Farsi too?"

"I took some classes. For my old job."

"Henry, what are you saying? You're going back there?"

Henry remained stone-still, staring oddly. "Uh—I think so."

"But not in the military?"

"No. No, of course not. I'd be—I'd be—I'd have to be, sort of, um, *undercover,* you could say."

"What? Like as a missionary?"

"Sort of. I mean, not outright, of course."

"Henry, it's still a war zone. And that'd probably be the least of your worries. It's not like they're exactly 'Christian-friendly'."

"I know." He sat back and lifted his hands. "I just can't shake this feeling. Maybe God's behind it."

Tom stared in silence a moment. "Oh, man. It's kinda nuts. It's—like—I don't know. Nuts."

"Right. It's nuts, but…" He shook his head. "But I might be the most qualified person around. Maybe one in a million. Or a billion." Henry sat forward. "Think about it. I know the area. I know the people. They're good people, Tom. Not all, of course, but in general, they're amazing people."

"Yeah. I guess."

"And God loves them."

Tom half-heartedly shrugged. "True."

"And I know how to move, where to go, where *not* to go. I'm dark. I can blend, especially with these Uzbek features."

"Yeah."

"Heck, I'm not even American. I'm officially Mexican. Did I tell you I checked? My Mexican citizenship is still valid. They never even knew I left the country."

Tom showed surprise. "What?"

"I'm keeping it that way. They think I now live in Cuernavaca. I'm going back down there next month to get a Mexican driver's license."

"Hold on." Tom narrowed his eyes. "So you're really serious? You really want to go back to the Middle East? I don't…" He never finished.

"I'm not sure. Thinking hard about it."

"What would you do?"

"It'd be difficult. Quite difficult. I'd have to really plan. I know I couldn't enter as a missionary. Aid worker, perhaps." Henry stood and began to pace, staring intently through the floor. "Yeah, perhaps. No way I could be supported by churches. Couldn't be associated with a missions organization. I'd just have to make it happen somehow."

"But what would you do? You mean like refugee camps? Feeding the hungry?"

Henry shook his head almost imperceptibly as he paced. "Probably not. I'm thinking long term."

Tom laid his head back and stared at the ceiling. He gently placed his hand over his incision.

"I have connections." Henry remained deep in thought. "I know people who could hook me up. Like my friend Victor. He's even a Christian. And getting in would be no problem. Staying in would be tougher. Especially if I'm to be in contact with the locals." He glanced at Tom with an odd grin. "That's kinda the point, isn't it?"

Tom shrugged. After a few moments he said, "Isn't there like a zillion orphans over there now?"

Henry stopped in front of the window with one arm crossed and the other hand on his chin. "Yeah, that's true. Plenty enough, anyway."

"Listen, Henry…oh, no, there it goes again." He gritted his teeth waiting for the wave of pain. Finally he settled. "Listen, I know better than to try to talk you out of it. You're kinda dauntless, you know."

Henry grimaced and showed a weak shrug.

"You'll have to become convincingly non-American."

"Uh huh." Henry stood still looking at nothing for a long time.

At last Tom announced, "Enrique, I'm really gonna miss you."

CHAPTER EIGHT

Tom watched from the driver's seat of the Scout as Henry bounded down his apartment stairs. Henry tossed his bag into the back and climbed in.

"Hey Chief, where's the fire?" Tom chuckled.

"What?" Henry pulled his seat belt across.

"Nothing. You just look like you're in a stinking hurry all the time."

"What? Is that weird?"

Tom eased onto the road. "Not weird. Just intense. You run hot, I guess."

Henry shrugged and grunted *I don't know.*

"Thanks for coming."

"Of course." Henry looked over. "Whoa!" he yelped. "What the heck, Tom?"

"What?"

"Your eye."

"Oh, yeah." Tom chuckled. He pinched open his eye and showed Henry. "Got stung by a bee."

"On the eyeball?"

Tom smiled awkwardly. "Yeah. Hurt pretty bad. It's better now. Not even blurry anymore. Tatiana had to pick out the stinger."

"Tom," Henry muttered, shaking his head. "Tom. Tom. Tom. You must have broken a lot of mirrors."

Tom and Henry headed up to the mountain house, talking nonsense a few minutes before the topic turned earnest.

"It's just that," Tom said, "I'm not too sure anymore. I feel like a spectator rather than feeling—uh, I don't know—connected to God. What they call 'worship' makes me feel disengaged from reality. And I don't mean from physical, material reality because I'm engaged with the spiritual; more the exact opposite. As if I'm supposed to feel all amped about God, but the focus ends up on how amped I'm supposed to feel." He shrugged. "But I'm probably the one who's weird."

"You are weird. Sometimes that's good, though."

"Don't get me wrong—the church does a ton of good. Good people engaged in good things. You know, working for God's kingdom."

Henry nodded.

"And I want to do stuff for God too. I really do. I've always been such a selfish pig. Never did more than talk the talk. Though—there's not much I can get out there and do now." He chuckled. "Except maybe give money. I may be dry in spiritual gifts, but at least I'm drowning in mammon."

Henry laughed. "It's a dirty job…"

"In fact, I've been giving a good amount there. I'm sure they're stoked." Tom stopped at a red light and looked over. "But I'm not all that thrilled about it anymore. I'm less and less a 'cheerful giver'."

"Huh. How's that?"

"Well, for example, it goes toward art, landscaping, slick brochures, full-time staff with titles like 'Children's Events Coordinator.' They just renovated the atrium with all this stuff; don't get me wrong—it's gorgeous, but…" The light turned green and they started moving. "They even bring in professional musicians to liven up the worship, trying to make it more dynamic—more 'spirit-filled'."

"People are like that, I guess," Henry said. "They don't notice a lightning bolt until you hang tinsel on it."

"To be honest, now that I'm actually a Christian, I'm a lot less cynical about it. I see the point of a lot of stuff I used to think was just stupid.

Yet—somehow—I feel like I learned more about real Christianity in a few hours with you than I did in decades of attending the spectacle."

Henry cut in. "Listen, sir. Don't deceive yourself about that. Some plant and some water. It's the Bible that changes people, and you know you didn't get much of that from me. For years, God used them to plant his thoughts in your head, and it's God who made sure his words didn't come back empty."

"Okay. I suppose. But it's still a lot like watching a machine."

"And don't let yourself fall into a different trap. Don't overcome your cynicism about one thing only to grow cynical about something else. Don't forget that 'machine' is God's. Just because your personality doesn't jive with their style doesn't mean God can't use that stuff to do good things."

"Yeah. Makes sense."

"And if you don't learn there's no perfect place on this planet, you'll go your whole life hopping from one disappointment to another."

Tom hesitated and nodded weakly.

Henry cocked his head. "But of course you shouldn't support a thing that really grates against your spirit—given your spirit is brought up right."

"Brought up right?"

"Means you pick up a Bible, read it, and do it."

"Okay," Tom mumbled. "Okay. Makes sense. But—do you like the idea of dumping money into decorations and entertainment?"

"Heck no. But I'm not gonna sit here and waste my life figuring out how me and my clique are superior to other brothers and sisters."

Tom became silent and kept his eyes out the windshield. "Okay. I see," he said quietly.

They rode along a minute or so before Henry added, "You could try visiting the church I've started going to."

Curiosity crossed Tom's face.

"But be warned: It might freak you out. It would be quite, uh, different from what you're acclimated to."

The aspens flanking Tom's house had put on a little height since their planting the prior spring. Their tiny leaves already quivered just like they would in a few weeks as broad spades. Slate clouds had spread overhead, driving a breeze upslope and driving Tom and Henry indoors. Tatiana had driven to town.

"My whole life," Tom said, "I've felt like I've been waiting for the bus."

Henry looked puzzled.

"Stuck at a bus stop, unwilling to venture out because the bus is just due to arrive. But it never did. Year after year. I waited for something to happen that would make my existence make sense, that thing that would show me why I was created. But the bus never came. When I had legs, I also had a family, so I couldn't just say, 'Oh, to heck with waiting,' and drag them out into the rain. And I certainly couldn't abandon them at the bus stop and go do my own thing. And then after… How's a guy supposed to brave the storm in a wheelchair? Besides, any spirit of adventure I had was stripped from me."

Henry chuckled. "Crackin' analogy, bro."

Tom glared. "Whatever, Crumpet. You know, before the Scout, I spent a lot of time at bus stops."

"Ah. Okay."

"Yeah, but that wheelchair—God used that curse to make me a lot of money. Too much, really. And now I realize the money's not for me. I'm just one guy. A guy who could live on a slice of pizza for a week."

"Well, that's good, I guess."

"So, what I'm saying is, I think I know why I'm here. At least a little."

Henry watched him, waiting.

"You won't need support from a mission board."

Henry cocked his head and twisted his face.

"I've got this," Tom added.

"What? You've got what?" His eyes widened as it dawned on him. "What? Paying for my…."

"Yeah. Sponsoring you. To start. Other stuff too, as it comes up."

"Tom…"

"First, I'm going to liquefy all this..." he whirled a finger around toward the house "...wretched excess."

"Oh, no way. You love it here."

"Yeah, so what? I've gotta do something while I have the chance. I've only got so much time left to do something worthwhile."

"You don't know that."

Tom sat back in his chair. "And I've got more money sitting in other places. My patents are worth a ton."

"Tom, no. You..."

"Look, man. I've got no heirs."

Henry held his tongue.

"I gotta be smart, though." Tom furrowed his brow like he did when designing. "Create some instant cash, but keep enough cash flow coming in and redirect funds wisely. Try to increase my revenue stream. Maybe sell Verve and license the patents. I don't know."

Henry shook his head. "You gotta stay at Verve. You're the brains."

Tom grimaced. "The brains—yeah, right. I said I don't know. Maybe sell but stay on board and take a salary. I'm still just brainstorming."

"This is crazy, Tom."

"Not as crazy as you."

Henry nodded, then a wide grin spread across his face. "It's crazy. But kinda exciting too." He suddenly sobered up. "But I'm not asking you to dump money into my..."

"You can stop right now. It's gonna happen."

A tiny hand-painted sandwich board sat in the grass in front of a little old stucco homestead.

"Ig less yuh day chris toe new estro salvador," Tom read as he drove past. "What's that mean? Christ something." He searched the tree-lined neighborhood for an open curb to park by.

"Iglesia de Cristo Nuestro Salvador," Henry corrected. "It means *Church of Christ Our Savior.*"

"Oh, so it's a Church of Christ?"

"No, it's Catholic."

"Look, here's a spot—wait—Catholic?" Tom stared at him. "Really? Oh." His eyes darted about.

"Don't worry." Henry laughed. "It's not strictly Catholic, not in the sense you're thinking. Does that look like a cathedral to you?"

"Well, no." He put the Scout in park.

"Listen, it's hard to start a work in this neighborhood if it's gonna slap everybody's tradition in the face. Almost everybody around here goes to *Our Lady*. Hermano Luis—not *Padre*, mind you, *Hermano*—had a little falling out with the archdiocese some years ago because he started teaching unconventional stuff. He still teaches it, though he has to introduce things cautiously. People are slow to awake to things they're not used to, but they do awake. Wouldn't happen at all if they thought he were a *Protestant*. So it's a good thing he's not. You might call him an *Independent Catholic*."

"That sounds goofy."

"It is. Trust me." Henry opened the passenger door. "You ready?"

Tom looked unsure. "I guess so."

Henry came around the truck and waited for Tom to lower himself with the mechanical arm. "Hey, don't be surprised to discover a lot of genuine brothers and sisters in unexpected places."

Tom nodded.

"In fact, you'll find more true believers in imperfect churches than you'll find perfect churches—there aren't any." Henry motioned toward the stucco building. "No way they've got everything nailed down perfectly, but then again, there's no way I do either. But so far I'm okay with it; I've found a lot of good here. I guess God's still in the business of people and not religion."

Tom nodded again. He pressed the button to retract his robot arm and turned his chair toward the church. "Wait, is this going to be in Spanish? You know I don't…"

"Don't worry. They know you're coming, and agreed to give it a try in English. Only Mamá Jimena doesn't know any English, but she said it's okay."

Tom exhaled a nervous breath and began rolling himself down the street. As Henry strolled alongside he said, "At least you'll find out what it feels like to be a minority."

Tom shot him a look. "You ever spent time in a wheelchair, pal?"

"Touché."

When they entered the church, Tom discovered that it was indeed a house—*somebody's* house, with couches and shag carpet and a TV and an out-of-date kitchen that smelled wonderful. Fifteen or so people milled about or sat on folding chairs, conversing. A man, smiling broadly and wearing a clerical collar, approached Tom with hand extended. "Good evening. You must be Tom. I'm Brother Luis. Welcome. We're so glad you came."

"Thank you. I'm glad to be here."

Luis glanced at Henry. "Hola, Enrique."

Henry lifted his chin and shook Luis's hand.

Luis turned back to Tom. "I hope you're hungry. It's Ana's tamales today."

Tom grinned nervously and glanced up at Henry. Henry gave him a slow nod and looked away, smiling from ear to ear.

CHAPTER SEVEN

Floor-to-ceiling windows made up most walls of Tom's office at the far end of his mountain house. But if that ever felt too claustrophobic, he could roll through double doors onto his giant east deck. And if he wanted no walls at all, he could follow a gently winding walkway through ponderosa forest to another, smaller deck overhanging a steep draw at the northern boundary of his property. This was the only spot on Tom's land where he could see another structure on his side of the valley: the rooftop of a neighbor's house almost a mile away down the northeast slope. After about eleven o'clock, this little deck remained in pine shadow the rest of the day, and regardless of how hot the day became, a breeze nearly always made it more than tolerable.

Tom and Henry found themselves on the north deck during this kind of day. An early heat wave had crept up, yet the grassy slopes below were still verdant and freckled with blossoms from spring rains.

"Hey, how do we have Wi-Fi way out here?" Henry looked up from the computer on his lap.

"Oh, yeah. I just had a line run out here a couple weeks ago. I thought it would look good in the property description on the website. Buyers sometimes get nervous about connectivity way out in the mountains; I sort of wanted to blow them away."

"Good grief, Tom." Henry wagged his head. "You sure you want to leave this place?"

"Have to eventually anyway. It's the best way to get our plan off the ground quickly."

Henry sighed and gazed over the valley a moment. "Alright, where were we?"

"Mexico City."

"Right." Henry hunched over his computer and typed a little, then he looked up. "So, an organization in Mexico City should be able to transfer funds directly. I doubt it'll raise too many eyebrows, especially since you know that over there they'll scrape off a chunk for themselves."

"How do we make sure they don't get too greedy—start dropping threats unless we line their pockets?"

"There are ways."

Tom raised his brows. "Okay. So you're sure a real orphanage should be in place in Mexico City first?"

"Absolutely. And why not? This is a real charity org, and every proof needs to be there. Victor already started working on scouting some locals to come on as full-time staff. And the donors need to look real too. And probably not Americans. Not many at least. For you, we'll set up a few legit international accounts, but I'll have my people create some pseudonyms for you. And the more additional donors we can recruit, the better. Even if they're donating pennies."

"Not churches?"

"Probably not. Keep it private individuals. This can't be a Christian charity. A real, international humanitarian operation."

Tom began to type some notes, but stopped and squeezed his eyes shut. Henry didn't notice but continued to read his own screen, chin in hand.

"Hey, Henry, I'm gonna need to do something about this pain. It's just real bad today."

He looked up, concerned. "You sure?"

Tom didn't quite make solid eye contact. "Yeah, just gimme a couple minutes." He wheeled forward. "Here, set this on that chair for me." He handed Henry his laptop.

Tom rolled down the path through the trees. Henry watched him, a bit sad, until he passed out of sight.

Five minutes later, Tom reappeared through the trees. After he locked his wheels, Henry passed him his laptop.

"So, handing out Bibles would be among the riskiest things," Henry announced, leaning back. "As much as we can distribute electronically, we should. You can't deny hard copies found in your house."

"Don't get your head lopped off," Tom said grimly.

"It won't happen, I promise you. Not with me alive, anyway."

Tom stared at him awhile, shaking his head. "And you won't even tell me where you're going."

"I don't even know where I'm going. Not exactly. But if I did—no, I wouldn't tell you. We need to remain as detached as possible. You need to be fully convinced you're sending money to a charity in Mexico. And all you'll ever know is Victor is spending it wisely."

"Alright," Tom said unconvincingly. "You're the expert."

They talked and schemed and argued and strategized for another half-hour before it became clear that Tom's work day was done. He became increasingly spaced out, and started to talk half sense and half nonsense.

"Alright, buddy," Henry announced, standing up. "Let's call it a day."

"Why?" Tom said vaguely.

"I don't think we'll get much further today. You should probably rest. We'll pick this up tomorrow."

"No, I'm good," Tom slurred as Henry began to push him toward the trail. "No, I'm good."

"No, we're done." Grief creased Henry's face. "You're gonna take a nap."

Tom didn't answer.

By the time Henry got Tom to his room, it became necessary to clean and change him before he could tuck him in bed. Tom barely noticed. Tom fell asleep nearly instantly. Henry told Tatiana to take some money from the drawer and go have fun. She did. He remained in Tom's room for hours, working on his computer, praying, ensuring that the sound of Tom's breathing remained constant.

CHAPTER SIX

Again glass separated Tom from the universe. Again he lay in a hospital bed, yellowing leaves out the window barely able to draw his gaze, for Henry sat by his side.

"I'm really excited," Henry said. "It's all coming together."

"Yep," Tom said. "Even if you weren't returning to Asia, it's still great. To already have three little Mexican kids before the place is even finished…"

"Yeah," Henry said. "Yeah, it's good. Victor called yesterday. Said that the director of the state facility has got about twelve more orphans they can't keep. Once the beds arrive, we'll get the final inspection, then we can probably take them right away." He nodded blankly, staring. "But I'm returning. I'll probably be ready before the end of the year."

"That soon?" Tom shook his head. "I can't believe how little red tape they have, even compared to Mexico."

"Yeah, well. It's been as much battlefield as civilization for decades. There's hardly even a real government. That's good for us, though."

"It's about time." Tom looked pleased.

"What?"

"That it's good. That God is doing something. You know—that I'm useful for something. Heck, I never was, even before the accident. It's good that God is finally using me."

"I'm sure he's been using you," Henry said. "Maybe now it's a bit easier to see."

"Ha."

"You act as if you can know what he's thinking."

At last Tom's gaze found its way out the window. "You ever felt you were meant for something you'd been denied?"

"Besides citizenship?"

Tom didn't hear him. "I asked Kate that one time. She had no clue what I was talking about. I told her I felt like I had no more purpose in life than our pet hamster, racing my heart out on my little wheel to get nowhere." He turned back to Henry. "It feels good to be doing something."

Henry answered his phone.

"Henry." It was Tom, sounding strained. "Is there any—oh, hold on, unnghh…"

Henry stood and strode briskly from his desk, phone to his ear. "Tom, what's up? Tom?"

"Henry." Tom panted. "Is there any way you could come to Verve?" He paused. Henry heard a groan away from the microphone. "I could really use your…" More panting. "…use your help."

"What? Do you need an ambulance?"

"No, it's not that." Tom's voice reverberated as if he were in a small space.

"I'm at work" Henry said.

"I know. I'm sorry. Could you come?"

"Can't you get somebody there to do whatever it is you…"

"No, no, no. Unnghh. No, they can't know." Tom paused another moment. Henry heard scuffling. "Please?"

Henry glanced around his little office. Only two other employees were at their desks at the moment. "Okay, I'll be right over."

"I'm in the bathroom by the back. The one near…" Another groan. "…the one near my desk."

Several minutes later Henry entered the door and warmly greeted

Eileen, but quickly passed by to avoid a conversation. He made it to the bathroom and knocked. "Hey, it's Henry."

There was a long pause. "Yeah. Come in." Tom's voice came weakly through the door.

Henry tried the handle. "It's locked."

"One sec." Several seconds later the handle clicked.

Henry opened and passed in, closing the door behind him.

Tom slumped in his wheelchair, flushed and sweating profusely, his nose running down his face. "Take me in your car. Okay? Take me."

"Where to?"

"Anywhere. Sneak me out."

Henry wheeled him out the back and around. After excruciatingly moving him to the passenger seat and cramming the chair in the back, he drove out to the street. "Do you need to go to the ER?"

"No. I told you." He moaned. "Just go park."

Henry stopped under a shady tree on a side street.

"Lean my chair back."

Henry hopped out and went around and slowly lowered him, gripping his arm.

"Okay." Tom was still panting. "That's a little better."

"What's the deal, Tom? You're dying here."

"No. It's not that."

Henry returned to the driver's side and climbed in. He watched Tom, waiting.

Tom lay with his eyes squeezed tight and his hand on his forehead, chest heaving. "It's withdrawals."

"Huh?"

"I needed you before it gets any worse." Tom looked at him weakly. "I quit my painkillers. Last night. Flushed every last one." He groaned and lay still a moment. "I can't let those devils get in our way." He shut his eyes and turned away, lying still except for his trembling hands. "I need you to make sure…" He caught his breath. "…make sure I don't call anyone. No more of that stuff. Never again."

Henry took his hand. "Alright."

CHAPTER FIVE

The eastern horizon appeared under light so faint it still carried no color, and a fingernail moon hovered among the stars. Late autumn chill suffused the sleeping morning air.

Tom wheeled himself along the walk toward the driveway with Henry a step behind, a single carry-on bag slung over his shoulder. Tom stopped by Henry's car and began to raise his wheelchair to standing.

"You didn't have to see me off," Henry said as he opened his car door.

"I wouldn't miss this. Besides, you know I don't sleep."

"Alright, well." Henry set his bag on the seat and cautiously leaned over to embrace Tom in his askew stance. "I'll see ya. Take care of yourself."

"Yep. You too. I'll miss you."

Henry turned about, taking in the view of black pines silhouetted against the night and the lights of the city far below. He breathed deeply through his nostrils. "Okay. I'll text you when I get to Mexico City, and of course whenever I can get word to Victor that I've arrived, he'll let you know."

"Thanks."

"Stay in touch, okay?"

"Okay. Bye, Henry."

Henry climbed in, started the car, and slowly pulled away with a wave and a sheepish grin.

Tom watched the dark lane through the trees until he no longer heard the engine. Until he could no longer see the tops of pines catch the headlights.

He dropped his head into his hands and wept.

CHAPTER FOUR

New glass hung in the crooked family picture, and the picture hung on the same old nail on the dining room wall. Tatiana had straightened it twice before giving up.

"You don't give me moneys enough to live in tiny slum house," she grumbled as she passed into the kitchen. Tom remained hunched over his computer at the dining table. He didn't see that the look on her face meant she meant it.

"Ha ha. It's not a slum; it's perfectly fine. You even get to sleep in my son's old room."

"It's slum."

Tom swiveled toward the kitchen. He couldn't see Tatiana, but he heard her banging around under the counter. "When's the last time I gave you a raise?"

"Too long," came her muffled voice from below. She rose into view with a saucepan in her hand. A loud metallic crash made her jump and lift a hand to her heart. She glared toward the floor. "Stupid, small kitchen." She clanged the saucepan onto the laminate counter and sunk out of sight. Tom heard pots and pans clattering back into the cupboard.

"Well, I'm sorry. I'll give you a raise."

She reappeared, smiling coyly. "Okay. What if a bonus too? Big Christmas bonus."

"Christmas is over."

"So? Why do a bonus must come *before* Christmas?"

Tom raised his brows, wondering it himself.

Henry's former colleague, Victor, ran Tom's international aid agency. He worked in its Mexico City headquarters managing day-to-day operations, routing funds, and traveling to supervise missions. But because purse strings are tied to puppet strings, Tom maintained ultimate control, receiving frequent reports from Victor on everything from balance sheets to bathroom cleanliness. Henry's confidence in Victor proved accurate, for Victor turned out to be a solid ally: passionate, honest, reliable, well-connected, savvy with government officials, and shrewd under the table.

The agency was funded solely through donations, and though the donor list had grown to a few thousand, seven of these donated the lion's share. These seven were actually Tom.

Operations had expanded rapidly—far beyond Tom's expectations. The orphanage in Mexico City opened its second location, staffed by several workers drawn from the first facility. Three additional orphanages were underway in other countries, but the one dearest to Tom's heart was somewhere he still didn't *officially* know—though he had discovered it was near an international border, and in a mountainous region, and American troops sometimes passed through, and Henry couldn't speak to them in public.

Victor referred to Henry's orphanage only as *Number Two*. He had surprising connections in the area, but all Tom ever knew was what he learned from one cryptic conversation with Victor: "I've got people over by Number Two," Victor said. "They keep an eye on stuff. Know the area. Know everyone."

"What kind of people?"

"Don't worry about it. They don't exist. We'll call them 'Billy.' Just know that they can get hookups for Henry and can feed us info. I'll be 'tipping' them for their service, so to speak, just so you know."

Tom's aid agency also began providing food and supplies to victims of war, famine, natural disasters, and shoddy governing. These shipments typically went to places closed to Christian missionaries, and they typically were accompanied by clandestine bundles of literature; chief among them sections of Scripture or disguised Bibles.

Tom also heeded Henry's advice to pursue electronic distribution. He headed up the development of an app that allowed underground churches to share the Bible as encrypted files, with the app randomly morphing its facade through updates. Tom considered this work probiotic rather than viral.

A text from Tom: *Hey Victor. My software is broken. Can you help? Thanks.*
Victor's reply: *Right. I forgot your update. Uno momento.*

A few minutes later Tom's email inbox chimed. The subject line read: *Hey.* The content read: *He sounded good on the phone last week. Pretty excited.* Below that were three photos of Mexican kids mugging for the camera. In the background of each photo was a different product from three different companies. Tom then found the logo of each company on its website, sampled the color for each logo, and scribbled the hexadecimal codes onto a scrap of paper. He entered the eighteen characters into his decryption software and loaded a file named *hay-sauce-012.* Henry's message now appeared in plain English.

Tom texted Victor: *Okay, I'm good. Thanks. Good to hear. Talk to you soon.* He turned to Henry's message.

Hi Tom. Received that last transfer. Thanks. I can't tell you how much we needed to buy those blankets and coats. Winter here doesn't want to quit.

I'm sure one of the kids would have died without our help; I found her in town lying in a pile of garbage in an alley, hypothermic and starving. Crippled, too. Poor thing would have been dead within a few hours, no doubt. But she's doing better. Moving about now—best she can: she's beyond crippled, she's quite the—uh—anomaly. Looks like her fetal development took place in a waffle iron. But probably the bravest soul I've ever seen. And don't forget the people I used to work with. So far she's great; not an unkind bone in her body. So, you saved a life.

Anyway, thanks so much. Sorry this is so short. Miss you. Take care, sir.

Tom sat back, an odd smile on his face. "A crippled girl," he muttered, shaking his head. "Of course."

CHAPTER THREE

"No, man…" Tom spoke into the phone. "No. It's been well over a year since I heard a peep from her."

His former brother-in-law, Jonathan, was on the other end. "Alright. I guess she's really skipped out."

"Why, what's wrong?" Tom said.

"I think your sister and the low-life might have left the country or something." Tom noticed Jonathan's refusal to say the name *Emily*. "I'm pretty sure the alimony kept her from ever officially marrying the slime-ball. But I attempted a new case to recoup some of that; there's this common-law marriage alimony exception or something. So my lawyer sent them a note, and *poof.*"

"What, you never heard back?"

"Worse," Jonathan said. "Bank accounts cleaned out, AWOL at their jobs, their rental abandoned, half their junk just sitting there."

Tom was quiet a few seconds. "I'm telling you, it's like I don't even know that person."

"No kidding."

"Well, I'm sorry, Jonathan. I don't know anything. She just stopped answering her voicemails, responding to texts, and then her number went out of service. A while back I sorta gave up caring. I've only got so much bandwidth for caring, and Emily sorta became packet loss."

"Hmph," Jonathan grunted. "Okay then. You know—it's strange. I feel almost relieved—maybe I can start to stop caring."

"Yeah. Sorry, man. And I thought my lady troubles were a bummer." Tom chuckled grimly. "Apparently you don't even need to be in a relationship for a woman to break your heart and run off with the money."

"How do you mean?"

"This'll sound like a joke to you—but Tatiana, my live-in nurse that was with me for years, did that a few months ago. I really liked her. She was good. But she started getting all bent out of shape over money, talked me into more pay and a bonus, and then vanished. She even took off with all the petty cash I kept on hand for household expenses and stuff. No note, nothing. Just *poof*. Never even answered a single text message."

"Women..."

"I think it's just *people*. People can be pretty rotten."

"Yeah. No doubt," Jonathan muttered. "I assume you've got new help?"

"It's been tough," Tom said. "The lady I've got now is horrible. She's just..." Tom sighed. "...*real bad*. I think because I'm disabled she thinks I'm also dimwitted or something. Talks to me like I'm a child. 'How are we feeling today? Did we have a good nappy? Let's not forget to eat our peas.' As soon as I find a replacement, she's done. I think I know how I'll break it to her: 'How would we like to be unemployed today?'"

"If that naproxen isn't helping, we could try some hydrocodone to see if..."

"No," Tom snapped at the nurse. "I said no narcotics." He heard himself and softened. "Sorry. I'll be okay. When I said I was in pain, I was just answering your question. I'll be fine. Really."

"If you're sure," she answered sweetly. She then finished up her task and left the post-op room.

Tom retrieved his phone from the side table, but he kept his head on the pillow and held the phone above him as he worked. A few minutes later an email arrived from Victor: *Attachment from Hay Sauce*. Tom's eyes lit up. He decrypted the file and began to read.

Dearest Mr. Ericson,

Victor said you have another surgery coming up. Big surprise. Hope it helps. We'll see, I guess.

So, good news: we have a convert. At last! You know that disabled girl I told you about a few months ago? The one I found half-dead? Well, it's her. I'm not surprised she's the first one...

Tom lowered his phone, annoyed. *Seriously, God?* he thought. *All this time, all this effort, millions of dollars, and all we get is one convert, and it's some useless crippled girl in the middle of nowhere? What's she supposed to do for your kingdom?* Tom sighed, returned his phone above his face, and scanned for where he left off.

...not surprised she's the first one. She's my jewel. My little jacked-up jewel. I don't know if I've ever been so happy. Not sure if this is how it feels to be a parent; you know how they say they love their child, no matter what? But maybe that's a different context. This girl, deformed as she is, might be the most amazing person I've ever met. Hard not to love. I have to scold the other kids all the time for being cruel to her and shunning her, but she simply chooses to smile. (Tries to smile—what you might call her "face" doesn't quite cooperate.) She always compliments them and tries to play with them and helps them learn their lessons. She's really smart. She's picking up reading twice as fast as any other kid. And man, she's tough. She might even top your record for suffering. She even has constant pain in her spine. Hey—maybe she's your long-lost sister! Ha ha. You two should start your own little wheelchair club. Except, she couldn't even use a wheelchair; she just slithers along or drags herself around on this little dolly I made her.

She's older than the other kids, so we talk late when they're asleep. Her story is brutal, but I practically had to yank it out of her; she holds no bitterness or guile for how she's been treated.

We talked real late tonight, and as always we talked about the gospel, and tonight she just broke. Believed it, prayed, cried. I just want to clap my hands right now, but the kids are asleep. She's asleep now too. On the ground—that's what she's used to. Crazy girl. I wish you could meet her.

Anyway. I couldn't wait to tell you about my jewel. I know you'll be as thrilled as I am. Take care, and survive your surgery, okay, sir? Keep that

money coming... :)
   From Whom It May Concern

Tom's eyes filled. *God, I'm sorry.* He squeezed his eyes shut and the tears spilled. *I'm so sorry.*

The insurance machine began to turn its cold eye toward Tom. For many years, Tom had drawn from the well that his fellow policy holders had somewhat voluntarily dug for him. But some different folks—who preferred a gusher over a well—got tired of watching their surplus guzzled up. Desperately ill and injured people were drying up their profits. When the machine discovered that some multi-millionaire in Colorado had tapped into its vacation fund, it turned on him. Tom was grateful he had enlisted some smart lawyers along the way, but they still had to contend with the might of the mega-corporation. It unearthed the minutest detail from his medical history, his fiscal records, his business practices— anything they could assert had resulted in unjustifiable claims. Tom hemorrhaged money just to keep his legal team in the game, and still they lost several expensive battles. Fortunately, he spared his charities from their drilling, but his donations suffered nonetheless.

To make matters worse, one of Tom's wheelchairs had broken the arm of a customer—or so the lawyer claimed. Verve also found itself in court, pointing out the clause in its customer agreement stating that their wheelchair's standing feature must only be used on a flat, level, stable surface. Nevertheless, they ended up settling before it was over; they wanted to maintain their stellar reputation, and a gag order was easier to obtain via a hefty payoff.

Letter from Henry:

Tom, thanks for your last letter. I really needed it right now. A horrible thing has happened: my Jewel went missing. It's been a couple days. I've looked everywhere, asked around, tried to get some help, but nothing. I'm dying here.

I doubt it was foul play. For three reasons: Nobody would want to kidnap her. Her dolly is gone. She's crazy enough to try heading out on her own. For several months now she's been talking a lot about her people needing the Gospel, but I told her that it's not time yet. I told her I couldn't risk us heading out there. But she may have just attempted it without me. She's brave. Too brave, it appears.

I keep blaming myself. So pray, please. I'm at my wits' end.

And truly, I really appreciate the words of wisdom you sent. You've encouraged me to try to trust God in this.

Please, please pray.

And you know I'm praying for you. I'm sorry to hear about another lawsuit. The leeches will gun for every penny you've got, doesn't matter if you've got a wheelchair to prove you're legit.

—H

Tom slammed his laptop shut and pushed himself back from his dining table. "God! What are you doing?" He buried his head in his hands and began to shake, half in despair and half in rage. *God, why this, why now? You just keep—you just keep—what? Crushing us. Or something.*

"Tom, you alright?" a voice called out from down the hallway. Antonio, Tom's latest full-time nurse, appeared at the opening, looking worried.

Tom looked up, his face red. "Sorry, Tony. Yeah, I'm fine. I just got some bad news. About work. I'm just really ticked off is all."

Antonio looked at him sideways. "Okay, cool. Let me know, alright?"

"Sí," Tom said, attempting a pleasant look. Tony disappeared.

Tom collapsed again. *You trick me into giving away everything for just one lousy crippled girl to trust Christ—and we can't even hang onto her. Henry's pride and joy, you know. What, you gotta start doing this to Henry now? What? Just because he associates with me? I'm sick of this.*

A few minutes later, Tom was in his bedroom with the door shut. He had dragged himself onto his bed and put his face in a pillow so Tony wouldn't hear him bawling. *Forgive me. Forgive me, God. Please. I don't know what to do. I'm so sorry. I can't keep doing this to you. Help me.*

———————————

Carly rushed up to Tom's desk at Verve. "Tom. Tom," she tried to whisper, but it came out more as a croak. Her face was white and her eyes wild. "You haven't heard about Justin?"

Tom showed confusion. "He was out yesterday. I don't know why."

Pain swept her face. She leaned down to his ear. "Janie just called me. Justin committed suicide."

His mouth dropped open and he raised his hands. No sound came.

Carly began sobbing violently. She dropped to her knees and buried her face against Tom.

Letter from Henry:

Hello there, Agent 99.

Remember how I told you some of the kids were coming around? Well, since my last letter, Gawhar, Naima, Ramin, and Naji believed in Christ, all within a couple of days. I think as soon as one broke, it encouraged the others. So, that makes five now. And I think three more are real close. I was really losing heart there for awhile, but I guess our timing and God's don't match. Maybe we've finally breached their defenses. Apparently, a monotheistic culture wasn't quite enough of a foundation for these kids; I just had to start at the beginning. Street kids never had much family to teach them anything. But wow, perhaps we're over the hump.

In more depressing news, I've finally stopped searching for my Jewel. She must be dead. Or rather, with God. I do take comfort in that.

The new heat is working great. Just in the nick of time, too: winter is back in full force. Thanks for all that equipment. Best in town. And hooking it all up was easy, even for me.

I've really gained the trust of a few of the locals. I think they may be willing to listen to the gospel. I'm considering how and when. Help me ask for wisdom, okay?

Looking forward to hearing from you. I'm sure you've been busy, but I crave your letters. Alright then, take care of yourself.

Agent 86

Email from Victor:

Tom, I hate to have to say it, but we got hacked. Oumar in Mali didn't receive the last transfer due to "insufficient funds." I looked into it, and the account is almost at zero. The records show that over six days, 39 transfers were made to an Argentine bank. They claimed the account the money went to belongs to us, but it's at zero now too. I'm awaiting word from them to see if they can track what happened.

I froze our other accounts for now until I can find the breach. So, until we get this cleared up, we're out almost half a million. It's a major goat rope. I'm really sorry. Hernando is researching our legal recourse to restore the funds, and Verónica and I are working to locate the perpetrator and protect our remaining assets.

Sorry for the brief note, but I wanted to let you know ASAP. I called, but didn't want to leave a voicemail about this. I'll call you tonight, or as soon as I hear anything, or you can call me as soon as you get this.

V. R.

Tom sat in his wheelchair at his desk at Verve with his head hung and his hands lying inert in his lap. He almost imperceptibly rocked forward and back. A pair of springy ladybug antennae from a Halloween costume stuck up from the back of his chair, wobbling gently.

God, he thought, *I don't want to be ungrateful. What you do is up to you. But I'm not sure I can keep it up. You've gotta help us. We can't do this if you're not going to show up strong for us. I don't know why you wouldn't protect this work we're doing for you.*

Tom raised his eyes to the ceiling. He looked worn; almost stunned.

Forgive me. You have been good. You've helped us get the work overseas rolling, and we've even started hearing some good news. I really am eager to see what you're doing through us. I trust you're up to something.

And you've let me live longer than I should. And you've kept Verve going strong. And you've given me... You've given me...

Tom sighed audibly. His colleague George glanced over.

I guess that's what I'm wondering. Can you help me be happy about it? I feel like I should feel—I don't know—'joy' or something. I'm just—I'm just— I'm so tired of being alone. I wish I could see Kate just one time. Just for a little while. He rubbed his chin and returned his hand to his lap. *I know that's a dumb request. I'm sorry. Maybe if you could just tell her 'hi' for me. If you're allowed to do that.*

He sat up. "Oh, gosh." He chuckled a little. "That's even dumber."

George glanced over.

CHAPTER TWO

Text from Victor: *Tom I need to call. Talk in 15 min?*
Reply from Tom: *I can talk now. I'm not busy.*
From Victor: *Give me a few. Try to get alone please.*
From Tom: *OK*
Tom wheeled himself to Coby's bedroom door and knocked. Antonio called out, "It's open."

Tom peeked in. "Hey Tony, I'm going for a walk."

Tony paused his TV. "You need me to come?"

"Nah. I'm just going around the block a couple times. Need some air."

"Bien."

Tom stopped on the sidewalk in the shade of a little tree and stared at his phone. The longer he waited the more anxious he became. At last it rang. "¿Qué onda, Victor?"

"Sorry," Victor said. "I had to get on a different line."

"No worries."

"Tom, I got bad news."

Tom wilted and looked toward the sky, then he put the phone back up to his ear. "What?" he groaned.

"Okay." Victor exhaled. "Billy found out why Henry's been offline."

266

Tom's heart began to pound. "Okay...?"

"Henry's dead."

"What? What?" Tom's insides climbed into his throat. "Victor, no."

"It's true. Billy is..."

"Oh!" Tom squeaked out. He dropped the phone in his lap and covered his mouth with both hands, staring.

Victor waited a while. "Tom?" He gave him a few more seconds. "Tom? Tom, you there? Tom?"

"Sorry. I'm back."

"No problem. I'm really sorry."

Tom made a choked little sound. "How'd it happen?"

"Shot." Victor sighed. "Probably an AK, based on the noise the neighbors described."

"Dear God," Tom rasped. "They know who did it?"

"Nobody knows for sure. Somebody told Billy they thought it was the father of one of the orphans. Found out Henry was a Christian missionary and took him out."

"Oh, no. Oh, no." Tom went silent, staring, shaking his head. "Wait—orphans don't have fathers."

"Well, that's what they said. Trust me, the whole place is *un desmadre*."

Tom remained silent.

At last Victor spoke. "Our kids were all there. They witnessed it."

"Oh, no, no!" Tom's voice broke. "Are they safe?"

After a pause, Victor said, "I think so. The cops were out there, of course, but not for like two days, I think. I've been trying to contact them. It's the middle of the night over there."

Tom remained silent.

"Don't worry, Tom. We'll figure something out. I'm on it, okay?"

More silence.

"Okay, Tom?"

"Yeah, okay," Tom answered. "Sorry. I'm kinda stunned."

"I know. It's bad."

"Alright. Thanks, Victor. Anything else you need right now?"

"No, we're good. Just keep praying. I'll be in touch right away. And Tom—I'm sorry."

"Yep. Me too." Tom paused. "See you."

"Okay. Bye, Tom."

———————————————

Antonio finally began to worry. He found Tom around the block, staring, sitting in full sun a few feet beyond the shade of a little tree.

CHAPTER ONE

Victor located twelve of Henry's orphans. He never found the other two, nor did he hear another hint about Jewel. He smuggled the twelve to orphanage Number One in Mexico City. Because he was the only Mexican he knew who understood some Pashto, Victor personally began teaching them Spanish. It proved a harder task than he imagined. Having been thrown together at the crossroads of many diverse, warring cultures, these children had barely learned to trust each other in Asia, let alone willingly adopt a new, alien culture in Mexico.

The stolen money was never restored. The deeper Victor dug, the more fearful he became that he would blow the cover for all their operations. Tom agreed to let the money go. They decided to cease the aid missions and divert remaining funds to keep as many orphanages operational as they could. Regardless, over the following year and a half, they had to close works in Sudan, Laos, and Mali. Only two other works outside of Mexico remained open, because they could fund them overtly as Christian orphanages.

This allowed Victor to hand over the agency to people with no experience coordinating covert operations. For years he had desired to live a normal life and devote more time to his family. Though he would miss Tom's generous salary, he finally stepped down from his role.

In the meantime, Tom faced three additional surgeries to remove intestinal gangrene. As his weight continued to drop, he began supplementing his meager diet with partial parenteral nutrition at home each day. He never felt other than starving. Antonio had to administer Tom's I.V. first thing in the morning, preventing Tom from showing up at the Verve office until ten at the earliest, or, depending on how Tom felt, much later in the day, or not at all. This became too frequent.

Tom chose to sell Verve and all of his patents. He established a fund to trickle his patent money into his charities over several years, and he placed new leaders in charge of finances and operations. He donated the Scout to Verve as a demo vehicle, and he sold Verve Engineering to his employees for a total of $77.82, split unequally according to seniority; he ensured that Justin's widow received an appropriate share. Carly became Verve's new President and CEO. Within a few months, many of the original Verve Fabrication employees sold their share and retired. Verve began its decline. Within a few months, the medical corporation that had purchased Tom's patents would end up buying out Verve, and it would auction off the Custom Conversions division and its associated patents. The Scout would be parked among fleet vehicles and, lacking a driver's seat, would never be driven again. Within three years, the Verve name would cease to exist.

Tom lay on his side, curled in the corner of a concrete room. The only light streamed through a ragged, decrepit shutter covering the window on the opposite wall. He dimly perceived a number of other figures lying on the floor, all of them as he was: disabled, twisted, suffering. A lone figure silently walked about, occasionally stooping to care for one of the moaning patients. She kept passing by Tom, but never stopped to tend to him. He tried to call out to her, but his effort only created flaming agony in his lungs and stomach. The woman finally crossed in front of the window, and the thin blades of sunlight passed over her face. It was Kate.

Tom awoke suddenly. He inadvertently tried to sit, but pain in his gut tore at him. He lay back, his eyes flitting about. The dream had vanished, leaving only sterile hospital walls around him. He touched his forehead and found it wet and clammy.

Oh, God. Oh, dear God. Help me.

Tom lay still a few moments, trying to avoid moving the muscles in his torso. His thin breath came almost as a flutter. In and out. Pause. In and out. Pause.

God. I suppose you have your reasons. You create, you destroy, things come and go. I guess I don't need to know why. You made me and you gave me dreams. And heart. And skill. And desire. But perhaps you didn't need them much. I guess that's your business. But I really had hoped—I had hoped I could have done something bigger, more valuable, with it all. Did I wait too long with my talents buried? I'm sorry. I'm really sorry. Well, no more chances to change that. I guess that's your business. A remote, long-buried fear appeared in his eyes. *Just hold my hand now, please. If you don't mind.*

The pain spread from his guts to his lungs. His eyes stayed dry, remaining unfocused on the white above him. His breath fluttered weakly in and out.

You're good though. I know that. Even if I wasted my whole life running on a little hamster wheel...

Tom lay still a few moments. He swallowed with much effort around a tube down his throat.

I'm sure that's not exactly true. You don't do anything for no reason. I'm sure I meant something to you. Ah—I just wish it weren't over. I wish I had more time. But maybe you were satisfied enough with what little I offered.

Thin, raspy fluttering.

At least I'll rest soon, and all the tears will be over. It's been a hard road. But you've been good. I know I didn't deserve any better. Thank you for what I had. Thank you for you.

Another slow swallow. A tiny smile flickered across Tom's face.

Thank you for you.

CHAPTER ZERO

Another night in a hospital room. Another leaden, lumbering night in his black cell seen only by countless colored lights on the fronts of machines, the world on the outside of the glass as dark as his prison. Another endless night lying awake because he only slept when he succumbed to the temptation of narcotics. Another night floating sometime between last and first daylight, Tom was alone again. Enormously alone again. This night it began.

A weight—an anvil or an engine block or a grand piano—rested on his chest. It steadily grew heavier and heavier, as if it hung from a slowly growing vine. His lungs, his arteries, his cells all began to cry out, he knew not what for, for his mind was full of fog. The only thing clear to him—the only unmistakable thing—was the hurting. Then also an irritating sound: a steady, piercing tone, inorganic and lifeless.

At once his dark room became white, a white that burned into his brain. Through the cloudy brightness a figure hastily approached, calling his name. A woman's voice. She was by his bedside, and he thought he felt her touching his hand. Her gaudy uniform told him she was a nurse. Her face leaned close to his, and her muffled, echoed voice came a bit nearer. It was the Indian woman, the nurse with the beautiful smile and the long name he couldn't pronounce, the one who brought him ice in a tiny paper cup. It must have been she who had flooded the room with light.

Then she was gone. It might have been a week or an hour or a few seconds, he couldn't tell, but suddenly she appeared again rubbing and slapping his hand and saying, "Tom. Tom. Tom. C'mon Tom. C'mon Tom." A moment later another nurse was on his opposite side, but her back was toward him and her face toward the machines.

It seemed someone was slowly dimming the lights. *Ah—thank you,* he thought. *But why would they dim the lights? And who?* His pain was subsiding, but he noticed it less than he noticed the growing darkness. The nurses were now just silhouettes garbling and moving about like black nightgowns hanging from a clothesline on a breezy night.

Suddenly another woman entered the room, but unlike the others, she wasn't filmy and shadowy and haunting; she was bright and clear. She was dressed not as a nurse or doctor or civilian; what she wore differed from any costume Tom had ever seen. Her clothes were made of silk and gold and light and the sound of distant singing, and the woman seemed to illuminate them from within. The garments streamed out away from her as if she moved through gently flowing water. Her face was inexpressibly lovely, wide and fair-skinned and crowned with rich auburn hair woven throughout with gilded ribbons. And her blue eyes smiled at him, unlike the tortured eyes of the shadow nurses beside her. The shadows simply mumbled away and worked on the machines and worked on the body on the hospital bed, and they paid no heed to their strange visitor.

"Kate," said Tom to her.

"My precious darling," Kate replied.

"I keep dreaming of you. Usually we're in strange places, though sometimes we're at home or in the car. This is the first dream you've come to me in the hospital."

"It's time to stop dreaming. Instead you shall go home. You see, I've been given a great privilege: I've been sent to accompany you there."

"I'm being released? Why don't they at least wait 'til morning? And—and I still don't feel very well." He narrowed his eyes at her. "And why would they send you? You're... You're..."

"It's morning at our home, and I was sent by a better doctor, you might say. We have a new home, a better home. That's where we're going."

At this Kate drew alongside him, seeming to pass through the foot of the bed. She reached out and lifted his limp hand off the sheet and slid her other hand under his frail, emaciated legs and effortlessly drew him up into her arms.

He felt her warmth, and the last remnant of his pain fled from him. He gazed up into her perfect face. That moment his mind awoke.

"Are you ready, my dear?" she whispered.

"Oh, Kate!" he cried. "Kate! It *is* you. My beautiful Katherine! It's really you. What...? How...?" Before he said any more, he buried his face against her and wept.

He shook and sobbed; she simply waited and cradled him, running graceful fingers through his hair and tenderly kissing his head.

"Kate! My darling Kate!" he cried. The tears came heavy, but they seemed to vanish when they touched her. She alone heard his wordless cries. She understood perfectly.

"Yes, my dear. It is I." She kissed him a time or two more. "Tom, my love. It's your time. You shall go to him."

But he wasn't yet prepared for the thought. He could do no more than weep and hold her tightly and cry her name between sobs. "Beautiful Katherine. My wonderful wife. How I've missed you. I can't describe how much."

"Precious Tom. All is well. All is now well. Your commencement has arrived."

"The children, Kate? Our children?"

"They will no longer seem as children to you. Yes, they await you. But there is one better who awaits you as well."

That silenced him. He lifted wide eyes to her. "But I'm afraid."

"Don't be afraid." She showed a broad smile. "There's a kind of fear you shall keep, but not that fear. Don't dare call unclean what he has cleansed. Trust me that he longs for you. He's the one who sent me."

Tom collapsed into tears once more. Kate waited and rocked him. Soon he settled enough to look up again. "You're an angel, then?"

"Oh, no." She gently laughed. "Not the kind you imagine. Unless you mean *messenger,* then sure, today I'm an angel. But no, I'm as much human as you are."

"So, I'm…" He paused. *"Dead* isn't the right word, I'm sure. I don't know what to think. This is—something. It's quite new for me. I suppose you understand."

"Yes, I remember. The night you don't remember, upside down in that silly old car." She kissed his forehead and smiled down at him. "Neither am I your wife, as you said. Of course you know that already. But it's no matter: we're far closer than husband and wife now, and shall forever grow closer still. We're now brother and sister, and we remain companions and friends—though far better. We're no longer bound to each other, but bound to Christ alone. Does that satisfy you?"

"Sister…" he whispered, but not to her. He then lifted his eyes. "Yes, my sister. I certainly love you more today than ever. I can't be dissatisfied with that. And him…" Tom's eyes swam, searching for words. "To be bound to him! But his satisfaction at being bound to me—I can't understand it."

"I know," Kate said gently. "Don't worry about that. You'll understand when you see him." She kissed him again. "Shall we go?" And she began to lower him to the ground.

"I can't," he protested. "Surely you know about…" but he looked down and found himself standing on his own legs, restored and strong. He was clothed as she was, but not entirely, for his garments were suited for him as hers were for one lovely and feminine and fair. He spun around to find the shadow world gone: the hospital room, the worried nurses, the machines blinking their lights, his own useless, crumbling body inert upon the bed of dingy white sheets. He wouldn't see the doctor arrive. And he wouldn't fret a moment over the useless heap they would lay in a box and cover with dirt to be forgotten in less than a generation. But one day it would be remembered by someone greater than them all.

"Where are we, Kate?"

"This isn't a place. But I'm here to lead you to a place, our home—though neither is that yet a 'place' in any sense you now understand. You must simply continue to walk and trust."

He looked down at his feet. "Walk and trust—ha! I haven't been doing either very well. But I'll try."

"Your only duty was to try, not to berate your efforts. There is one with that authority, and you shall hear what he shall judge. But don't be afraid—I know him. We talk about you." She smiled broadly at him. "And many, many others feel about you as he does, those who also love you, those who met him through you. You shall meet them all, for our home is their home. But first you shall see the one who loves you most of all—he who was injured that the lame may be healed."

Some, upon finding themselves healed and restored, have been known to dance and leap for joy, spinning, shouting, clapping their hands. That moment was soon to come for Tom Ericson, and when it did, it would bury itself deep inside him and stay with him forever.

He now found himself sinking to his knees, eyes glistening. His hand still in hers, he drew her down to her knees before him. She grasped both his hands and held them close to her.

"Oh, Kate. I am nothing, and I've done nothing. When I finally started to serve him, I was too late. Very few met Christ through me. Really, none did. A friend of mine actually did the work. It's not of me."

"Of course it's not of you, nor is it of your friend. It's all of Christ. But the same must be said of the many who met him through you. It's all of him; we only help."

"But there weren't many," Tom protested.

"There are tens of thousands." She paused, letting it sink in. He shrunk back a little. "They await you. They want to meet you."

Tom shook his head. "Tens of thousands? But..."

"Who gives the increase?" Kate said sharply. "Not you. Not Henry either. He merely sowed. You merely watered."

"You know about Henry? But you were gone before I met..."

"My love," she interrupted, smiling. "I *know* Henry."

Tom froze, realization dawning in his eyes.

Kate continued, "What you did, what Henry did, what Victor and the others did—these were not vain, futile, random acts that took the Master Gardener by surprise. A seed grows underground, does it not, dear Tom? What you did, what Henry did, even what his Jewel did— these merely helped set things in order in the Master's field. His seed grew underground for decades, spread its roots beneath the feet of people not yet ready for it, until at last it could go unnoticed no longer, for the land itself had changed underneath them."

Tom shook his head. "It can't be. Henry only began his work a few years ago, not decades."

"This underground kingdom continued to grow for decades after your death."

His stunned response came slowly. "But I just died, only a moment ago."

Kate smiled and tilted her head. "Just as you're not in a place, neither are you in time. A moment here doesn't equal a moment there. When you see their grateful eyes—when you have no end of kisses and embraces from those whose spirits were born after your body died—you will believe."

"But how could they get here before me?"

"Who said they were here before you? You won't understand until you walk and trust. In some ways it's still beyond my understanding, though I've walked here far longer than I did there."

This perplexed him even more, but she spoke before he could ask.

"Tom, don't assume that as the days crawled by for you, or that as the decades raced past you, they did so for us. While you spun round and round on your little ball of clay, your speck of a planet, watching the sun rise and set, merely trying to survive each day, we've been living—truly living. You'll soon know what I mean. And this life isn't marked by time as you know it."

"I…" Tom started, with a little shrug. "I suppose…" He could think of no other objection to raise.

"Shortly before your body failed, you said, 'I wish it weren't over. I wish I had more time.' Do you remember?"

He nodded anxiously.

"Ah, dear Tom—as if a few decades was all he had to work with. You've only started serving him, loving him, enjoying him."

His eyes widened. He began to slowly nod his head.

Kate continued, "This life, not that life, has been his objective from the beginning. It's here that no promise of his goes unfulfilled."

"I understand."

Kate reached out and gently touched his cheek, then she returned her hand into his. He looked up to find her gazing deeply into his eyes.

She said, "Watching day after day pass, you felt—we all did to some degree—that our lives were slipping through our fingers. Time seemed a cruel tyrant, hurling us against the end of our brief lives before we could achieve our most meager desires, before we barely started to comprehend why we existed. We pitied ourselves that we didn't have the slightest power to make the fleeting moment of our lives worth something. And indeed, in that way we were inert, because the power to make our lives 'worth something' was never given to us in the first place. The one with that power asked us merely to walk and trust. Neither our impotence nor the brevity of our lives were obstacles to him to make our lives worth something. And his 'worth something' is something of immense value, not just for us, but for him also, as well as for all those he loves. Our idea of a life worth living was typically quite short-sighted and selfish, but he wanted for us a life worth living forever. That short, painful moment gave birth to it."

"What a fool I am." Tom stared at her, stunned. "What a fool. If only I would have walked and trusted."

"Tom, you did trust. Imperfectly, as I did. Trust isn't measured by how we feel, but by what we do. It's like courage."

"But I..."

"And you did walk. Imperfectly, as I did. Yet he had the foresight to account for our wanderings. You assumed you only ran in circles; you didn't know you were on a journey of billions of miles: the earth around its axis, its orbit around the sun, the sun hurtling through its galaxy, the galaxy through its neighborhood. All of these whirled us around their axes toward some distant, glorious place waiting for us. But none able to reach their destination without a gigantic, invisible power spanning them all, propelling them, coordinating them, guiding them."

"Wheels in the middle of wheels," Tom whispered.

"And here we are," Kate said, a gleam in her eye. "Pinpoint accuracy."

"I'm ashamed." Tom sighed. "Down in the trenches, it seemed so hard to trust him with it all. But—but his view is so much higher than that."

"It was hard. It was supposed to be hard. You know, mortality has its purpose: it provides tools—tools such as faith, patience, self-denial, suffering—that are so effective at producing a man of utmost worth to God, they're only needed a short while. He quickly strips away that life so we can enter life far, far more abundant. And it's true: life's trials will seem so small when you see him."

He stared off distantly a moment, then whispered, "I believe that."

"Look at yourself, Tom," she added. "You lost nothing: not your family, not your legs, not your money, not your friends. And as you'll soon see, you shall gain a hundredfold more, to say the least. Our brothers and sisters love you and want to thank you for helping them—people you never even met until today."

"I would very much like to meet them," he said. "And I'm dying to see the kids." He caught himself. "So to speak..."

"Ha!" She cocked her head and showed a crooked smile.

Tom rose smoothly to his feet and stretched out his hand toward her. "In that case, please finish the task you were sent to do."

Kate took his hand and stood, then she nodded toward the light. "Shall we?"

With his hand still in hers, he turned, drew a deep breath, and took his first step.

Kate beamed as she watched Tom enter. It was as if he passed under a waterfall—but this waterfall was made of colored light streaming from every direction. His mouth fell open, his eyes grew wide, and his hands fell to his side. He slowly sank to his knees. "What?" He looked up at Kate, delight on his face. "What?"

She lowered herself by his side cross-legged and waited, immersed in pleasure just watching her brother.

He lifted a hand to his mouth and began slowly shaking his head, tears filling his eyes. "No. No. It's…" He never finished the thought, for at once something swept over him. His face lit up with joy and wonder.

As if all he needed were a gentle nudge—a modest yet incontrovertible reminder that *this* one: the power behind the universe, the holy sovereign, the thundering lawgiver, the adamantine judge, the creator of all things good, the source of all happiness and pleasure, the humble servant who played with children in his lap, the man of flesh tempted by every human failure, the undefiled lamb—that *this* one had suffered to make him spotless—suddenly Tom Ericson was wholly and immutably amended.

And his life began.

TOM'S STORY CONTINUES IN *THE SEVENTH AGE*

I pondered that mysterious prophecy about the Creator living on earth as a man, ruling as its king for a thousand years. The sparse details intrigued me to endless speculations:

What would 'reigning with Christ' entail? What predicaments arise when resurrected saints live alongside mortal men? What would it look like for the lifeless curse of Eden to revive? Why would an iron scepter permit a mutiny? At death, don't saints have all their tears wiped away and enter everlasting, untainted bliss?

These questions prompted my first novel, *The Seventh Age*. In it, I had inadvertently written Tom's continuing story before it dawned on me that he was perfectly suited as the main character in another book I was writing: *Moment of Inertia*.

Told in the style of an epic fantasy, *The Seventh Age* explores these speculations as Tom finds himself engaged in even deeper philosophical and metaphysical ruminations.

To obtain a print or electronic copy of *The Seventh Age*, visit:

WWW.VERSEFIVE.COM

There you'll find free samples of *The Seventh Age* and *Moment of Inertia* in PDF format. Also, go to versefive.com to stay abreast of news about upcoming books or other projects.

ACKNOWLEDGEMENTS

Londa, my best friend, the one who "divides the sorrows and doubles the joys" of my life. She reads my books before they're good but she tells me they're good and how to make them better.

Also, Jim Hutchinson and Steven Hileman. Friends, mentors, artists, inspirers, patient reviewers.

And all the writers and speakers and thinkers who have dedicated their lives to enriching my life and the lives of others. Your fingerprints are on every page.

ABOUT THE AUTHOR

Jason makes designs and pictures and particular groupings of words to trade for food and shelter, and during his free time he makes designs and pictures and particular groupings of words just for fun. And sometimes he goes outside, since it's quite nice where he lives.

Made in the USA
Middletown, DE
06 February 2020

84218529R00175